# TIL DEATH
# DUE US PART

# TIL DEATH DUE US PART

JIM CHANCELLOR

Columbus, Ohio

Til Death Due Us Part

Published by Gatekeeper Press
2167 Stringtown Rd, Suite 109
Columbus, OH 43123-2989
www.GatekeeperPress.com

The cover design, interior formatting, typesetting, and editorial work for this book are entirely the product of the author. Gatekeeper Press did not participate in and is not responsible for any aspect of these elements.

ISBN (hardcover): 9781642378726

# Dedication

THIS STORY COVERS the entire span of human emotions... from the heart-felt innocence of puppy love, childhood friends and young lovers; to the gut-wrenching heartbreak of the tragedies of war. All born from impulsive, life-altering decisions.

Chances are, all who have served, or are still serving this great country, have navigated that span of emotions . . . as have their families and loved ones. For those reasons, this book is dedicated to you.

It is further dedicated to all who were tragically taken on the battlefield; and to the ones they left behind to hear the sound of 'Taps' while crying over a flag-draped coffin . . . and asking God 'Why?'

It is dedicated to all who survived, but continue to fight the demons of their experience, and the fear of what awaits them each night.

It is dedicated to those whose fate remain a mystery; and to their loved ones whose only consolation is a merciful sense of closure.

It is for all who celebrate the great majesty of this country, and the heroism of all its warriors who have fought to keep it that way.

This story is your story. To all of you . . . I salute.

—*Jim Chancellor*

# Contents

## Part III: The Long Road Home

## Part IV: The Reunion

# Foreword

Jimmy, Katie and Bobby were a trio cut from the fabric of Americana.

They were the three amigos. They were James Stewart, Donna Reed and Gary Cooper. They were 'One for all, and all for one.' They were the Hardy boys meet Shirley Temple. Then, they became Americana meets Vietnam.

*Til Death Due Us Part* takes the reader through a trilogy of dramatic and unsettling contrasts. It begins in the Norman Rockwell tranquility of small-town America, complete with all the images one might expect . . . baseball, hot dogs, apple pie, best buddies and boy meets girl.

With little forewarning, their story shifts from the idyllic heartland of Middle America to the savagery of war in the jungles of Vietnam. Tranquility meets brutality. Yet, even when the author takes us into the deathly trenches of warfare, he continues to tease us with the anticipation of a heroic happy ending.

Only to then be thrust into an equally traumatic tragedy of a post-war transition that rivaled the horrors and dilemmas of war itself.

In the spectrum of human emotions, there is no greater contrast than the tranquil setting of small-town America colliding with the horrific struggles of jungle warfare. If there is, it would be the range of emotions experienced when true love is confronted by circumstances that beg for that love to die.

*Til Death Due Us Part* is a mixture of all of that, and more.

The misspelling of the title is not a misprint. It is not the miswording of one of the most well-worn phrases in the English language. Instead, it is the expression of the hopes, desires and expectations these high school sweethearts had for each other and for themselves. They were *due* to reunite and spend their lives together. They were *due* to know the happiness that everyone around them had anticipated. Given all they had encountered, they were *due* to live happily ever after. Would it happen?

Their *due* was an expected return to the life they once knew from one of the most horrific interruptions known to mankind.

There is an expression that says, 'It takes a village.' In this case, the combination of love, tested by the savagery of war, threatened to destroy that village.

Love stories typically have both heroes and villains. They invariably distinguish themselves with white hats and black hats. But, what happens when they don't wear hats? Or worse, if they change hats in mid-stream? What happens when life after the war is as horrible and tragic as the war itself?

As for Jimmy, Katie and Bobby, which among them are the winners and who are the losers? Are there any winners?

This their story.

—*G. Ross Kelly*

# PART I

# The Three Amigos

# CHAPTER 1

# The Legend Begins

"TIME OUT" CAME a booming voice from the Black Oak All Stars dugout. Through the chatter of the crowd noise, the sound was like a huge clap of thunder on a steamy summer's night. Out of the dugout walked a towering figure. He was Sam Elliot, the coach of the All Stars. Sam was a big man, 6'3" or maybe 6'4" and he was huge! Not fat by anyone's description . . . just big, but everyone that knew this man knew his heart was as big as his chest and the team loved him. As Sam walked to the pitcher's mound, he motioned for the entire infield to meet him there.

These were Little Leaguers, but they and their coach were as intense and serious about this game as college or professional athletes. They were the Black Oak All Stars, but in their minds, they were the Chicago Cubs or the New York Yankees. A conference on the mound with their coach was not to be taken lightly.

Once everyone was gathered on the mound, "Big Sam" looked at his pitcher and said, "Doug, it looks like you're having a little trouble, are you tired?" The coach didn't wait for Doug to answer. He already knew what he was going to do. "Jimmy, you're pitching. Doug you're going to shortstop. Everybody else be ready for a play at home plate or first base. We have one out to go."

Jimmy Wrann had been playing shortstop the entire game, but with the game on the line, Big Sam made the change. Jimmy was brought in to try and get the last out for his Black Oak All Stars. His team was leading by a run in the last inning, but their bitter rivals, the Junedale All Stars had runners on 2nd and 3rd with 2 outs.

Junedale was a neighboring community that seemed to always beat the young boys from Black Oak. They seemed to take pleasure in consistently beating their neighbors, especially on their home turf. And here it was, on the verge of happening yet again. The game was on the line and Junedale's best hitter was patiently waiting in the on-deck circle. He had a look of confidence on his face, almost smirking.

Before heading back to the dugout, Big Sam looked at his young relief pitcher and said, "Don't worry son, I know he's a pretty good hitter. Just do your best."

When Sam departed for the dugout, only two people were left at the pitcher's mound . . . Jimmy and his catcher Bobby Bowers. Jimmy and Bobby were the only 10-year-olds playing on a little league All Star team which mainly consisted of 11 and 12-year-olds . . . just like the Junedale squad. Black Oak's hopes for a victory now rested on the shoulders of their young superstar.

With Sam back in the dugout, Bobby quickly glanced towards home plate and the hitter now standing in the batter's box. He looked back at his best friend and said, "Are ya scared, Jimmy?" Jimmy shot back quickly, "Heck no I ain't scared! I ain't scared of nothing . . . now get back there and let's get this thing over with."

If Jimmy wasn't scared, the rest of his team was not quite so confident. The Junedale players had history on their side. They were licking their chops. A young 10-year-old, they thought, was no match against one of the best hitters in the area. The players from both teams and the onlookers seemed resigned to the possibility that this would not end well for the Black Oak team. If recent history was any indication, the best hitter in the area would get a hit and knock in both runs, once again, delivering a victory for the Junedale squad.

Except, Jimmy was never much for history.

He settled himself, looked in at Bobby and reared back to fire his first pitch. It was right down the middle. "Strike one," yelled the ump. The batter didn't flinch . . . he didn't look at the ump, or even to his coach for encouragement. He just stared directly at Jimmy with a devilish grin.

He took the next pitch just like the first one, right down the middle. "Strike two" yelled the ump again. It almost seemed the like this guy was setting the stage for a big finish. After the second strike the batter stepped out of the batter's box but never took his eyes off of Jimmy. The frail 10-year-old pitcher didn't blink. Both the Junedale fans and the fans from Black Oak were on their feet screaming and cheering wildly in anticipation of the next pitch.

Jimmy and Bobby's moms were in the stands, standing together and holding hands, praying that Jimmy could somehow win this battle. Their Dads were also on their feet and whispering to themselves "The curve ball Jimmy, throw him the curve".

Jimmy's infielders were nervously chanting their support to their pitcher. He was facing the most feared Little League hitter in the area and they've seen their rivals sneak out a win too many times.

"Hey batter Hey batter" came the chatter from the Black Oak third baseman they called "TK." The second baseman, Larry Bristoff, chimed in with his encouragement as well, "Come-on Jimmy . . . you can do it!" Bill Chancellor, the slick fielding first basemen, kept repeating over and over to himself, "Not this time. Please, not this time!"

The player's nerves were on edge and the noise and the anticipation from the crowd had risen to a mad crescendo. It seemed the whole town was screaming. David had Goliath down to one swing. "One more strike" everyone yelled. "One more strike." Then came the curve ball.

"Strike three you're out!" yells the umpire.

The batter looked at the umpire in glaring disbelief. His Junedale team was in a state of stunned silence. As they were frozen from their astonishment at what had just happened, Jimmy's teammates were rushing to the mound as if it were the end of Game 7 in the World Series. The Black Oak onlookers were jumping up and down in jubilation. The yell of the umpire's call of, 'Strike Three, you're out' was still lingering in the air.

With that one call, a legend was born.

Jimmy Wrann was no longer an undersized 10-year-old Little Leaguer. From that moment on, throughout the community and the area, he was the kid who took down a rival. From that moment on, he was 'Jimmy.'

The game was over, but the fun filled celebrations were just beginning. Jimmy was a small thin cotton top kid and possessed the heart of a lion. Bobby was stocky and somewhat overgrown for his age and had the heart of a Teddy Bear.

They were a perfect twosome.

Long before this game, the two friends had established a tradition at the end of every game when Jimmy pitched, and Bobby caught. Mimicking the major leaguers they followed so closely, if the game ended with a strikeout, which it did quite often, Bobby would throw down his mask and glove and rumble toward the mound. He would then jump into the arms of his pitcher and best friend, and the two of them would go tumbling to the ground, giggling and laughing.

Observing the rambunctious celebration between their two sons, Bobby's Mom said, "I really wish Bobby would lose some weight. I am afraid someone is going to hurt somebody doing that."

"Oh, don't worry about it" Jimmy's mom said with a smile. "How long can they do this? They're only young once" she continued. "It would be too embarrassing to do in high school or even in Babe Ruth league."

Jimmy and Bobby viewed themselves as lifelong friends. They were born on the same day, at the same hospital, and were seldom seen apart. They were kindred spirits. They couldn't imagine anything separating them from each other, especially at times like this.

# CHAPTER 2
## The Dare

As JIMMY AND Bobby were brushing themselves off from rolling around on the ground, still enjoying the sweetness of their victory, they heard a shrill voice from the stands. "You'd never be able to strike me out like that." The friendly taunt did not come from the opposing dugout. It came from a skinny girl from behind the dugout. Were it not for her dirty old ball cap and her ponytail sticking out the back of it, she could have been mistaken for a boy.

"Who is that?" Jimmy asked Bobby, as they walked toward their parents with their arms around each other. "Oh that's Katie Hankins. She's a girl that wishes she was a boy so she can play little league." "Well is she any good?" asked Jimmy. "I heard she was pretty good as a girl, but I have never seen her play. She just moved here a couple of months ago" said Bobby.

Katie Hankins had just relocated with her family to the Black Oak community from the town of Richmond, Indiana. Richmond was a couple rungs up the social ladder from Black Oak, and Katie was still adjusting to the move. Black Oak, despite its small town charm, didn't have the same activities of Richmond, she felt. She was still upset from leaving her friends and the activities that Richmond offered.

In his best flirtatious taunting reply, Jimmy responded to the young girl. "You're just a skinny little girl who couldn't hit me in a million years." Jimmy was right about one thing. Katie was a small girl and skinny as a rail. She had reddish blond hair and blue eyes, and had a spunky attitude. She had always wanted to play little league baseball and had the talent to do so. However, in those days, girls were supposed to be playing with dolls, not challenging the local stud pitcher to a show down right in front of everyone, including his parents and his best friend.

Not expecting a response, Jimmy was surprised to hear Katie yell back, "Oh yeah, I dare you to pitch to me right now. Cause if you do, your fat little catcher won't be running to the mound when we're done!"

Wow, a double whammy. She was trash-talking both Jimmy *and* Bobby and didn't seem to care who heard her. Despite her gender, her age and her size, this little girl was talking some smack! Jimmy was being called out, by a girl, and in public, no less. His and Bobby's baseball prowess was being challenged by a girl who looked barely big enough to hold a baseball bat, much less hit his pitching. He couldn't let her taunts go unanswered.

"You're on!" Jimmy replied. "Just name the time and place! And, I'll pitch to you left handed. How 'bout that?" "No way." she replied. "I want your best stuff, so you'll have no excuses."

What Jimmy and Bobby had initially interpreted as a joking taunt was now a serious dare that they couldn't let pass. It wasn't that day, but the following Saturday when the dare was answered. They met at the same field as promised and Jimmy laid down the ground rules.

"Alright, I will pitch to you and Bobby will be both catcher and umpire. He'll call 'em fair and square and what he calls goes! You'll get three strikes and if you don't get a hit in those three strikes, you're out and we win. OK?"

"That's fine with me" Katie said.

Given the playful nature of her challenge, Jimmy kept waiting for Katie to lighten up, but to no avail. This girl had on her game face and was not going be intimidated by these two stud 'wannabees.' She was determined to prove that she belonged on the playing field just as much as the two of them did. It may have seemed like a joke to the two little leaguers, but she was deadly serious.

As Jimmy took the mound and proceeded to throw some warm up pitches, Katie donned a batting helmet that was too big for her head and picked up a bat that looked like the size of a major leaguer's. When Jimmy pronounced himself ready, she stepped into the batter's box. Jimmy still found it difficult to take the girl's taunts seriously, but with her demanding his 'best stuff,' he was going to give her just that.

As she settled in to the batter's box, Jimmy suddenly realized he had a smaller than usual strike zone to work with. His first pitch was high and outside. Katie momentarily stepped out of the batter's box, but just as quickly, stepped back in. The second pitch was right down the middle. Katie swung and missed.

"Strike one," Bobby yelled with a little chuckle.

"You got lucky . . . come on throw it again" goaded the tomboy. The third pitch was also down the middle and Katie made solid contact. But it was foul. "Strike two . . . one more and you're out" Bobby said. Holy crap, Jimmy thought, this girl really can hit. He better bear down, or he would never hear the end of it.

The next pitch was wild. Two balls, two strikes! As he watched Bobby reach for the errant pitch, Jimmy realized they had made no provisions in the ground rules for the possibility of a walk. "What would happen if I walk this girl? Jimmy thought to himself. "That would be as bad as her getting a base hit!" Rather than raise the specter of that possibility, he decided to keep that thought to himself. He toed the rubber and let the next pitch fly.

Again, she made solid contact, but again it went foul. This was not turning out to be the laughing matter Jimmy or Bobby had envisioned. This girl had game! Jimmy decided he would have to resort to his killer pitch, the curve, to finish this little bet. Nobody hits the curve ball. Especially a girl.

Jimmy's curve was supposed to start out going right toward the batter's mid-section. Not wanting to be hit by the pitch, the batter would jump out of the way, and the ball would then curve back over the plate for a strike. This time, however, the pitch started toward the middle of the strike zone and began curving to the outside. "Strike three you're out! " said Bobby.

"NO WAY!!!" screamed Katie. "That ball was outside." Feeling like she had been robbed, she threw the bat down and yelled again "That ball was outside!"

But it really didn't matter to Bobby what Katie thought . . . he had already thrown down his mask and catcher's mitt and was already rumbling his way to the mound for their traditional celebration. This time, however, Katie was determined to disrupt their silly tradition. She followed him step for step. Bobby was laughing but Katie was furious.

Bobby's speed reminds you of a 300-pound lineman that has just snatched up a fumble on the 10-yard line and is trying to return it 90 yards for a touchdown. About halfway to the mound, Katie had caught the rumbling catcher, and began swatting at him, yelling "NO FAIR!!! That ball was outside."

I don't know if Bobby made it to the mound or if he staggered and fell into Jimmy, but they all three ended up piled on the ground. The three of them looked like a scrum in a rugby match. Katie was protesting, almost angrily. The angrier she seemed, the more Jimmy and Bobby seemed to be enjoying it. She was a girl, but she was fighting and acting like a boy.

Somewhere in the midst of the frenzy, even Katie started laughing. The three began laughing at each other and the absurdity of the situation. They remained on the ground, but soon the wrestling and the laughing was now just an occasional chuckle. As they lay on the ground glancing at the sunlit skies and occasionally at each other, Katie stated once more, this time as if she was talking to herself in a muffled voice, "It was outside."

To this day no one knows if that pitch was a strike or a ball. But, it was that day that those three ten-year-old souls melted together. From that moment forward, Jimmy and Bobby were no longer an inseparable twosome.

The twosome was now a threesome.

Throughout the rest of that summer, the three friends were inseparable. From more pick-up baseball games, to family cookouts, to just hanging out at the local recreation area at Griffith Lake, they were truly three amigos. And it didn't seem to matter that Katie was a girl. She could play baseball with the best of them. She was fearless. And she had a spunkiness that immediately diffused any issue of her being a girl.

Except for that long blonde ponytail that stuck out from the back of her baseball cap, she was as much boy as Jimmy or Bobby. Her previous hometown of Richmond, Indiana was becoming a distant memory.

As summer became fall, the threesome prepared for their new school year, Katie's first at the new school. With her two buddies leading the way, she had no problems making new friends. Jimmy and Bobby were sort of the junior high equivalent of the 'in crowd' and as their running mate, she was automatically inducted.

The truth is, with or without the assistance of Jimmy and Bobby, Katie would have automatically become a popular addition to the school. She was cute. She was smart. She was engaging. And had a bubbly personality. She just happened to also be tomboyish and athletic.

With the arrival of the new school year, baseball season turned to football. And just as they were on the baseball diamond, Jimmy and Bobby were center stage on the football field. Katie was in the stands with their parents rooting them on. Even in junior high school, Jimmy's talent was apparent to all. He was the quarterback on the local midget football team, and already, he had the high school football coach salivating.

Bobby was not as talented as Jimmy on the football field, but he was developing the perfect physique to become a dominant lineman. Off the field, Bobby was Jimmy's best friend. On the field, he was his best protector.

As they made their way through junior high school and prepared to become high schoolers, they were taking different classes and involved in different school-related activities, but their friendship remained intact. Katie was clearly the more polished of the three academically. She began taking courses that put her on a track that eventually could lead to attending a major university. Jimmy and Bobby had signed up for college bound courses, but they were not in the same league as Katie.

The good news in all of this is that Katie was the perfect homework companion. If either Jimmy or Bobby was experiencing difficulties with any of their assignments, chances are Katie would either know the answer or know where to define the answer. Just as the three of them were partners on the athletic field, they were perfect partners when it came to class work.

Those bonds that were forged between the three of them as mere children were becoming stronger as they became adolescents. Their parents had bonded, just as well. Gatherings among the six of them were becoming as commonplace as those of their children. When together, the parents talked about their work, the community, politics and the general state of affairs, but their conversations always invariably drifted back to their children. They appreciated the closeness the three shared, their school activities, and even the occasional scrapes that occurred between them.

Once Katie refused to speak to Jimmy and Bobby for more than a week because of a joke they made about another girl in their class. The two boys and others referred to the girl as 'Ms. Suck-Up', because she was always the first to raise her hand in class when the teacher asked a question. It was an innocent juvenile comment, but they had also referred to the girl as 'Four eyes' because the wore glasses and other adolescent comments.

In defense of her female classmate, Katie felt the boys were being critical 'just because the girl is smart.' When the boys were persistent in their teasing, Katie had heard enough. She didn't speak to either of the boys until they apologized more than a week later.

Overall, despite their inevitable differences and occasional clashes, the three maintained a tight bond which their parents appreciated. "They're going to need each other as they grow older and deal with the normal challenges of life", Bobby's mother once said.

Whether at school, on the playgrounds or in the community, the three were dubbed by their friends and the town folks as everything from the 'Three Musketeers' to 'Mutt, Jeff and Katie', to 'the Kingston Trio', in reference to a popular folk group of earlier times.

Whatever they were called, the three were indeed, 'All for One, and One for All.'

# CHAPTER 3

# The High School Years

As the years progressed and Jimmy, Bobby and Katie became high schoolers, their friendships, as did Jimmy's legend as a three-sport star continued to grow. He was an all-state quarterback, the ace pitcher on the baseball team, and the go-to guy on the basketball team. As a baseball pitcher, his earned run average his senior year was under 2.00. As the point guard on his basketball team, he averaged 18 points a game. And as the quarterback on the football team, he led his team to the state finals. His name was well-known among sports circles, not only in the community of Black Oak, but in the entire area.

Bobby had grown taller and still possessed that catcher/ lineman physique, as well as his teddy bear persona. Jimmy was the classic All-American quarterback, and Bobby was his protector, both on the football field and as his wingman off it. He did not possess the All-American good looks that his best friend had, but his heart, his loyalty and his character were solid. Bobby was the classic 'do the right thing' kind of guy.

Katie had retained her athletic interests and that same spunky attitude that endeared the two boys to her on that Saturday morning on the baseball field. In every pick-up baseball and basketball game that Jimmy and Bobby played in, she was right there with them, never failing to remind them that girls can play too. Given the right circumstances, she didn't hesitate to join the boys in their pick-up games.

Well into her teens, Katie was also becoming an attractive young woman. She had begun to attract attention from other boys throughout her high school years, but her interests and her loyalty remained with her two sidekicks. She was becoming a woman, but she was still that little girl tomboy at heart.

High school football and basketball games in the Black Oak community were major events. Championship tournaments or playoff games were even more special, virtually closing down the town's sidewalks! With his sidekick, Bobby, as his protector, Jimmy was becoming a three-sport superstar. In their junior season, they engineered a season for all seasons. They led their Calumet Warriors to the state finals where they would face the hated Lowell Red Devils.

Enduring the deafening sounds of their opponent's continued chant, "RDP" "RDP" "RDP" (Red Devil Pride), they fought valiantly but lost the game. The mere sound of 'RDP", to this day, remains a gut-wrenching reminder.

Though they lost a hard- fought battle for the Championship, Jimmy's legendary status continued to grow. He was already beginning to attract the interest of multiple colleges. He was an athlete with great all-around skills.

As for Katie, she never missed a game, cheering wildly for both Jimmy and Bobby, often times sitting right between the Bowers and the Wrann's. Win or lose, she was always the first to greet them after the game. Afterwards, the three of them would then go back to Jimmy's or Bobby's parents, whichever ones were hosting the post-game gathering.

By this time, the three sets of parents shared the same friendship as their children and followed every one of their three children's activities. While they always enjoyed their time with their growing teenagers, the parents also enjoyed their times without them.

As parents so often do, those times gave them the opportunity to reflect on their own lives in addition to their children. Just as their children were to each other, the parents had become each other's sounding boards. They discussed everything . . . from politics, to the civil rights movement, to the growing conflict in Southeast Asia.

As always, however, their conversations invariably came back to their children.

Katie's parents talked about their move from Richmond and the adjustments they went through with their daughter. They were especially appreciative of the friendship she established with Jimmy and Bobby not long after they had moved, characterizing it as their 'saving grace' to getting her integrated into the new community. They wondered about how life would fare for their children after high school. They wondered aloud if the three would try to go to the same college and if they would eventually drift apart if their lives took them in different directions.

Jimmy, they all concluded was going to be a star athlete and would have his pick of colleges, be it Purdue, IU, Notre Dame or an even lesser known college. They also agreed that wherever Jimmy went on an athletic scholarship, Katie would follow based on her academic performance. Bobby, they concluded, probably wouldn't have the same options. But if the other two chose schools nearby, they thought, they could see the three of them sticking together with the same closeness and devotion to one another, right through their college years.

They enjoyed fantasizing about what the future would bring for their children. They even engaged in 'What if . . . ' games. What if the three of them went to the same university and worked in the same company? What if they all became coaches and coached the high school's football, basketball, and softball teams? What if Katie married one of them? Which one would be a more suitable match?

Their 'what if' speculations also caused them to consider opposite scenarios. What if they go to different colleges and drift apart? What if Katie meets and marries someone new? Would her new husband accept her closeness to Jimmy and Bobby?

They talked of close friends they had when they were in high school that they now saw only at class reunions. They talked of childhood sweethearts whose relationships never lasted beyond high school. They acknowledged their conversations were no more than hypothetical fantasies, and always came back to marveling at how their children were growing up so fast. They counted their blessings for how smart and well-adjusted they were becoming.

The parents' conversations ranged from how crazy the world was becoming, to the local gossip in town, and invariably back to their children. And each time, they seem to come to the same conclusions . . . they had been blessed with wonderful children; they were growing up too fast; they were grateful that their children had each other and were such good friends; and, they were thankful to be in their quiet little hamlet, insulated from the craziness of the goings-on in the country and in the world.

It was all about grown-ups playing grown-up games about their children who were becoming grown-ups much too quickly. These were special times which the parents wished would never end.

'Oh, to have them remain children forever', they fantasized.

# CHAPTER 4

## The Love Story Begins

I THINK IT WAS probably Bobby who first knew Jimmy and Katie were in love. He would kid them frequently, but they would always deny it. The friendship that started years ago from a childhood dare and had been building for years, culminated into a full force love affair one day after a pickup basketball game.

Griffith Park, a local community parks and recreation area, was a favorite hangout for locals...especially high schoolers who enjoy playing sports. It had athletic grounds, recreation areas, picnic grounds, camping areas and a small lake. It was also where the high schoolers gathered to play basketball, softball, football, or just hang out.

On this day, they had gathered to play in a pickup basketball game that would pit Jimmy against the neighboring community's local bad boy they simply knew as *Bobby Lee*. Bobby Lee was from the adjacent town of Glen Park. He was three, if not four years older than Jimmy and equally talented on the basketball court. In fact, he prided himself as being the best and the baddest basketball player in the area. And he loved nothing more than proving it, especially against the up-and-coming golden boy from Black Oak, Jimmy Wrann.

Bobby Lee was taller than Jimmy and a good basketball player, but he was not a good sport. He had never been accused of being a gracious winner or loser on the basketball court. To him, losing meant fighting, and given the level of competition between him and Jimmy Wrann, he took his aggression to another level. Perhaps, the only thing that deterred him from trying to provoke a fight with Jimmy Wrann was knowing that Jimmy's friend, Bobby Bowers, was always close by. And, Bobby Bowers certainly wasn't going to let anything happen to his close friend, especially against someone as thuggish as Bobby Lee.

Bobby Lee was the kind of guy that you wanted to see get taken down a peg or two. And, if there was anyone who was capable of doing that on the basketball court, it was Jimmy.

Every time Jimmy would get the best of Bobby Lee even during the game, if Jimmy stuffed him or beat him with a step back jumper, Bobby Lee's temper would flare, and he would want to kick Jimmy's ass. I'm not really sure who would win in a fist fight. Jimmy was not the fighting kind, but his friend Bobby never stepped back from one.

So, when Bobby Lee would lose his temper and begin pushing and shoving and trying to start a fight with Jimmy, he would glance around to see where the guard dog was. And, as expected, he would find Bobby close by with that Clint Eastwood, 'Make my day' grin on his face. Bobby didn't have to say a word, but Bobby Lee knew exactly what he meant . . ." Don't be stupid, Bad Boy."

Thus far in their ongoing rivalry, despite his age and height advantage, Bobby Lee had been unable to consistently stop Jimmy. They both had wins and losses against each other, and each game came down to the wire. This one would be no different.

These were two players with comparable skills and of the same intensity. They were both accustomed to winning and both accustomed to playing 'no holds barred.' Without an official referee to police the players, they usually played, 'no harm, no foul.' Translation: You can call a foul, but unless you're bleeding or something is broken, it should not be called. People in the state of Indiana took their basketball seriously, and these boys were no exception. Calling a nit-picky foul would get you ignored when it came to picking teams in future games pretty quickly.

Since Katie was right there with them, they initially discussed her being the referee, but the other team was certain that Katie would have too much of a rooting interest in Jimmy's team, so they abandoned any further thoughts of that option. They would police themselves.

Knowing the intense rivalry between Jimmy and Bobby Lee, Katie knew this would be a fight to the finish and had no interest in being a referee anyway. She would rather be *playing*. Though she had clearly blossomed into an attractive young woman, she still possessed that tomboy spunkiness she had always had. On this occasion, she withheld her urge to be on the court with the boys and was content being a spectator/cheerleader for her favorite player.

There were only enough players to have four players on each squad.

This meant each team, with only four players, would be covering the same court usually covered by five players.

The game was hard fought from the very beginning and began with a series of non-stop fast breaks by both teams. No lay-up went uncontested. Blocked shots were body blows and drives to the basket resulted in take-downs. Despite the physical play, neither team had called a foul on the other. This was quickly turning into a brawl.

By the time the teams took their first timeout, the score was tied, 18-18, and both Jimmy, Bobby Lee and other players were already nursing scratches and bruises from their hard play. They were playing a fierce, if not violent brand of man-to-man defense, chest to chest and in each other's faces. Some of the players were on the high school basketball team. Others had tried out but failed to make the team, and it seemed those players, along with Bobby Lee, were the most physical. It was as if they had something to prove. But the key match-up was between Jimmy and his older, taller, out-of-town rival.

The more Katie watched, the more she was silently happy to be sitting this slugfest out, worrying someone was going to get hurt . . . especially Jimmy.

There was no clock so the teams had agreed that the first team to get to 50 points would be the winner. So far, it was neck and neck, and remained that way until Bobby Lee's team began to take a slight lead. With the ball back in his hands, Jimmy found an opening at the top of key and scored to pull his team back within 4 points.

The score was 48-44.

Bobby Lee was already talking trash to his younger rival. "Not yet, little boy. You ain't the king of the mountain, yet", he taunted. Katie was seething inside, listening to him talk to Jimmy that way.

The closer they got to the final score of 50, the more the pace slowed down from the earlier relentless back-and-forth's, and the more nervous Katie became. The teams were becoming more strategic and deliberate about how they best finish off their opponent. After Jimmy's basket, Bobby Lee was slowly bringing the ball down the court, determined to score the winning basket.

Jimmy picked him up at the half-court line, getting right in his face. After exchanging multiple passes back and forth between his teammates, Bobby Lee had the ball at the top of the circle. He saw a slight opening when Jimmy was moving back from guarding another player. Bobby Lee made his move toward the basket. Determined to block his progress, Jimmy moved over directly in his path.

In an official game, the ensuing collision could have been a foul on either player. Was it charging? Was it blocking? It would have taken a televised replay to determine.

But in this pickup game, it didn't matter. Just after shooting the ball, both players fell to the ground. No one called a foul and the shot went in.

Game over! Jimmy's team lost 50-44.

After the game, there was no anger, no name-calling, and no fisticuffs. There were just eight tired and bruised players collapsed on the bench and recalling different moments during the game. Jimmy graciously congratulated Bobby Lee.

As Bobby Lee and the other players gathered their belongings and began to depart, Jimmy remained on the bench with Katie by his side. He was still recovering, and said, "That was damn good game!"

Win or lose, Jimmy loved to compete.

Katie knew her sports and she knew the game of basketball. She was an astute analyst and pointed out several times in the game where it could have gone either way. She also knew Jimmy Wrann. She knew how seriously he took these games and wanted to console him after the hard-fought loss.

She gave him a kiss on the cheek and a big hug, sweaty body and all, and joked, "A referee would have called a blocking foul on you on that last play." As much as she cared for Jimmy, she could not resist razzing him, especially in moments like this.

Jimmy appreciated Katie. He appreciated how much she enjoyed sports and how much she supported him. And he appreciated her no-nonsense nature. She could get away with calling a spade a spade with Jimmy like no one else could. If he ever showed any signs of delusions of grandeur or signs of having a big head from all his athletic accomplishments, Katie always seemed to know what to say to bring him down to earth. With his head hanging down watching the sweat drip off his nose, he smiled. He hugged her back.

With everyone else now gone, he suggested they take a walk so he could ward off any stiffness that can sometimes follow these games. They wandered down one of the wooded paths which led to the lake area. All along the way, Katie was teasing Jimmy with lighthearted taunts about how she would have guarded Bobby Lee. He continued smiling at her relentless commentary.

Still wearing the same tee shirt which was wet with sweat from the game, Jimmy suggested they walk down to the lake where he could rinse it and himself off. Once there, he took his shirt off and drenched it in the lake water and began to wring it dry. Now shirtless, Katie gave him one of her taunting dares Jimmy knew all too well.

"If you want to get clean, why don't you just go in the lake to wash off?" she teased. The temperature was mild, but Jimmy had already felt the water temperature. It was not quite swimming weather. "Yeah, right." he responded. "If you're so brave, why don't *you* go in the lake?"

"I don't have a bathing suit" replied Katie. "Well neither do I" Jimmy shot back. The friendly banter between the two of them continued. They were now both in a light-hearted mood. Meanwhile, Jimmy was still shirtless. With his freshly lake-cleaned but still wet tee shirt, with Katie following, he walked over to a nearby picnic table. Heeding the lessons his mother had taught him, he spread the shirt out on the picnic table to dry.

Katie's eyes could not help being drawn to Jimmy's muscular frame. She had seen him shirtless before, but something about this time was different. The sweat he had built up from the game was not offensive, but now somehow alluring. She wanted to feel his body.

"What you need after your hard-fought game, is a good shoulder rub" Katie said. "And even though you lost the game", she continued only as she could, "I'm willing to give it to you. Sit down here and let me take care of those tired, game- losing muscles" she laughed. She sat on top of the picnic table and motioned Jimmy to sit between her legs on the bench.

Deciding to play along with her, Jimmy sat down, as directed. As his bare shoulders were touching the inside of her thighs, Katie began to massage his shoulders, all the while professing her prowess as a masseuse. "I'm a great masseuse", she said. "I've given my Father and Mother great shoulder and backrubs. I'm so good, they even pay me. They think I would make a great sports trainer."

As Katie continues to ramble about her great massaging skills, Jimmy is quiet, thinking to himself how good it feels to have Katie touching his body this way. These two have been friends since they were ten years old. They have wrestled each other, tackled each other in sandlot football games, fought over who has the better team, the St. Louis Cardinals or the Chicago Cubs. Jimmy and Katie have been as physical and as playful as Jimmy and Bobby.

But in his silence, Jimmy is thinking this is different.

In fact, he's not thinking. It is his *body* that is telling him this is different. As Katie continues to chatter on and rub his back and his shoulders, Jimmy is increasingly aware of his shoulders touching the inside of her thighs. He feels her budding breast press against his back with every forward motion. He feels her breath as he positions himself slightly closer. With her legs straddling his shoulders, he raises his arms around each leg, pulling them more forcefully against his body.

As Katie senses Jimmy's movements, she is feeling the same sensations as Jimmy, but attempts to continue her chatter, as if to pretend nothing out of the ordinary is happening. Jimmy has transitioned from using his upper arms to squeeze Katie's legs, to stroking her legs with his hands. With his arms still outside Katie's legs, his hands begin to reach further up her thighs. Katie has stopped talking.

As Jimmy continues to gradually move his hands further up the inside of her thighs, Katie is experiencing a sensation she has never felt before. In her silence, almost sub-consciously, she transitions from rubbing his back with the deep strokes of a masseuse, to stroking his back with the gentle caress of a lover.

Attempting to hold on to the façade of innocent conversation and her earlier jokes as a masseuse, Jimmy looks for the excuse to turn around and face Katie. "You seem to be slacking off", he said. "But whatever you're doing, keep it up. It feels good." Her face was inches away from his. He could feel her breath. He could sense the softness of her face, her lips. He wanted to kiss her. Katie wanted the same thing. She drew closer to him.

Katie's non-stop chatter was now reduced to a nervous confession, "Jimmy, my mother told me this could happen."

"Mine too," he responded softly.

From the awkward sitting position, Jimmy stood up and turned toward Katie. He gently placed his hands behind her neck and pulled her closer. Katie was still trying to muster some innocent conversation.

In mid-sentence, Jimmy interrupted her and kissed her. It was not the playful kiss of childhood friends or even adolescents. He kissed her deeply and with a passion that had been bottled up in the two of them for years.

After their prolonged kiss, the two embraced each other for what seemed like an eternity. Without ending the embrace, Jimmy said to her, "Katie, you have been wonderful to me." he said nervously. "And I will probably never be able to say what I feel. But thank you, for all of it."

With those words, he kissed her again and gently guided her to a more remote section of the picnic area, a few feet away. He held her tightly against his body, continuing to kiss her. Each kiss came with more confidence, with more forcefulness, and with more passion. Katie could feel the pulse of Jimmy's surging body. As they continued their embrace, Jimmy gently guided the two of them to the ground.

Using only a towel from his gym bag and his still damp tee shirt to protect her body from the ground, he crafted a makeshift mattress and proceeded to make love. Ignoring the awkwardness of their inexperience, they relied on their natural urges to guide them. Skin to skin, the childhood friends consummated their friendship into a loving relationship that all had assumed was theirs all along.

Having just given themselves to each other as they never had, the two continued to lay on the ground in each other's arms. As they silently gazed at the sky, Jimmy started laughing. "What?" Katie asked.

"Aw, its nothing", Jimmy responded.

Now her curiosity was piqued, almost embarrassed at what the answer might be. "WHAT??", she asked again. This time with more emphasis.

Jimmy hesitated for a moment and then said, "You remember the first time we met? When you were razzing me and Bobby as we were coming off the baseball field?"

"Yeah", Katie responded, not knowing if she wanted to hear the rest of his story.

"When I first saw you, I thought you were a boy!" he said as he resumed laughing.

"You thought I was a BOY?" Katie repeated, now needling Jimmy playfully in the ribs. "Well, do you think I'm a boy now?" she asked sheepishly. She was not sure he would say what she wanted to hear.

"Not in the least!" Jimmy replied in an exaggerated tone. "Not in the least!"

They squeezed one another tightly and kissed, only as lovers do.

That day, Jimmy took her breath away. With a body that longed to be touched, after a sweaty, steamy pickup basketball game, Katie became a woman. Their bodies became one just as their souls had done long ago.

From that magical moment, theirs was a different relationship. Jimmy, Katie and Bobby were still the Three Musketeers. Bobby was still their best and closest friend. But Jimmy and Katie had now become the item that everyone believed them to be all along. Every dance, every prom, every night, and every weekend, they were together . . . Jimmy, Katie, and their best friend Bobby.

Theirs was a relationship embraced by the whole community. At the checkout register in the local supermarket, the clerk asked Jimmy's mother when she would be announcing Jimmy and Katie's engagement. At football practice one day, Jimmy's coach asked him when the two would be married. Even "Red" the local barber would ask them every time he saw them "Hey when are you kids getting married?"

The entire community was living their fairytale romance with them. They were experiencing all that was alluring and quaint about two young people in love, in small-town America. In Black Oak, everybody knew everybody else's business, and in this case, the entire community seemed to know Jimmy and Katie's every move. But they didn't care. They had each other and the entire community behind them.

Everything was perfect.

Jimmy and Katie's love for each other continued to grow. This was expected and accepted by the entire town that watched them grow up. They were special, with a special bond, and they were loved by all. The happiest of the group seemed to be Bobby. His best friends are going to be married, and he will be Uncle Bobby to their children. Life was good for everyone.

All throughout their senior year, Jimmy's mailbox was being deluged with offers of athletic scholarships. From small 1-AA schools to major universities, Jimmy's legendary status was well known and sought after. He was the All-American kid with the golden arm. He was becoming a prized recruit. Jimmy liked the sensation of being recruited by so many colleges. But he was a small-town kind of guy and he loved his community. He had no interest in him or Katie venturing too far from home, that is, as long as the two of them would be going off to college together.

Bobby, in contrast to his friend, didn't receive any college offers, nor did his parents have the means for the growing costs of a college tuition. Everyone seemed to accept the fact that Bobby would just go to work instead of attending a college, and he seemed to be content with that path. As long as he was the best man for Katie and Jimmy's wedding when they returned from college, he told everyone, he would be happy.

Then life got in the way.

# CHAPTER 5

# Graduation

THROUGHOUT THEIR SENIOR year, the three friends were busy making their own and each other's plans for the future. Jimmy and Katie were busy helping Bobby with everything from writing his resume to delivering them to every possible employer in the town. They decided together that Bobby should work locally so they could all be together every time Jimmy and Katie came home from college for the weekend. They were equally busy figuring out which college would be most suitable for Jim and Katie. Jimmy was going to play football and study engineering. Katie wanted to be a special needs teacher.

When graduation came, Katie had been selected valedictorian of the class. In addition to his many athletic feats, Jimmy was also pretty smart. He was in the top ten percent of the graduating seniors. Bobby was in the top 30 percent. Everything was on track. It was all proceeding perfectly, just as it had been so carefully planned.

After graduation, the three had planned to spend their summer, in part to prepare for their future, and in part, to relax and allow themselves a well-earned vacation. Jimmy and Katie had selected and had been accepted to a college in southern Indiana and were determined to take some time off before leaving in the fall. Bobby had not found a job yet, but had his resume out to a variety of local companies.

Now, it was time to relax.

One Saturday, the threesome made plans to take a ride over to nearby South Bend and visit the campus of Notre Dame. None of them had the illusion of actually attending the prestigious university but thought it would be fun to visit the legendary campus.

On that Saturday morning, Jimmy and Katie stopped by to pick up Bobby at his home. As they rang the doorbell, Jimmy was sharing his enthusiasm about the possibility of seeing the Notre Dame Football team. It was summer, but that is when the football team is getting ready for the upcoming season. Maybe they could see them practice. They were in a lighthearted mood in anticipation of their road trip, and knew Bobby would also be excited at the possibility of seeing the much heralded Fighting Irish in action.

When Bobby answered the door, however, Jimmy knew immediately that something was bothering his friend. He knew that look. He knew the look Bobby had before a big football game. He knew the look when Bobby thought he may have failed an exam. It was the same look that he had when they were 10 years old and Jimmy had been called in to get the final out against the Junedale Little League All Stars. It was a somber look. It was a look that expressed a combination of worry and determination. That was the look Bobby had when he answered the door.

"Ready to go?" Katie asked. "I'm not going. Somethings come up." Bobby responded. "Something's come up?" Jimmy asked. "We've been planning this trip for weeks." he said. "Summer's almost over."

"Take a look" Bobby said, holding out an official looking letter. "It's from the Selective Service. I have to go in and take a physical. I have to take a physical for the draft!"

"Boy, they don't waste any time, do they?" Jimmy said.

They cancelled their trip to South Bend. Their visit to Notre Dame was now the last thing on their minds. Jimmy and Katie came in and joined Bobby and his mother in their musings about the war in Vietnam, the draft, and everything else that this stark reality provoked in their minds.

They spent the day looking up everything they could find about South Vietnam. They were studying the letter from the Selective Service. When was the physical? What would qualify as a deferment?

"Plenty of people are disqualified from military service because of health issues or physical problems," Jimmy thought. "Some people get disqualified because of poor eyesight, or poor hearing. I heard of one guy being disqualified for one leg being shorter than the other. Taking a physical doesn't mean getting drafted! This was just a normal procedure that everybody has to go through." he insisted, trying to lighten the gloomy nature of the conversation.

Jimmy and Bobby both turned eighteen during their senior year, and both registered with the Selective Service as required by law. But they gave it no more thought after that. It was the equivalent of getting a social security card, they thought. They knew there was a war going on in Southeast Asia, but that may as well have been on the planet Mars. Vietnam was a faraway place and was the last thing on their minds.

There was, however, something alluring about the notion of being in the military. Every kid, at some point in their childhood, plays Army. The marching, the guns, the battlefields. It all seems so manly, so macho. And the killing seems somewhat sterile. Maybe being drafted wouldn't be such a bad thing, they rationalized.

After declaring this was simply a pre-requisite to the draft and they should take first things first, they agreed they should just wait for Bobby's physical, which wasn't scheduled for another five weeks.

Having cancelled their visit to Notre Dame, the threesome and their parents tried to resume their summer plans, but the thoughts of Bobby's physical were never far away. Even when Jimmy and Katie tried to avoid the subject, Bobby would bring it up himself. "I guess I could always go to Canada." he once joked out of the blue.

"You wouldn't like it in Canada," Katie responded. "They're all bear hunters and flower child hippies. I don't think you'd fit in too well."

Following his friends leads, Jimmy joined in the fun, "Besides, you don't like ice hockey, and that's their national pastime."

On the day of his scheduled physical, Bobby reported as directed. He was told to bring any medical records with him that might be cause for disqualification from potential military duty. Having none, he arrived empty handed. Entering the building, he was greeted by sign that read, 'For all Selective Service physical examinations, proceed to Room 103', with a big red arrow pointing down a hallway. He proceeded to Room 103 where he was greeted by a clerk who, in a sterile voice, zero affect, and no eye contact, asked his name, Social Security number, and for his driver's license.

Bobby stated his name and social security number as he nervously fumbled for his driver's license. With license in hand, the clerk rifled through a thick notebook filled with a list of names. When she found his name in the notebook, she put his driver's license next to his name and confirmed that he was indeed Robert Bowers. Without making eye contact, she then gave Bobby a stack of forms and directed him to the adjacent waiting room to complete and return the forms back to her."

That was his first introduction to the Selective Service. His second awaited him in the adjacent waiting room.

As he walked into the next room, Bobby was confronted by what seemed like hundreds of fellow prospective recruits evidently going through the same exercise he was about to undergo. For such a large group of men gathered in one place, the room was eerily silent, interrupted only by the occasional command by a man in uniform who was obviously in charge of the process.

"Number 87" he yelled. An individual on the far side of the room stood up and responded, "Right here!"

"Take your number with you and proceed to Room 115," the man in uniform instructed.

As he surveyed the room, Bobby saw what looked like the most diverse group of men he had ever seen. They were black, white and Hispanic, short, tall, pudgy, thin, long haired hippy types, all American types, and ghetto types. He suddenly realized his gazing around the room made him momentarily forget his instructions. He proceeded to begin filling out the paperwork he had been given.

Once completed, Bobby returned the paperwork to the clerk who, after reviewing it for completeness, issued him a yellow card with a number on it . . . number 224. "Go back in the waiting area and wait for your number to be called," he was told by the clerk. "They will instruct you from there."

When Bobby returned home, his friends were there waiting to hear about his experience. Bobby said jokingly, "I spent four hours being poked, prodded, stuck, and examined, and not once being called by my name. From now on, I simply want to be known as number 224."

"I tried every trick in the book," he playfully continued," but I don't believe there is anything that will disqualify me." By the time he arrived home, Bobby had had plenty of time to reflect on what was seemingly an inevitable outcome. He was nervous but tried to stiffen his resolve for what awaited him.

Jimmy's situation was different. He knew that he would be able to get a college deferment from the draft, but he didn't like the possibility of losing his friend to the Army. That night, the two of them, without Katie, went out alone. The evening gave each of them time to reflect. "Bobby", Jimmy said in a tone Bobby had not heard from his friend before, "do you realize this is possibly the first time you and I might be a part since that time we were kids? I'm not even sure what to think about it"

" Ahh", Bobby dismissively responded with the wave of his hand. "I'll go away and see the world, then I'll be right back here in no time."

"Even if I do go", he continued, "I heard if you get sent to Vietnam, you also get a paid vacation and can go to places like Hong Kong, Tokyo, or even Hawaii. If I'm going to see the world, I may as well let the government pay for it."

Bobby was being lighthearted about the possibility. Jimmy assumed beneath that cavalier attitude, Bobby was scared, just as Jimmy was.

As the realities of Vietnam began to creep into their lives, Bobby seemed more casual about the situation than his friends or his parents. They all knew that Bobby would pass his physical and then be drafted into the Army. They knew it would only be a matter of time. The path forward would be simple. The war was escalating and surely Bobby would be called on to serve in Vietnam.

The threesome struggled to regroup and look at the major league curveball they had just been thrown. One day while they were all talking about how they proceed forward knowing Bobby's future was in the Army, Katie came up with a radical idea. "Hey, what if we all put our lives on hold for 2 years while Bobby is in the Army? That way we can all go to college together . . . Bobby can use his G.I. benefits and I'm pretty sure you could still get a scholarship."

Jimmy, not sure if Katie was seriously proposing the idea or just throwing out random thoughts, was in a silent reflective gaze out the window. He remained silent and motionless, almost as if the other two were not in the room. Katie and Bobby continued talking.

Suddenly, Jimmy stood up and looked at the two of them and said, "That's a great idea!"

Katie and Bobby had moved on from her idea, covering a variety of other topics during Jimmy's silence. So, they were not sure what Jimmy thought was such a great idea. "What are you talking about?", Katie asked.

"You know. What you said! We take two years off from our plans. You know!"

Jimmy transitioned from his silent gaze to now take center stage in this conversation. And as he moved toward his Katie and Bobby, the two of them stopped their conversation to hear their friend's idea.

"And, I'll take the idea one step further." Jimmy continued, looking straight at Bobby. "What if I join the Army with you? We go in just like Katie said. We spend the next two years in the Army, then come back and we all go to college together. We can go in on the buddy system, just like the recruiters talked about when they came in and spoke to us in school assembly."

'He was serious', Katie thought to herself. She began to have second thoughts about even offering up the idea in the first place. She was torn. She hated the notion of the two lifelong friends being apart. And, she didn't want to see Jimmy give up all that he had worked for. But she knew how much the two meant to each other. Holding back tears, she said, "I'll support whatever you two decide, and I'll be here for both of you when you both return home." She emphasized the word 'both.'

While Bobby refrained from outwardly showing any emotions, inside he was jubilant at the possibility of his friend joining the Army with him. They've been through everything else in their lives together. It would only be fitting for the two of them to do this together.

Bobby and Katie both knew Jimmy Wrann didn't make decisions lightly. And he was never fearful of the consequences of his decisions. Bobby thought about the two of them standing on the pitcher's mound before Jimmy got the final out against the Junedale All Stars. Jimmy was seemingly the only person in the park that wasn't afraid.

He remembered when a basketball game against one of their rivals was tied with four seconds left and the coach looked at Jimmy during the timeout, and said, "Wrann, can you make the shot if we can get the ball to you in the corner?"

Jimmy didn't hesitate. "Just get me the ball."

And now, he was putting his life on hold to be with his best friend. Bobby was also close to tears.

"That's it." Jimmy said. "We're gonna do it. If they'll take us as a team, I'm right there with you Bobby. Now, I've just got to go and break the news to my parents."

The three of them hugged and each said, I love you, to each other. Jimmy and Katie then left Bobby's house to drop her off at her home, before he headed home to face his parents. Meanwhile, Bobby, bubbling over with excitement, went bounding in to the den where his parents were, and blurted out, "Guess what?"

The ride to Katie's house was largely silent. When Katie spoke at all, she just murmured, "I don't know what to say."

Jimmy reached over and took her hand as he was driving. He pulled it up to his mouth and kept it there as he drove. "I love you, Katie," he said. "Do you understand what I'm doing? And why?"

"I do, Jimmy. And I love you, too. I've just got to have some time to let this sink in. I'm proud of you. You and Bobby mean the world to me. I'm just scared."

"It will be alright, sweetheart", Jimmy responded. "It will all work out. Trust me."

When they pulled into Katie's driveway, Jimmy pulled Katie close to him. He kissed her and said, "I'll call you later." With that, he drove off to have a perhaps, much more difficult conversation.

Just as the three friends suspected, Jimmy's conversation with his parents did not go as well as he had hoped. As much as he had rehearsed what he intended to tell them, hoping they would understand and support his decision, it did not go as planned. He was asking them to understand and support giving up the opportunity to go to college, instead opting to go off to war. That would take a little while.

Ironically, when Jimmy arrived home, his parents were watching a documentary on television by Walter Cronkite on the rising tensions in Southeast Asia. That was not the best lead-in to his intended discussion. That notwithstanding, he told his parents he had something to discuss with them when they had a moment.

Sensing the seriousness in his son's voice, Jimmy's father turned off the TV and casually said, "What's up, son?"

Jimmy then launched in to his rehearsed rationale for why he had decided to join his best friend to enlist in the Army. His mother reacted the way any mother would react. She became highly emotional and pleaded with Jimmy to reconsider his decision. Jimmy's father was a little more reserved. In fact, his calmness added to Jimmy's discomfort.

After listening intently and taking it all in, Jimmy's father finally spoke.

He said very calmly, "Now let me get this straight . . . You are proposing to put aside the offers you've received to play football at the collegiate level, and instead go into the Army with your best friend. You are proposing to give up a college deferment that would be the envy of every prospective draftee in the country, to instead go and do what so many are trying to get *out* of doing."

Jimmy started to respond, but his father was not finished.

He continued, "You're proposing while others are considering bizarre and extreme ideas to avoid military service, from going to Canada to shooting themselves in the foot, Jimmy Wrann," saying his name with emphasis, "you are planning to join the Army with your best friend. Do I have that right?"

Trying to maintain the strength of his convictions, Jimmy responded to his father, "Yes sir. That's right."

Jimmy's father did not agree with his son's decision and expressed his disagreement forcefully, but he knew his son and had come to trust his judgment. Putting his arm around his wife, who was still crying, he said, "Jimmy, we have very different feelings about this, as you can see. But, we love you, we trust you, we support you, and we know what you and Bobby mean to each other. If that's what you and Bobby have decided, then that's what we'll support."

Through her tears, Jimmy's mother did manage to get in one other question: "Does Katie know what you're doing? Does she support this?"

Jimmy responded, "Mom, you may not believe this, but she is the one that came up with the idea. Yes, she supports our decision."

That simple idea, which took Katie less than fifteen seconds to offer during a free-wheeling brainstorming session, would alter the course of the lives of the three friends in ways that none of them could ever imagine.

After his conversation with his parents had run its course, Jimmy called Katie. "Did you tell them? What did they say?", she asked anxiously.

"They understood. They don't agree, but they understand and support what we're doing."

"You can certainly understand their concern, Jimmy. But knowing they support your decision means everything!" Katie replied. "It's late and we've had a long, emotionally draining day. Let's talk tomorrow. Love you."

"Love you" Jimmy replied. "Good night."

Jimmy had one more phone call to make.

When Bobby answered, Jimmy simply said two words, "We're on." Bobby responded with muffled excitement in his voice, "All right! I'll call the recruiter in the morning to make us an appointment. Good night, Jimmy. Here we go!"

"Here we go.", Jimmy repeated, and hung up the phone.

In less than three weeks, the pair would be on their way to boot camp, and most likely off to fight a war in a remote part of the world. They would be confronting an enemy few people knew we had, and even fewer seemed to understand why. The best they knew was that it had something to do with what was called, the 'domino' theory.

That 'domino' theory would become the centerpiece of these two young men's lives, and the life of the woman Jimmy loved.

# PART II

# The War

# CHAPTER 6
# Basic Training

"**E**VER BEEN TO Missouri?", Bobby asked the guy sitting next to him on the military bus. He spoke in a loud voice, competing with the roar of the bus's engine and the non-stop chatter of its apprehensive occupants.

"Naah", his fellow passenger replied. "The closest I've ever been to Missouri was when we came to a family funeral in Wichita, Kansas when I was in the 10th grade."

"Where are you from?" Bobby continued. Bobby engaged people easily. He was a lovable, teddy bear kind of guy and was embarking on the biggest adventure of his life with his lifelong friend, who was sitting in the row behind him. He was amped up.

"Montana" the fellow passenger responded. "A little town outside Billings. You?"

"Indiana" Bobby responded. "I'm Bobby Bowers" he continued. "Me and my friend back in the back joined on the Buddy System. We've been friends all our lives, so we decided, heck, we've done everything else together, we might as well do this together. What made you join?" Bobby continued.

"JOIN?", his fellow passenger responded in an animated cowboy drawl. Hell, I didn't join nothing. I was drafted!'

The two continued their conversation as the bus approached a sign saying, 'Welcome to Waynesville Missouri', and another that read 'Travel Historic Route 66, Highway to the Stars.' While his seatmate was a little more reserved, Bobby seemed almost excited in anticipation of the great adventure he and his friend were about to undertake. He was like a kid in a toy store, exploring every shelf and offering non-stop commentary.

As they drove through the town, he continuously looked back at Jimmy in the row behind him, commenting on his every observation. He was struck by the number of pedestrians on the sidewalks of the town that were in military uniforms, and the number of signs on the storefront windows which read, 'Military personnel 10% off.' He was also struck by the nature of the retail stores. "Good gosh almighty", Bobby exclaimed. "That's the fifth pawn shop I've seen so far. There must be one on every corner." Bobby was enjoying his discoveries and sharing them with Jimmy and anyone else that would listen.

Jimmy just smiled. He was taking it all in as well, but silently. He was thinking about what lay ahead and about Katie. He too, was excited about their upcoming adventure, but was much quieter and more reserved than his friend. Waynesville, Missouri was not only a new town in a different state. It was in a different world.

As the bus approached the military installation, the chatter began to die down. They were greeted by a large sign which read in bold letters, 'Welcome to Fort Leonard Wood, Home of the 5th Engineer Battalion.' Suddenly, it seemed, the reality of what they were about to experience, was upon them.

Once their bus was waved through by the gate guard, the chatter resumed. Jimmy and Bobby and the other passengers were now paying close attention to what seemed like hundreds of squads of soldiers marching in formation throughout their route. Many of them were chanting various sing-song phrases in unison with their marches and their squad leaders' commands. Others were marching to the repetitious commands. '*Your left, your left, your left, right, left.*

"Sounds like every group has their own song," Bobby stated. "I wonder what ours will be." He was impressed at the sounds of the marching soldiers' heels clicking in unison to the cadence of their squad leaders. "Listen." he continued. "Listen to how all their boots hit the ground at the very same time. It sounds like a big rubber mallet hitting a tree stump. I don't think our high school band ever sounded like that. I wonder how long it took them to be able to march like that?" Bobby asked to no one in particular.

Little did he know he would soon learn that it doesn't take long!

As the bus reached its destination, they were told to keep their seats. Within minutes, a trim, rough looking man dressed in starched military fatigues and a clipboard entered the bus and began to bark instructions to the newly inducted passengers. He introduced himself simply as 'Drill Sergeant'. He was not to be called Sir, or Mister, or Son of a Bitch, he said. Just 'Drill Sergeant.'

At the conclusion of his instructions, he asked in an emphatic tone, "Is that clear?" Hearing a chorus of mumbled responses, he asked again, this time with a little more emphasis, "You are now in the Army. And in the Army, there is no room for confusion. So, I'll ask again, Is that CLEAR???"

This time, he got his desired response . . . a more emphatic chorus of, "Yes, Drill Sergeant!"

With that, the passengers were told to disembark the bus and line up in formation as instructed. Some of the passengers required a little more instruction than others. In their nervous efforts to comply with their instructions, they were stepping all over each other. They were dressed in all manner of civilian clothing and still holding on to the travel bags they brought with them. Given the number of personnel around them who were dressed in military uniforms, the ragged busload of characters looked glaringly out of place. That would soon change.

In a matter of hours, Jimmy and Bobby were once again standing at attention in formation with their fellow passengers. Only this time, their heads were shaved, their civilian clothes were gone, and they were once again being addressed by the Drill Sergeant that seemed to constantly be in a bad mood! "Our recruiter back in Indiana was much nicer than this guy'" Bobby thought to himself as the instructor barked out his instructions.

This was not going quite how their recruiter back in Indiana said it would. They would have that same thought on multiple occasions before their basic training came to an end.

So here they were. In a different world, being yelled at by a man they already disliked, before they've even had a chance to do something wrong. Like on the bus coming in, Jimmy and Bobby were in different rows of their new Company formation. Bobby was upfront; Jimmy was two rows back. They were not arm in arm like when they were in little league, or when they were being yelled at by their football coach. This felt like some sort of out-of-body experience and knew they would have to rely on each other like never before.

Despite not knowing what was in store for them, they were kind of giddy and actually enjoying the experience. There was something macho about being tested, about being physically pushed to their limits. They were also learning it would be a test of endurance. Could they respond physically to the challenges that were being thrown at them, all while being verbally abused in the process? They both believed they could. It was sort of like summer football camp. They would make this a contest, like two kids playing army. Except this really was the Army and the stakes would be much higher.

They were immediately thrown into a series of physically strenuous activities. Jimmy responded well to each of them. He was in excellent physical condition and responded well to every drill. Bobby also liked challenges, but he was not quite the physical specimen his friend was. Where Jimmy was the trim, athletic quarterback, Bobby was the big, slightly overweight offensive lineman. He had a little more of a struggle with the physical drills.

One of the drills, for example, required you to carry a buddy over your shoulder for 40 yards. You were supposed to match up with someone your own size making it equally hard for each soldier. Even though Bobby was 30 pounds heavier than Jimmy, they teamed up to make it work, just like they always have done. Basic training did not allow the two to support one another the way they had done in the past, but any time Jimmy could be there for his friend, he was there.

After completing one of the drills, the squad was back in formation. The Drill Sergeant was silently pacing up and down the lines, studying his new recruits. When he came to Bobby, he paused to take a closer look. He inched up close to Bobby's face, so close that the brim of his hat was touching Bobby's face.

With somewhat of a smirk on his face, the instructor said, "You are a big boy, aren't you soldier. You look big and strong boy, you look like I could ride you as a tank. You're probably about as smart as a tank, too. I'll just call you 'Baby Tank.' Is that alright with you, boy? I'll just call you a baby tank who ain't got no rank. Sounds like a song, don't it Baby

Tank. Kind of fitting, too. A big old dumb tank trying to be a soldier, but ain't got no rank. Well, Baby Tank, for the next eight weeks, I'm gonna be riding you like a tank. You got me Baby Tank?"

The sergeant didn't let up. "You don't mind if I call you 'Baby Tank' now do you? Is that OK with you? I mean, I won't hurt your feelings if I call you Baby Tank, will I?" Not giving Bowers a chance to respond, the Drill Sergeant replies to his own question, "I frankly could give a rat's ass if you mind or not, Baby Tank".

"Yes, Drill Sergeant.", Bobby said, looking straight ahead and doing his best not to appear nervous.

All this time, Jimmy is cracking up, trying to keep a straight face as his friend is being put through the wringer. He knows any moment, he could be the subject of the Sergeant's ridicule, but he wasn't through Bobby just yet. Continuing, he asked Bobby, "Just, how much do you weigh, Baby Tank?"

"About 235 lbs., Drill Sergeant" Bobby responded.

"235?", the instructor repeated!!! "Yeah, well when I'm done with you, Baby Tank, you'll be lucky if you weigh *one* thirty-five. Can you sing, Baby Tank?" The sergeant seemed to be taking great pleasure in repeating the new nickname he had given Bobby.

"Not very well." Bobby responded, not knowing what this particular line of questioning had to do with losing weight.

"Well, I'm gonna start by teaching you how to sing, Baby Tank," the sergeant continued. "I'm gonna make you famous. Now, you pick up that pack, put it over your head and run around this entire company singing,

'Rub Dub Clank, Clank,
I'm a big old baby tank'

"SING Baby Tank! And I better be able to hear you!"

Bobby picked up his pack and proceeded as ordered, and every time he would venture beyond the Drill Sergeant's field of vision, Bobby would hear him scream, "I can't hear you, Baby Tank, Louder!"

Jimmy was silently enjoying this to the high heavens. Though he knew better than to show it, inside he was cracking up. Doing everything he could do to suppress his laughter, he was hysterical at the sight of his friend being tormented by the Instructor. Somehow, he managed to keep a straight face. He was just glad it was not him being ridiculed and abused in front of the entire squad. He still had to strain to suppress his laughter, however, every time he heard Bobby screaming, "Rub Dub Clank, Clank, I'm a big old baby tank."

Throughout basic training, that became a running joke. Every time Jimmy and Bobby had some down time, somewhere in the conversation Jimmy would say "Wait. What? I can't hear you, Baby Tank." It was just like when they were back in little league, laughing and ridiculing each other, when they would end up wrestling one another on the floor.

Then one night late into basic training, the worm turned. It was Jimmy's turn in the barrel.

It was after 'lights out' and he was caught sneaking into the Dayroom where he bought a Powerhouse candy bar out of the vending machine. The drill sergeant, ever vigilant of his troops seemingly 24 hours a day, was in the barracks at the time, and caught Jimmy in the act. 'Busted!!!', so Jimmy thought. He was shocked and totally unprepared for the sergeant's reaction, however.

In stark contrast to his normal demeanor, the sergeant was very calm and almost nice about it. He didn't seem upset at all. "Don't worry about it Wrann. It's late. Just give me the candy bar and go back to bed."

"Whew," Jimmy thought. He had dodged a bullet on that one. "That was a lot different than I expected," he thought to himself as he got back into his bunk. "Maybe the Drill Sergeant has a heart after all," he thought. He went to sleep that night thankful that he was in the clear.

The next morning, bright and early as the squad assembled into formation, the Company Commander was there with the Drill Sergeant and it was he that called the squad to attention. After the typical "Company, ten*HUT*", he then yelled, "Private Wrann. Front and center!"

"Oh shit, what is this about?" Jimmy thought to himself as he ran to the front of the company. "Sir, Private Wrann reporting Sir." He had remembered from the group's very first orientation, when you are addressing an officer you always begin and end with "Sir." However, he forgot another part of that protocol. It began to downhill fast from there.

His Drill Sergeant was standing right next to the Commanding officer and Jimmy, still wondering why he had been summoned, made the mistake of glancing over at his sergeant, as if he might get some clue. That's all the sergeant needed.

"Are you looking at me, Boy?" screamed the Drill Sergeant. In a complete turn-about from his mild reaction last night, the sergeant now seemed loaded for bear. "You piece of shit, you looked at me, didn't you?"

Jimmy quickly remembered that lesson from the first day they arrived, but in his nervousness, he slipped up. He made eye contact with the Drill Sergeant, violating a cardinal rule of boot camp. It didn't stop there. That was just the beginning of what would become a downward spiral. In responding to his Drill Sergeant's question, Jimmy nervously replied, "No Sir!"

Going from bad to worse, he then violated a second cardinal rule. Officers are called Sir! Enlisted men are called by their rank. So, in this situation, the Commanding Officer would be called Sir, but the Drill Sergeant would be called, as he so plainly informed them on the bus that day, 'Drill Sergeant.'

"What did you call me, you worthless piece of shit?" screamed the Drill Sergeant, drawing even closer to Jimmy's face. "Do you see any bars on me, soldier?"

Now, as if he were foaming at the mouth like a mad pit bull, his face about 2 inches from Jimmy's, spitting as he continued his tirade. Pointing to the chevrons on his sleeve, the sergeant said, "You see these, pretty boy. This is the only thing I better EVER hear out of your mouth! Do you understand me, pretty boy?"

Jimmy, mustering up his best game-face, trying to appear unfazed by his sergeant. "Yes, Si . . . , Drill Sergeant." He almost made the same mistake *again* before he sucked the 'sir' back into his mouth. The sergeant paused, continuing his up-close-and-personal inspection of Jimmy's face. Jimmy stood, stiff as a board, looking straight ahead.

After what seemed like an eternity, thinking this might be the end of the spectacle, he then gave an ever-so-fleeting glimpse toward his instructor to see if his sergeant was finished.

That little glance, however, that took no longer than a blip on a radar screen, launched the Drill Sergeant into whole new orbit of what he called 'whoop ass.' Now, he was even more animated than before.

"You just can't follow simple instructions, can you, Pretty Boy!" The sergeant got even closer to Jimmy's face. "You must like me because you obviously can't keep your eyes off me. Am I your type, Pretty Boy? Are you gettin' sweet on me? Is that it? Well, you better find yourself another boyfriend, Pretty Boy, 'cause if I catch you looking at me again, your ass will be mine. And not the way you want it!"

By this time, mercifully, the Company Commander intervened. He said to his sergeant, "Relax Drill Sergeant. You know basic is almost over and I want these men to remember me as a kind and gentle man." Though Jimmy was liking what he was hearing, that last part seemed a little sarcastic. Then he turned to Jimmy.

"So Private Wrann," the Commander continued, "you wanted this candy bar so bad last night that you were willing to get up after lights out to get it. And we want you to have it. So, go ahead, Private. Go ahead and eat this Powerhouse candy bar."

Things were happening so fast that Jimmy's head was now spinning, but he was now figuring out that this was all about last night. He was being punished for what he thought he had gotten away with! Thinking how calm and understanding the sergeant had been at the time, he was being presented that same candy bar by the Company Commander, with what seemed like a direct order.

"So, THAT's what this is all about.," Jimmy was thinking to himself, "That stinking candy bar!"

Assuming he was being directed to eat the candy bar right there on the spot, Jimmy cautiously took the candy bar from his Company Commander and said, "Sir, yes Sir." What he wanted to eat last night, he was now being ordered to eat in the presence of the entire Company. Jimmy slowly began to unwrap the Powerhouse candy bar, but then realized the Drill Sergeant wasn't done with him yet.

"Did you hear the Commander say anything about unwrapping it, Pretty Boy? I don't think I heard him say a fucking thing about unwrapping it soldier. He just said *eat* it!" Now realizing he was being ordered to eat the candy bar AND it's wrapping, Jimmy hesitantly bit into the Powerhouse candy bar, complete with paper and cardboard wrapping. He chewed and chewed, trying to dissolve the collection of chocolate, paper and cardboard, but the more he chewed, the bigger it seemed to get in his mouth.

This time, it was Jimmy's turn to catch the crap, Bobby thought to himself, as he quietly witnessed his friend being ridiculed and dressed down in front of the Company. This time, it was Bobby's turn to be the observer and not the victim of what they were discovering was the typical type of harassing treatment everyone endures at some point during their military boot camp experience.

As Jimmy continued his efforts to swallow each bite of his morning concoction, he slowly lowered his hand with a portion of the bar still uneaten. The Drill Sergeant was quick to ask in his familiar sinister voice, "You think you're done, Pretty Boy? UMM *UH*, that Powerhouse bar must be good. Go ahead, Pretty Boy, finish it up." Jimmy grimaced and swallowed the remainder of the candy bar in one piece, contorting his face as it went down. Uncertain of how his digestive system was going to react to what he had just consumed, Jimmy was ordered back into formation.

Now, each of the two friends had been on the receiving end of boot camp harassment. And both had survived. By day, basic training was a combination of harassment, classes, physical drills, and military training, all under stressful conditions. By night, however, it was a chance to relax and engage in razzing and adolescent horseplay that would be typical of a bunch of guys who had been thrown together from all parts of the country. Over this period of weeks, complete strangers would become lifelong friends, all being subjected to equal opportunity harassment. Rednecks with ghetto types; hillbillies with Hispanics; it was a complete melting pot.

No matter what they endured during the day, at night they would sit together telling jokes, singing songs, and talking about life back home.

When they first arrived for basic training, the common observation was how different everyone was. The more time they spent together, however, they began to realize how much alike they were.

Some were from the country; some were from the city; and some, like Jimmy and Bobby, came from the heartland. Some were white; some were black; and some were Hispanic. Some liked country and western music, while others liked rock and roll. The blacks loved their blues or Motown, as did several others in the barracks, as Motown was becoming mainstream.

Under ordinary circumstances, very few of these recruits would have been friends or would have even acknowledged each other. Under these circumstances, however, this collection of complete strangers slowly became their own band of brothers.

In the evenings, while polishing boots and preparing for the next day's activities, it was not uncommon to tell jokes, tell stories of home and even break out in song. One night as a Temptations song was blaring on the radio, several of the recruits began to sing along with the music, complete with the hand gestures and choreographed steps the group had become famous for. Jimmy and Bobby were cheering them on and clapping their hands to the music when Jimmy decided to join in.

As Jimmy tried to blend in with the group, they all stopped singing. One of them looked at Jimmy and exclaimed, "Are you kidding me? That's how come white folks get such a bad reputation, man! That's *terrible,* man." The others laughed and continued clapping to the music. Jimmy reverted back to singing quietly to himself.

In the military you grow very close with the people you serve with, and this group was no exception . . . They were indeed becoming the buddies they would need to be to survive the journey that lay ahead of them. Though they knew it paled in comparison to the closeness that the two them and Katie shared, Jimmy and Bobby and the rest of their company had created a bond.

"Maybe that's what it's all about." exclaimed one of the recruits one evening, as they were sitting around in the barracks. "They treat us like crap to force us to join together against the man." he continued. "Maybe that's their idea of team building." he said.

"They sure as hell have a funny way of team building," another responded.

'Yeah, Jimmy thought to himself as he listened to the conversation. 'Maybe that's what all this is about.'

Through it all, Jimmy and Bobby's conversations invariably would always go back to Black Oak and Katie. "Hey Baby Tank, I can't wait to tell Katie about your singing lesson." Bobby would then counter, "Hey, Pretty Boy, I can't wait to tell her about your favorite late-night snack. How was that Power bar, by the way? It seemed to really go down well."

Oh, how they missed Katie. It felt so strange going through this extraordinary experience together without having their friend with them. How could they ever explain it all? After eight weeks of putting up with all they endured in Basic Training, there was more to do before they would see her or their families. Basic training was followed by what the Army called Advanced Individual Training or 'AIT.'.

THEN, they would get go home on leave before embarking on their permanent assignment. Knowing what that would be, they were looking forward to enjoying those precious 30 days back home before heading 'across the pond.'

Joining the Army on the Buddy System, Jimmy and Bobby were assured to serve together and then get to go home together. However, they were assigned to different jobs (MOS's or Military Occupation Specialties, in military lingo), which meant they would go to different bases for their advanced training.

Upon graduation from boot camp, Jimmy was assigned to Fort Eustis Virginia to be trained as a crew chief/door gunner on a UH-1H helicopter. He was excited about his assignment and the next round of training. Bobby was given a different job, however. His was what most people think of when they think of the Army. He would be an Infantryman . . . a 'Grunt.' He would be fighting in the trenches, on the front lines. His was a very different form of advanced training, and in a different location.

As the conflict in Southeast Asia continued to escalate, the Army needed grunts more than anything. And now, Bobby would become one.

Jimmy and Bobby were clear about what was at stake and what their future would be. Instead of waiting to be told, they decided to volunteer for Vietnam. It was a country they knew nothing about and, despite the training they had received, they still didn't fully understand why the U.S. was even there. They knew it was about stemming the rising tide of communism, and both assumed our government knew what they were doing. So, the lifelong friends were planning to do their part.

*"We must always believe in three things. We must never lose faith in the Lord, our country, or our families. If we can keep these beliefs alive, and be there for each other, then we will all survive this and get back home."*

# CHAPTER 7

## Till Death Due Us Part

AFTER THEIR AIT was completed, Jimmy and Bobby received thirty days leave before they would depart for Vietnam. Having completed their training in different locations, the reunion was as much for the two of them as it was with Katie and their families.

When the three of them got together, Katie often felt like the odd man out listening to Jimmy and Bobby recount their experiences in their various training programs. The conversations were riddled with the two of them constantly saying things like, 'Remember the time we had to complete that obstacle course in the rain? Or, 'Remember that short Puerto Rican kid who kept bragging about his girlfriend.' Looking at Katie, their discussions frequently ended with, 'You shoulda been there.'

Katie obviously had not been there, and the more they talked, the more she realized how much she missed the times the three of them had together. The more she also realized how much she missed Jimmy.

"I really missed you guys'" she blurted out during one of their times together. "And I sure missed you, Pretty Boy!" she said to Jimmy, alluding to the story they had shared about Jimmy and his candy bar episode. "You guys have been away for less than six months, and it felt like forever. I don't know what I'll do for a whole year. I may have to send you a case of Powerhouse candy bars when you get to Vietnam just so you'll remember who I am" she laughed. "That may be your most favorite thing to remember me by when you're over there."

"I'll tell you what he *really* needs to have when he's over there," Bobby responded. "He needs to have a wedding ring! *That's* what he needs to have" he repeated.

Jimmy and Katie laughed. They truly loved each other and were both struggling with the reality of being away from each other for so long. But marriage? They were kids for crying out loud.

"I'm serious" Bobby persisted. "You both love each other and who knows what our lives will be like in another year. Why wait?"

In his own subtle and innocent way, Bobby had a gift for stating the obvious. Jimmy and Bobby now knew a little more about Vietnam and the uncertainty of their futures. The more they kicked around the idea, the more it went from being ludicrous, to becoming, "Why not?"

In the same manner and in the very same room where they were months ago when Jimmy decided to go into the Army with his friend, they came to an even more profound decision. Jimmy looked at Katie and without saying a word, he raised his eyebrows, as if to say, "Whadda you think?"

In the same non-verbal fashion, Katie responded, as if to say, "I'm ready if you're ready!" Jimmy broke through the momentary all the body language to make sure she was saying the same thing he was saying, "You're SERIOUS?"

"I am if you are" Katie responded.

Watching the entire verbal and non-verbal exchange happening in front of him, Bobby excitedly jumped out of his chair as if he had just discovered a snake in his chair and blurted out, "I think I just heard a wedding proposal. Did I?"

"You did", Jimmy responded.

"Yes, you did," Katie confirmed.

"Then it's agreed" Bobby said. "Then, let's get to work. We've got a lot to do and not much time." Bobby was engineering this as if he were the parent of the bride or something.

This was déjà vu, all over again. The threesome had made the second life-altering decision since graduating from high school, and they now had a second surprise announcement to make to their parents less than a year after their first surprise announcement.

The world was spinning and so were the lives of the three best friends. They had less than 30 days to arrange and consummate a marriage that had been years in the making. After kissing Jimmy like she never had before, Katie scrambled to get her things together to leave. "I've got things to do" she said. "I've got to start by telling my parents. I am sooo happy" she said as she rushed out the door.

Jimmy had to do the same thing. When he broke the news to his parents, his mother once again, predictably, began to cry. The last time Jimmy had a surprise announcement, she cried tears of fear and apprehension. This time, they were tears of joy. She had waiting for this day for a long time. She was just surprised at the suddenness of the decision.

Jimmy's father was also happy. He was even happier when Jimmy told him Bobby had agreed to be his best man in the hastily arranged ceremony. It was only fitting. From little league to marriage, the three amigos would be together.

"He has grown up quickly," Jimmy's father said to his wife as their son walked out the door to meet his future bride to plan their wedding. "From high school star quarterback, to the Army, and now this, all inside a few months."

"I'm nervous," his wife responded.

"Yeah, me too." he said. "But they're not kids anymore."

"I miss those days" she said, gazing out the kitchen window, at nothing in particular.

The hastily arranged plans fell into place. It would be an outdoor wedding held in the town park. It would be informal. Through telephone and word-of-mouth invitations the entire town was invited. There would be no RSVP's, no gifts, no dressing up. This would be a come-as- you-are event to celebrate the wedding of the town's favorite sweethearts, with their best friend right beside them. It was if this would be a marriage of a threesome!

In many ways, it was.

They decided that all three, the bride, groom, and the best man, would speak during the reciting of the vows. Jimmy, and Bobby as his best man, were dressed in their Army Class A uniforms, proudly displaying their first ribbon on their chests, which they received for completing their training.

Katie was wearing the same wedding dress her mother wore some twenty-five years earlier. She had prepared her wedding vows and had practiced them hundreds of times in the privacy of her bedroom. Now, she would say them for real in front of hundreds of onlookers.

After dozens of write's and re-writes, Jimmy was prepared with his vows, as well.

Katie went first. The chatter of the crowd had reached a dull roar by the time the ceremony commenced, but as Katie began to speak, it drew silent, the way an Army barracks does when the Company Commander walks in. The crowd strained to hear the nervous bride. Both Katie and Jimmy's mothers were already in tears.

"I, Katie Wrann, pledge to you my husband Jimmy Wrann, and to my best friend Bobby Bowers, that for better or for worse, in sickness and in health, I will always be there for you." She said the name, Katie *Wrann* out loud in public for the very first time. It felt good. It felt good to Jimmy as well. He would go next.

"To my beautiful wife, Katie Wrann, I pledge to be there for you under whatever circumstances God presents us. For better or worse, for richer or poorer, in sickness and in health, and in peace and in war, I, Jimmy Wrann will love, cherish and protect you until the end of my life." He then looked out into the audience and directly at Katie's Mom and Dad.

"And, to you, Mr. and Mrs. Hankins. Thank you for welcoming me into your and your daughter's life. With the gift you've given me, I pledge to love, honor, cherish and protect your daughter until my dying breath. She will be loved and honored just as you have always hoped she would be."

"And finally, to the best friend anyone could ask for." Jimmy looked at Bobby. "Bobby Bowers, you have been there for Katie and me just as we have for each other. And I thank you from the bottom of my heart. And for that, I pledge to do the same for you."

Jimmy turned back to Katie. They were beaming as they looked into each other's eyes, briefly forgetting Bobby was to speak also. They then looked at their friend who was already holding back tears. He cleared his throat as he nervously prepared to speak.

"To the new Mr. and Mrs. Jimmy Wrann," he began. "To the best pitcher I have ever caught, and to the prettiest girl I have ever seen, I Bobby Bowers pledge to each of you that for better or worse, for richer or poorer, in sickness and in health, I will always be there for you."

Trying to maintain his composure, even the presiding pastor was a little choked up. He was well acquainted with Jimmy, Katie, Bobby and their families, and turned to the adoring crowd, and said, "Ladies and Gentlemen. I present to you Mr. and Mrs. Jimmy Wrann, AND their best man, loyal overseer and guard dog, Mr. Bobby Bowers."

Each of them then took a glass, arranged for them on a small table for the occasion, raised it to the onlookers, and said nervously, naively, yet defiantly, the words that would haunt them more than they could ever imagine. "Till death *due* us part."

The presiding pastor announced to the assembled crowd, "And now, we welcome you all to join us in the celebration of this blessed event with the food and festivities that have been arranged. Let the celebration commence!"

The disc jockey from the local radio station had positioned the station's mobile unit next to the pavilion in the park to provide music for the occasion and assumed the master of ceremonies duties for the remainder of the occasion. He encouraged everyone to enjoy the food that was there before the partying began.

The couple's parents and townsfolks had hastily arranged for a picnic styled collection of fried chicken, potato salad, beans, macaroni, sandwich fixings and desserts. A group of cafeteria-styled tables covered in white cloths served as their buffet. It was like a carry-over from the town's 4th of July picnic, which had been celebrated weeks earlier.

Katie and Jimmy did not eat. They were too consumed with the hugs, kisses and well-wishes that followed the ceremony. Bobby, however, didn't hesitate to find his way into the buffet line. Having not eaten before the ceremony, for fear of 'losing his lunch', he was starving. Jimmy was reminded of an occasion during basic training when Bobby did, in fact, lose his lunch after an endurance run.

After the guests had had a chance to get their food and drink, the radio personality wasted no time in kicking off the festivities. "Ladies and Gentlemen. Please join me in welcoming to the dance floor to have their first dance as bride and groom, our guests of honor, Mr. and Mrs. Jimmy Wrann."

As the crowd applauded and parted to allow the newlyweds access to the dance floor, the sounds of Elvis began to flood the pavilion, with his classic, 'I Can't Help Falling in Love With You.'

Jimmy was more agile on the football field and basketball court than he was on the dance floor, but he was geared up for this special occasion. With their arms wrapped around each other's waists and their heads resting on each other's shoulder, they sank into the music as if there was no one else there. Other than repeating to each other, 'I love you' as they danced, the two were mostly silent in their solitude, reflecting on the events of the day. As they sway back and forth in each other's arms, the crowd watched silently and glowingly as the Wrann's celebrated their first dance together.

About half way through the dance, Katie began to search for Bobby, and finally spotting him somewhat hidden by the crowd with tears in his eyes. With Katie being Katie, she thought it only appropriate to have their best friend with them on the dance floor. She sprinted to him and grabbed him by the hand and then returned to her husband. The three friends finished the song with Katie's face buried in the chests of the two men she loved most in the world.

Bobby felt a little silly being on the dance floor with another guy, but this moment seemed to block out any self-consciousness the three of them may have felt. For Katie, this was a dream come true. For Jimmy and Bobby, they were swept away by the specialness of the occasion . . . three friends forever, til death due us part! They laughed and danced as if they were the only three people in the world.

As they held each other on the dance floor, Katie's Mom whispered to all 3 sets of parents, "My God . . . these kids really and truly love each other, don't they!"

Bobby's Dad agreed, "I am pretty sure they would die for each other." He thought back to the vows the three made to each other an hour ago, 'Till Death Due us part.' Little did he know just how prophetic those words would become.

When the song came to an end, the disc jockey immediately went into another wedding favorite, Bobby Vinton's 'You Are my Special Angel' and asked Katie to remain on the floor to be joined by her father for the traditional Father-Daughter dance. As the two passed on the dance floor, Mr. Hankins jokingly said to Jimmy, "Mind if I have a last dance with my little girl before you take her away from me.

Approaching his daughter, he said, "Remember how I taught you to dance when you were a little girl?" Now nodding, laughing and crying all at the same time, as if overtaken by the memory, she immediately knew what to do. She removed her shoes and placed her feet on her father's shoes just as they had done since she was a little girl. She followed as he glided the two of them around the floor, swept away by the moment and the music.

The more they danced, the more they laughed, and the more Katie began to swing back into 'Katie' mode. She was Daddy's little girl and had just married the man she had dreamt of marrying since grammar school. But she was also the same spunky, outgoing girl she always was. Not bound by convention or tradition, this was Katie's night and there would be nothing conventional about it.

At Katie's urging, the two began to dance toward Jimmy. Seeing the two headed his way, Jimmy began moving toward Katie and her father. But as he got within an arm's length, he stopped, and dropped down to one knee as a knight would to a queen and looked directly at Katie's father, as if he were asking for her hand in marriage. "Mr. Hankins, I meant every word I said earlier. Nothing within my power will come between me and your daughter. I will love her til 'death due us part."

With her head resting on her father's chest and tears in her eyes, Katie listened to the emotional exchange between the two men. Her grip on her father's hand grew tighter as she listened. As Jimmy finished and began to rise, Katie was still holding her father's hand in one hand and twirled around and reached out to Jimmy with her other hand.

Her father silently mouthed to his new son-in-law, "Take care of her" and then to the two of them, "I love you." With that he gently bowed to the two of them and moved to rejoin the crowd.

She was now fully in the grasp of her new husband. The rite of passage was complete.

With that the music of The Spencer Davis Group's, 'Gimme Some Loving' began to blare over the speakers, and the DJ proclaimed, "OK, let's get this party started!"

The music was loud and upbeat, and swaying to the rhythmic sounds, Jimmy picked up his new bride and began swirling her around the floor. The crowd quickly joined in. Bobby, no longer bound by the nervousness of the earlier wedding ceremony, was leading the pack. The emotions of the day, combined with the music and alcohol, put him in a jovial mood. With the moves and rhythms of the oversized, not-too-agile, white guy he was, he began a conga line around the dance floor. Jimmy and Katie, along with what seemed like the entire town, joined in.

As the party continued into the evening, Jimmy, Katie and Bobby managed to sneak off for a private moment, retreating to the edge of the park to take a break from the non-stop celebrations. They were joined by the bright, yellowish moon that was rising over the small lake. The three quietly contemplated the day's events and the uncertainty of their future. Katie was thinking to herself, 'Everything is perfect. This has to be what love is . . . If only it could stay like this forever . . . Thank you God. . . . Thank you for everything you have given us.' Standing in between her two friends with her arms around each, she squeezes both.

With the celebration winding down, the disc jockey announced the last song. Just as he had done with the first song of the evening, his selection was all too appropriate, especially for the bride and groom and their friend. The sounds of Peter, Paul and Mary began to ring through the speakers, 'Well, my bags are packed, I'm ready to go . . . ' As the lyrics continued to the song, 'I'm Leaving on a Jet Plane', Jimmy looked at his new bride, then at his friend. They were silent. They knew all too well the significance of the lyrics. Still arm-in-arm, they hugged each other ever more tightly as they sang along to the lyrics, 'I don't know when I'll be back again.'

As the crowd began to disperse, they rejoined the party to say their goodbyes. Jimmy and Katie again hugged their parents and began to mingle throughout the crowd, thanking them for coming and receiving congratulatory hugs and well wishes. One of the town folks said to the couple, "I've been waiting for this day for a long time. I just didn't realize it would happen so soon!" Another asked Bobby, "OK, now when are *you* getting married?" He responded playfully and with the effects of the alcohol evident in his speech, "Heck, I can't get married. I have to go fight a war and watch after these two."

As the newlyweds made their way through the crowd of well-wishers, Katie continued to think silently, 'We really did this. We really did it. And I'm going to have to let him go in a matter of days!'

She thought of the unfairness of it all.

After the day's events, Katie and Jimmy were exhausted. The ceremony itself took less than twenty minutes, but the eating, talking, and partying with the town folks lasted over four hours. Eventually the newlyweds left the festivities to go to Jimmy's house to thank his parents for their support and all they had done. They then went to Katie's house to express the same to her parents.

Exhilarated, exhausted and still reeling in amazement at what they had actually done, they were now finally alone. Jimmy's father had reserved a suite for that evening for his son and new daughter-in-law at the local Holiday Inn. After spending hours with well-wishers and their families, the newlywed couple settled in for their wedding night.

These two had been best friends since childhood. They knew each other's every move. They completed each other's sentences. They knew each other's biases, fears, aspirations and dreams. Yet on this evening, they were both nervous, unsure of exactly how to proceed. Somehow, as much as they knew each other and had been intimate with each other, this evening felt different.

They were no longer high schoolers that occasionally made out in their parent's living rooms when they could steal a few moments alone. Nor, were they the two virgin lovers that found one another after the pick-up basketball game in Griffith Park that day. They were Mr. and Mrs. Jimmy Wrann. They were married. And even if they only had days together before Jimmy would have to depart for Vietnam, they were *together*, til death due us part!

After finally eating a specially prepared room service dinner, the two made their way to the bed as husband and wife for the first time. Katie, still reflecting on the day's events and what was to come, had mixed emotions as they held each other. She was a combination of joyful, tearful and aroused at the prospects of making love to her new husband whom she concluded was decidedly more fit and muscular from the effects of his military training.

Jimmy had momentarily forgotten about the emotions of the evening. He was just plain aroused!

The two made passionate love throughout the evening, interrupted only by cat naps and times of quiet reflection. There were long moments where they simply stared at the ceiling, contemplating the whirlwind of events since they were high school sweethearts, and what lay ahead. There were questions, many, many questions. 'What if . . . ?' What would you want me to do if . . . ?' There were hundreds of questions and issues that lingered in their minds, but so few answers.

"All we have is tonight and our love and dedication for each other. The rest will take care of itself" Jimmy said.

"And Bobby" Katie said.

"What?" Jimmy said, still silently consumed by all the unanswered questions.

"And Bobby" Katie reminded him. "We have each other, *AND* Bobby."

"Right" Jimmy responded. "Thank God for Bobby." With that, he pulled Katie to him and the two, once again, made love.

Little did they know that on this evening, the couple would conceive a child. On this, their wedding day, a day that was clearly the most eventful day in either of their lives, it would become even more meaningful with the conception of a baby. That baby would be a son, born at a time when both his father and God Father would be fighting in that war.

His name? Jimmy Wrann of course, but he would lovingly be called Little Jim in honor of his father.

"We must always believe in three things. We must never lose faith in the Lord, our country, or our families. If we can keep these beliefs alive, and be there for each other, then we will all survive this and get back home."

# CHAPTER 8

# Vietnam

VIETNAM IS BEYOND belief. As soon as Jimmy and Bobby arrived in the country, they would quickly learn, soldiers in Vietnam were concerned about one thing... survival! They had a twelve-month tour of duty in a war-torn land that was about as far from home as they could get. They just wanted to do their twelve months and get home! Survive, and in the process, do what they could to help their country win a war. Those were their priorities, in that order.

The indoctrination into their new home went quickly for the two friends. They were separated into their respective units. Jimmy's was a helicopter company in Pleiku whose assignments were combat assaults, resupply missions, emergency medivac and whatever else the troops might need. Bobby, being a 'grunt', was assigned to a unit that would be fighting in those battle situations on the ground.

For the soldiers, including Jimmy and Bobby, this was the same war, but being fought from two entirely different perspectives. It was like a tale of two cities. From the air, as a helicopter gunner and Crew Chief, Jimmy saw the beauty of the land... the water falls, the beautiful beaches, the tropical forests and the lush green jungles. From the air it had the beauty of a vacation getaway. Also, when the helicopter crews returned their base camps from a mission, they had hot meals and their own bunks to sleep in. That is, if they were lucky enough to make it back to their base. Jimmy had heard that the life expectancy of a door gunner during a fire fight is 19 seconds... 19 seconds!

For Bobby, the landscape and the living conditions were quite different. That beautiful landscape Jimmy saw from the air was full of many things that could kill you. Besides the enemy soldiers, those lush green jungles brought with them torrential rains, unbearable heat, leeches, bugs and all sorts of deadly wildlife. From elephants to many species of reptiles, some as big as a motorcycle, and poisonous snakes that can kill humans with a single bite.

One of the most feared was the bamboo viper, or as the locals called them, the Step and a Half. It was said that if you were bitten by this small green snake, you would be dead in about a step and a half.

Besides the constant threat of the enemy, soldiers learned quickly about the deadly wildlife in the Vietnamese jungles. As one soldier with a deep southern drawl reminded Bobby, "If one don't get you, chances are, the other one will."

The living conditions of the ground forces were no better. The food the grunts ate were rations that came from a can. Theirs was a steady diet of some sort of spam-like concoction that was designed to provide all the vitamins and minerals one would need to survive in bivouac conditions (military jargon for camping out), but it tasted like stale porridge or oatmeal that had gone bad. If anything positive would come from this experience, Bobby surmised, he was bound to lose weight during the ordeal.

Their sleeping conditions were about as good as their food, especially in the rainy seasons. Their 'bed' was sleeping on the ground under a poncho during the dark and raining nights trying to stay dry, picking the leeches off whenever they could. Sleep was a rare commodity in the jungles of Vietnam.

But when push came to shove, who knew who had it worse? The grunts were constantly in the line of fire on the ground, yet when helicopters were flying in and out of battle zones, the helicopter's door gunner was a juicy target for enemy fire. The grunts would tell you they wouldn't trade places with the man in the door (door gunner) for anything because once the shit starts, they say, everyone is shooting at the man in the door, not the grunts on the ground.

Conversely, not too many door gunners wanted to be on the ground, living day in and day out in the jungles of Vietnam with all its dangers. The harsh reality was, both were living the horrors of war. Maybe those realities were from a different point of view, but they were the same harsh realities.

The fears and apprehensions of war are seldom talked about amongst the fellow soldiers in the trenches or in the camps back on base. Like in boot camp, there is a macho-like environment that the soldiers maintained with their fellow soldiers. Their conversations were seldom about their fears or their concerns, but more about the adventures and the near misses of the day. Who got hit . . . who almost got hit . . . how many enemy soldiers they took out . . . getting out of a fire zone by the skin of their teeth . . . that was the nature of the local chatter amongst GI's.

Fears, concerns, anxiety about the dangerous conditions they were living under? Those were topics reserved for the most intimate conversations with fellow troops. The letters they sent back home to their loved ones were self-assurances that they were OK, and not to worry.

If you want the truth about war, they told their families, don't rely on the press. The press, they said, was all about ratings, posting the most gruesome photographs or stories they could manufacture.

The stories of returning veterans, though at times exaggerated for affect, would reveal what was really happening. It was their stories that brought the realities of war home.

Jimmy and Bobby were quickly thrown into mix of those realities. They learned military strategy. They learned of the tactics being engaged by the enemy and the tactics to be used against that enemy. They learned the 'rules of engagement' . . . when you could fire at the enemy and when you shouldn't fire. They learned those rules of engagement were not always fair and practiced equally by both sides. They had rules. The enemy did not.

Theirs was not a conventional war. It was termed a 'guerrilla war.' There was no certainty about who the enemy was, or when and where they would show up. Vietnamese civilians could be harboring the enemy. They could be supporting the enemy. They could *be* the enemy. Under any conditions, there is a natural anxiety that accompanies war. But in an unconventional, guerrilla war situation, that anxiety gets heightened further.

Jimmy and Bobby were learning quickly. Sometimes, their best training was not occurring in the classrooms, but in the trenches with their fellow soldiers. In a matter of weeks, the two had transitioned from being green newcomers, to becoming hardened combatants. Life moves fast in a war zone, except when you're counting the days before you go home.

Once Jimmy was in a free fire zone, which meant if you received any type of fire you could automatically return fire without calling in for permission to return the fire. The helicopter was hovering just above the trees when they received fire from a small village in the distance. The small village appeared to contain maybe 7 or 8 hooch's (the thatched huts of Vietnamese villagers). Steve, the aircraft commander banked hard to the left to give Jimmy visibility to the village to return fire.

Once he started returning fire, Jimmy quickly realized that he could start the hooch's on fire with his tracers from the machine gun, which would quickly wipe out the entire village. In those frantic moments, that is exactly what he did. One hut went up in flames, quickly followed by a second. In a matter of minutes, the entire village was in flames.

Consumed by the adrenalin rush, he didn't let up. He unleashed as much carnage and destruction as he could. When all was said and done, Jimmy took out his little 35mm camera and took pictures of a village that once was home to a small group of Vietnamese peasants but now a rubble of burning ashes.

When he returned to base in Pleiku, he recounted his story to the old salty dogs that had returned before him. When Jimmy was done telling his story he was expecting some praise or "hell yea" from his fellow gunners. Instead one of the crew/chiefs that had been there longer than most said, "Sit down Wrann, let me tell you what you really did"

The VC (Viet Cong) from the North would go into the villages of South Vietnam to ambush or attack American and South Vietnamese soldiers. Since they were the only ones with weapons, the villagers were at their mercy and essentially held captive.

The VC, maybe 6 or 7 . . . maybe more, maybe less, would enter the village and disguise themselves as villagers and wait for opportunities to attack the enemy. When a patrol or helicopter entered the area, they would open fire.

The crew chief looked at Jimmy with a bleak, somber expression, and proceeded to lecture him on the realities of just what had happened.

"By the time you banked and began returning fire, the VC's were gone, leaving only those innocent villagers to die. So, did you do battle with the enemy today? Did you take it to the bad guys? No Wrann, you destroyed an entire village of people that only wanted peace. A village of innocent farmers, mothers, fathers and entire families. That is what you accomplished today.

With the force of a 2x4, Jimmy had just been broadsided with the realities of this war, and exactly how it was being fought. These were not toy soldiers and some game. These were innocent families being caught up and destroyed in some senseless war. And now, Jimmy was an active participant.

You could have heard a pin drop when the Crew Chief finished. Jimmy said nothing. He slowly stood up and began walking toward his bunk, hiding his tears from his fellow soldiers. He was a soldier in the ultimate macho environment. But he was also a human being coming to grips with where he was . . . and who he was . . . . a mere teenager who had been thrown into the ugliest of situations. It was perhaps at that moment when the realities of war began to change him, sucking from his soul all the love and innocence he once knew.

Back at his bunk, he began to argue with himself, finding any argument that would allow him to live with himself and what he had just done. 'This is war, right? Innocent people have to die, right? I was just doing my job, right? It wasn't my fault . . . was it?'

As much as he tried to rationalize his actions, the other side of his brain was speaking louder. 'What are you doing? If you were ordered to kill women and children, would you do it? Well, that's just what you're doing. Who are you, Jimmy Wrann? Would Katie even recognize you today?'

As he lay on his bunk and eventually began drifting off to sleep, the rationale that finally came to him, which would allow him to continue, was the thought, 'This is *where* I am, but it is not *who* I am.' By morning, a different man than he was the night before, he was back at it.

Like Jimmy, every soldier that set foot in Vietnam had to find ways to rationalize their presence in the country and doing the things they had to do in this war. Anything that reminded them of home and the sanity they once knew, diversions from music to sports, were many times the sources of their salvation.

Jimmy, being a natural leader, started a baseball team on the base at Pleiku. And spearheaded by his talent, they were pretty good. They would play, and usually beat, just about any team from other units that would play them. From impressive displays of talent and skill, to the amateurish bumbling's of players not so talented, the games were entertaining and competitive. They were just what was needed to the soldiers' minds off the hellish war they were experiencing.

Pranks and adolescent horseplay were another form of diversion.

In the military, and in Vietnam especially, there was an invisible wall between officers and the enlisted men. They certainly fought together but were not to engage one another socially. This rule allowed officers to issue orders and commands to enlisted men without being influenced by friendships or emotions. They slept and socialized separately, but they fought together.

In any type of combat situation, however, such as with a helicopter crew for example, that rule didn't apply. Officers and enlisted men alike flew together and trusted each other with their lives. They weren't concerned about what the government thought. In wartime, some of the tightest lifelong bonds occurred between the pilots and the enlisted men.

And as in combat, officers and enlisted men were equal opportunity pranksters when it came to what our parents described as, 'boys will be boys.'

One night, Steve Warren, Jimmy's pilot and an officer who bunked in the officer's barracks, threw a smoke grenade into Jimmy's hooch. It wasn't a danger to anyone, but it certainly sent Jimmy and his fellow enlisted men scrambling. Overall, the prank was taken in good humor, but could not be without some form of retribution for their superiors.

But, as they say, 'Payback is a bitch.'

A few nights later, Jimmy and his buddies returned the favor, and upped the ante in the process. At the opportune moment, around 2:30 in the morning, Jimmy threw a CS (training grenade) into the officers' barracks, and then he and his buddies sat back to enjoy watching their officers scrambling from a dead sleep.

However, he may have gone a little too far. A gas grenade can cause real problems and is not to be taken lightly. Twenty minutes into the practical joke, the base siren went off, causing everyone to have to fall out in full formation . . . at 3:00 o'clock in the morning. As everyone was struggling for fresh air to breath, there stood Jimmy Wrann in his underwear, wearing a government issued gas mask. Knowing nothing more serious had happened, he silently enjoying his retribution.

When it came to diversions, from the baseball games to the pranks and practical jokes, none was as effective or as enjoyable as daily mail call. Cards, letters and packages from home were the ultimate anecdote to the horrors and insanity the soldiers were living through on the other side of the world.

Katie, just as she said she would do, wrote religiously to Jimmy and Bobby, sending them packages including photos, non-perishable foods, and even Jimmy's favorite Powerhouse candy bars. Hers and the letters and packages from their parents were their only connection to what was going on at home. Who won the football game? Who got married? What was going on in the high school they were recently a part of? Though he could not physically be with his newlywed wife, he and Bobby both felt her presence and the presence of home through her almost-daily letters and packages.

However, little did Katie or anyone else back home know, Jimmy and Bobby were no longer the fresh-faced teenagers she said goodbye to weeks ago. By the end of their first month in the country, they had both been transformed from the happy-go-lucky local high school football heroes they were back in Indiana, into hardened, battle-worn soldiers, jaded by the harsh realities of a war they were just now beginning to understand.

For both of them, this was just the beginning.

# CHAPTER 9

## Dak Seang

BEING IN SEPARATE units, Jimmy and Bobby had lost contact with each other during their early days in Vietnam. They would soon discover, however, that all along they had been in the same area of operations (or 'AO').

In the Central Highlands area of the country, an increasingly deadly battle was taking place called Dak Seang. The remote base in the northern part of the Central Highlands had been under siege for its ninth consecutive day. They had already lost 9 helicopters during the siege and the occupants of the base were trapped. The US had F4 (Phantom fighter bombers) fixed wing aircraft bombing the surrounding mountains just to keep the VC from over running the camp.

Bobby was with the battalion that was at the heart of the siege, and on the verge of being overrun by the Viet Cong. They were outgunned and outmanned, and in dire need of support.

Jimmy was a door gunner with the 119th Assault Helicopter Company and had been flying in and out of the area for several days. His captain and aircraft commander was a guy named Steve Warren. The co-pilot was named G.W. McDermott. Jerry Clapp was his fellow gunner on the helicopter. Jimmy manned the left side of the craft, Jerry the right. They were a tight crew. On base, the officers and enlisted men were separate; in the air and in combat, however, they were blood brothers, one for all and all for one. These were Jimmy's blood brothers.

Dak Seang was surrounded on three sides by mountains, making it a little hairy to maneuver a helicopter in and out of the area. That always made for an adventurous ride, especially in combat situations.

On this particular day, the crew received a distress call announcing that infantrymen were trapped in the area and needed an emergency evacuation. Jimmy's crew was in the area and quick to answer the call.

"This is Gator 28. Estimated time of arrival is 2 minutes . . . will need exact location of extraction."

As the pilot headed toward the destination, he reminded his crew, but talking specifically to Jimmy as he talked, "Now you keep your ass in the ship, do you hear me? This place is hot, and we don't have any guns (gunship support) with us. We're going to get in, get as many out as we can, then we're getting the hell out of there. Got it?" He then repeated the question with added emphasis to Jimmy, "You got it Wrann?" Jimmy didn't have to respond. All knew what Jimmy would do.

By this time, the crew had flown dozens of missions together and trusted each other with their lives. Steve, the helicopter commander, knew Jimmy would do whatever the situation called for, even if it meant risking his life. He seemed to ignore the danger of the situation, always opting to do whatever he thought was the right thing to do. Jimmy had already developed that reputation.

Everyone knew they were headed into a dangerous situation and began gearing up for the action. Nothing more need be said. They were silent, listening only to the chopping noise of the helicopter blades, but soon began hearing the sounds of small arms fire and explosions as they got closer to their destination.

As they approached, the chopper banked hard to land and both gunners went hot, protecting their approach and landing position. Only when they touched down did they realize how dangerous this extraction was going to be. Jimmy began returning fire with his M-60 machine gun, but quickly realized he was out gunned.

They were getting hit with small arms fire from multiple directions, and from a 50-caliber machine gun coming from the tree line that bordered the open field. Jimmy concentrated his fire on the on the 50 caliber that was coming from the trees, and at the same time, he was screaming at the soldiers they were attempting to rescue, "Come on!!! Come on!!!

From the moment they hit the ground, the crew knew they were in a major firefight. Dak Seang had been under siege for days. The enemy was well armed, tremendously mobile and supported by the North

Vietnamese. Now, in the middle of that firefight, Jimmy and his crew had the task of rescuing as many of the remaining infantrymen as they could.

The adrenaline was pumping and every second counted.

The small arms and machine gun fire from the enemy was now being accompanied by artillery fire. One of the shells from the artillery volleys landed close to the chopper, blowing several soldiers into the air, mortally wounding some and severely injuring others. Soldiers were dying and being literally blown to pieces right in front of them, as they were attempting their rescue. They knew they would be next if they didn't get out of there in a hurry.

Wounded and dead soldiers were strewn about the area around them. Some of those who were still alive could not make it to the chopper on their own. They would need help. Acting on instinct Jimmy bolted from the ship determined to drag wounded soldiers to the ship.

"Mayday, Mayday this is Gator 28", screamed the aircraft commander. "We are under heavy fire and need gun support now!" "Jimmy!" Steve screamed to his gunner. "Get back here!" The aircraft commander was trying desperately to keep his crew inside the craft, but Jimmy had already left the aircraft.

"Mayday! Mayday! My crew/chief has left the ship to assist survivors. Under heavy fire. Mayday, Mayday." The commander was frantic. He knew he had only seconds on the ground and was desperate to execute a rescue without losing his crew in the process. His focus was to get his ship and his crew out of there while they were still in one piece, but Jimmy was already twenty-five yards from the chopper, focused blindly on the rescuing anyone he could.

Knowing he has mere seconds, Jimmy realizes he can only retrieve one of the wounded soldiers. He runs to the soldier closest to him. The soldier's left arm is blown off below the elbow and his leg is mangled and nearly gone. But he is breathing and conscious. Jimmy, focused on the severity of the soldier's wounds, did not see the soldier's face. He was trying to figure out how to lift the soldier without making his injuries more severe than they already were. As he makes the effort to lift him, the soldier, still conscious and screaming in excruciating pain, looks at his rescuer in amazement. "Jimmy, is that you?"

In the midst of the gunfire and explosions happening around them, Bobby, not knowing if he was in shock and hallucinating, realized it was his childhood friend that was rescuing him. Bobby cried out, "Jimmy it's you . . . Jimmy help me . . . please help me."

Hearing his childhood friend's voice, Jimmy was equally startled and amazed at their surprise reunion, but he never broke stride in terms of getting his friend back to the chopper. He shouted back, "Yep, it's me, and I'm getting you the hell out of here. I'm going to heave you over my shoulder and we're going to get the fuck out of this place and go home." With that, Jimmy heaved his heavy friend over his shoulder as Bobby continued screaming in pain.

Through it all, the enemy artillery fire continued. The VC were 'walking in' the artillery, which means, depending on where the previous shell hit, they would radio in adjustments to be made for the next round. If the blast was beyond the target, they would adjust backwards and the opposite if it was short of the target. The VC were very good at this and able to adjust their targets quickly. Steve, the helicopter commander knew they were the target and that the next round would be even closer. He needed to get the hell out of there . . . but Jimmy was still out there.

The next round was indeed closer and nearly rolled the helicopter. Jimmy and Bobby were both blown to the ground. The three men that had already been rescued and in the chopper, immediately went to help. They picked up Bobby. Despite his size and the severity of his wounds, they got him back to the ship. Jimmy, however, remained on the ground, motionless and presumed dead.

Once back on the chopper, those who had been rescued were frantically screaming at Steve "Let's go! Let's go, Man! What are you waiting for? Get the fuck outta here!"

The enemy fire was getting hotter and had closed in on the chopper. They had the Americans on the run and were zeroing in for the kill. The grunts that made it to the chopper on their own continued to fight back with their M16's. Jerry Clapp, the right door gunner, moved from the right side of the ship to the left and was firing Jimmy's M60.

Steve's mind was swirling. He could hear nothing but screaming on the chopper, and he was looking at his gunner laying only yards away on the ground motionless. He was praying he was still alive and only unconscious from the concussion of the blast. Every second they stayed on the ground, was a second closer to certain death for them all. One grunt on the chopper grabbed Steve and screamed, "He's dead, man! There's nothing you can do for him. Let's get us the hell outta here! Let's go!"

In the midst of the chaos, as Jerry feels the ship surge in power as Steve begins to leave, he suddenly blurted out, "There is no fucking way we are leaving Jimmy. I'll get him!"

With that, he bolted from the chopper, head down, racing toward his wounded and unconscious friend. Steve now had *both* his door gunners off the ship facing enemy fire. Jerry didn't make it 20 yards before that enemy fire opened up with even more ferocity, all seemingly aimed at him. In a matter of seconds, before he got to Jimmy, Jerry took 3 or 4 rounds to the head and face area. His helmet and half of his head were separated from his body. He died instantly.

That same burst of gunfire also caught G.W McDermitt, the co-pilot of the chopper, in the head and chest. He was now laying wounded and motionless in his seat.

Though the entire flurry of events had taken place in a matter of seconds, it seemed to last forever for Steve. He was in a fog and everything around him was happening in slow motion. Jimmy was lying on the ground, either dead or unconscious. Jerry, his second door gunner, was dead. His co-pilot was also either dead or severely wounded. His ship had received heavy damage, flooded with a mixture of blood and hydraulic fluid spewing throughout the cabin. It was difficult if not impossible to see. And he had a severely wounded infantryman screaming in agonizing pain.

He was visibly struggling with what to do. Should he remain, in hopes that the guns he had called in would arrive in time to allow him to get Jimmy back to the ship? Or do they leave him and the remaining soldiers, not knowing if Jimmy's dead or alive?

The support choppers radioed they were no more than 30 seconds away, but those 30 seconds could be the difference between life and death for all of them. In a state of semi-shock, Steve concluded he had to get out of there, knowing he was possibly leaving a crew member behind. The enemy fire was closing in and the troops he had on board were screaming, "What the fuck are you waiting for . . . let's go!"

His training and instincts took over. Steve lifted the helicopter off the ground. He no longer could hear the plopping of the rotor blades; the screams of the soldiers were now muffled; he could not smell the smoke and hydraulic fluids that were leaking throughout the craft. He was in a fog, operating purely on instinct. The sounds seemed distant and muffled and everything seemed to be happening at half-speed.

Bobby was lying on the floor of the chopper, crying in pain and drifting in and out of consciousness. As the ship began to rise, he is conscious enough to look for his friend. Not seeing him, he began to yell in a near incoherent voice, "Where's Jimmy? We gotta get Jimmy!"

With the chopper gaining altitude, the rescued soldiers, looking through the open-bay door, got a bird's-eye view of the carnage they were escaping. The Guns had arrived and had begun to engage the enemy. In the midst of his shock and hallucinating, Bobby could see Jimmy on the ground. He was trying to move. He was still alive!

Not certain if he was hallucinating or actually seeing what he was seeing, he was certain his friend was still alive and crawling towards the place where the chopper had been. He could hear him screaming, begging for the chopper to wait. Bobby screamed at the top of his voice, "NO! NO! We can't leave him. NO! NO! Go back!"

It was too late. Steve had no choice but to escape the area to save himself and the remaining soldiers, yet Bobby, in all his agony, was certain his friend was still alive and being abandoned.

Jimmy was his childhood friend, his classmate, his teammate, and the closest friend he ever had. And now, Bobby was abandoning him. As the chopper gained altitude, he began sobbing uncontrollably. He kept crying out over and over, "Katie, I'm sorry. I'm sorry, Katie. I'm sorry." He could still be heard mumbling for Katie's forgiveness as he eventually drifted into unconsciousness.

As Steve continued piloting himself and the remaining soldiers back to their base in Pleiku, he was numb and glossy-eyed. He kept replaying the chaotic scene that had just taken place in his head. He could not shake the thought that he had left his crew member to die in the jungles of Vietnam. He recalled his last words to Jimmy . . .

*Jimmy! You stay in this fucking ship . . . do you hear me! This place is hot and we don't have any guns with us . . . the VC are all over the place . . . We're going in get and get out as many as we can, and then we're getting out of here . . . Jimmy do you hear me? Damn it Wrann, answer me!*

Then he thought to himself, maybe this whole thing was a dream . . . a nightmarish dream that would come to an end. It wasn't, and it didn't.

Drifting in and out of consciousness throughout the remainder of the flight, Bobby continued crying out. He was in agonizing pain from having lost part of his arm and had a leg that was in shatters; compounded by the anguish he was feeling from having left his best friend lying in the jungle of Vietnam. In his delirium, he thought to himself and to God, 'God, please, please, PLEASE, when he finally drifted into unconsciousness.'

It was when Bobby finally awoke that the real nightmare would begin.

# CHAPTER 10
## The Toll of War

I N HIS FIRST glimmer of consciousness, Bobby awoke to a blurry field of white. Through his grogginess, he could see white sheets, a white curtain, white bandages covering his arm and leg, and two individuals standing next to his bed, also wearing white. As he slowly began to regain his senses, he could tell he was in a hospital bed. He did not know where, did not know for how long, nor did he know who the people were that were standing over him.

"How are you feeling, Private Bowers" one of the figures asked? Bobby was now realizing from the tone of voice and shape, the figure was a female nurse. "You've been out for some time." While attempting to engage Bobby in conversation, the other figure, presumably a doctor, began examining the bandage on his leg.

"Private Bowers, I'm Doctor McMaster. You are in the base hospital in Cu Chi. I'll get right to the point . . . You're on your way home soldier, but unfortunately you have paid a very high price. You have lost your left arm from below the elbow and your left leg is badly damaged. We did what we could to save it. It will take months , perhaps years for you to walk again . . . if ever." Once your wounds are stabilized enough you will be on your way home"

With that sobering, matter-of-fact summary by the doctor, Bobby began to regain his senses and his memories of what had happened. The physical pain of his injuries was quickly trumped by the emotional pain of losing his arm . . . and leaving his best friend to die.

"Where's Jimmy" he asked?

"Whose Jimmy" the doctor responded?

"You know. Jimmy! Did he make it back? He and I came here on the Buddy system together. We came to Vietnam together, and we're supposed to go home together. Is he going with me?"

Bobby was still groggy from the medication and getting frustrated. The doctor seemed unconcerned about whomever 'Jimmy' was and urged Bobby to just relax and not move for fear of affecting his wounds.

"Well, before you go anywhere, you've got to get well. Meantime, let the nurse get you something to drink, and we'll find out about Jimmy when I come back." The doctor made an effort to comfort Bobby in his post-operative delirium, but Bobby was not comforted.

The doctor was now gone, and the nurse was offering him some orange juice. Bobby repeated to the nurse, "Did Jimmy make it back? He was still alive and moving. Did they get him?" Not knowing who Jimmy was or any details of the situation, she did not respond, and just said, "Try to get some rest, private."

When the nurse departed, telling Bobby she would be back to check on him later, he began to piece together the reality of the situation. He began sobbing. Was Jimmy alive? Was he dead? Had he been captured? What? He could not go home without Jimmy. Especially knowing he had been a part of the crew that left him lying there. How could he face Katie? How could he face Jimmy's parents? How could he face *anyone*?

After weeks of surgeries in the hospital, Bobby was strong enough to begin his rehabilitation. It would be long, painful and emotionally draining. He had to learn to walk again. He had to learn how to function with the lower part of his left arm missing. He was transferred to a military rehabilitation center to undergo the long and painful process of rehabilitation . . . all while living with memories and the pit in his stomach that he could not shake. The shame and torment he was feeling from seeing Jimmy being left behind that day would not go away. The government had declared Jimmy missing in action and presumed dead. Bobby, however, knew differently.

His months of rehabilitation were complicated and prolonged by the mental anguish and bouts of depression. There were days when he would do or say nothing, just staring at the ceiling for hours on end. There were nights he could be heard sobbing out loud. He had constant nightmares, reliving those final, horrible moments as the helicopter left Jimmy lying on the ground as they escaped from the firefight. One night, he dreamt that Jimmy was lying in the bed next to him, telling him how much he missed Katie and what they would do when he was back home. He awoke thinking he had just had a conversation with his friend, only realize he had been dreaming.

He was learning to walk again and manage without a left hand, but he could not learn how to forget. His thoughts constantly bounced around in his head like bumper cars. 'How could he leave his best friend?' 'Why couldn't it have been him that was left in that field to die, instead of Jimmy?' 'How would Katie ever look at him again?' 'How could he explain to her what happened that day?' 'Could he ever tell her the truth about what happened?' The mental anguish he was feeling far exceeded the physical pain he had experienced. He saw no way out.

In the final months of his rehabilitation, the prospects of returning home began to loom larger and larger. And the more he thought of potential alternatives. How could he return home and face Katie? He contemplated suicide. He contemplated not going back to the states at all. Maybe he would go to Australia, Canada, anywhere but back home to face Katie, or their families, or the rest of the community.

The medical staff was aware of his emotional state. They had seen it before. It was not uncommon given the nature and circumstances of their work. But they knew Bobby was in a dark place and they were concerned. One day, the doctor who supervised the rehabilitation unit in the hospital, followed Bobby back to his bed after one of the rehab sessions. "Got a minute, Private Bowers" he asked? "It's almost time for you to process out, and I want to make sure you're ready to go home" he continued.

"I'm ready as I'll ever be" Bobby replied in a dejected tone.

The doctor responded, "You don't sound very enthusiastic. Most GI's can't wait to get out of here. It's almost like you wanna stay here. You got troubles at home" the doctor asked?

"I *am* the trouble!", Bobby replied to the doctor. "I've got a problem I'm not sure can be solved", he continued. "But I'll deal with it. I'm sure it'll be alright" he said dismissively. He was not in the mood to spill his guts to a person he barely knew. He wasn't sure he could spill his guts to anyone.

The doctor simply replied, "There is no unsolvable problem if you surround yourself with God, family, and friends that love you."

Bobby whispered, to no one in particular, "They *are* the problem."

His terrible secret remained locked away inside, as did the tremendous burden that went with it. Bobby remained in a semi-depressed mood but did the best he could to put on a good face. He decided he had no choice but to gut through it. However, the man that he would become was a very different man than the eighteen-year-old, happy-go-lucky boy that came into this war merely months ago.

"What do you do" he would ask himself, "when people no longer accept you or love you when they know the truth?" You hide that truth, he concluded, and get as far away as you can.

The eyes that once revealed a boyish grin, now were beginning to reveal a man of uncertainty and cynicism. The face that was once filled with innocent smiles, became one filled with irritation and bitterness. The boy who would once engage complete strangers, became a man who was imprisoned by his secret, determined to let no one inside his walls. The tears he once shed from his injuries and the horrors of losing his friend, were being replaced by an emotional barrier, determined to allow no one to enter. His conversations which were once animated and childlike, were now hollow and impersonal.

He had already lost his best friend, and was convinced he would lose his remaining friends, if they ever knew the truth. He was determined to lose no one else by letting them in, for fear of losing them too. The only person who could possibly understand, he thought, was Katie. She would understand the horrors of war and be very supportive of him and what he had done for this country. But would she understand *everything?* He felt he knew the answer. The longer he was in rehab, the more those emotional walls were hardening.

Sayings like, 'Love will conquer all,' or 'Trust in God' were now just empty phrases to Bobby. He would do his rehabilitation in somewhat of a self-imposed isolation, and when it came time to go home, it would be to someplace other than the home he once knew and loved.

After more than 18 months dealing with rehabilitation and a sense of dread that would not go away, plans were made for Bobby's return home. The government, dealing with the war in Vietnam and its growing unpopularity back home, looked for any opportunity it could find to glorify the heroic actions of its soldiers. Bobby's return, they felt, would make for good PR.

They coordinated the homecoming with the state of Indiana, the Indiana National Guard, and the local officials in Black Oak to stage a hero's welcome befitting the first landing of the astronauts on the moon. Bobby reluctantly agreed, but he was a shell of the person he once was, both physically and emotionally.

A parade was held in Bobby's honor. The Governor sent a representative from Indianapolis to present him a plaque. The state legislature gave him a special proclamation. The local mayor gave him the key to the city. Standing in the very park where he had helped celebrate Jimmy and Katie's marriage just months earlier, Bobby listened to speaker after speaker give speeches about his heroism. Hundreds of friends and former classmates came out to welcome him home.

But through it all, Bobby never felt more empty, alone, and unheroic than any other time in his life. He was living a lie with a demon inside of him screaming to tell the truth. The last time he saw his friend, Jimmy was alive, not dead as the military had concluded. The government had convinced Bobby that keeping the prospects open that Jimmy may still be alive only prolonged the agony of mourning his loss. Get over it and go on with your life, they told him. Why prolong the agony, they argued?

Katie, more than anyone, was happy to see Bobby. She was thrilled that he was home, but she could see the change in his behavior. When asked about his time in Vietnam and his rehabilitation, instead of showing joy or happiness about being home, he would often have a blank expression on his face, as if he were still living the experience. At times, he would begin sobbing for no apparent reason. He was not the same, and no one could tell that better than Katie. But only Bobby knew why.

She was now the mother of a newborn son that she was eager to introduce to his Godfather. When she first introduced Bobby to Little Jim, however, instead of showing the joy she would have expected when meeting his new God son, Bobby held Jim to his chest and began to cry.

Aggravating the matter, Katie being Katie, had thousands of questions for her friend. What happened over there? Was it as bad as they say? What did Jimmy say about me? How shocked would he be to learn that he was a father? What would Jimmy think about his new son? How does the government know who's dead and who's just missing? What is their system for keeping track? Is our government being honest with us? Should we even be over there in the first place?

She had lost her husband and the father of her newborn son and wanted to know why. Katie was typically not in to politics, but she was now asking very politically-oriented questions. She had discovered other families around the country that had lost sons and husbands and were asking the same questions? How do we know he's not still alive and being held by the North Vietnamese as a prisoner of war? The term 'POW' was becoming a popular phrase around the country and Katie was using the term more and more frequently.

The gatherings with Katie and their families continued for weeks, but Bobby was already preparing his exit plan. He couldn't stay there with his family and friends, and Katie asking all the questions about Jimmy and about our government. He had put up the good front as if everything was hunky dory for as long as he could. It wasn't, and he had to get away from the constant reminders.

Bobby decided to move away. He would go off to college in the southern part of the state, just as Katie had suggested he, Jimmy and she would do one day. Except this time, he would be him by himself. No Jimmy. No Katie. Just Bobby . . . a wounded Vietnam veteran trying to get as far away from Vietnam as his mind would let him and get his life back together.

In college, he majored in Education with the intent of becoming a teacher and a coach. The studies gave him a temporary relief from all he had experienced and managed to graduate early. Upon graduating, he took a teaching position in a high school not far from where he went to college, which allowed him to continue his education toward his master's degree, while teaching school.

The new life Bobby was determined to make for himself was underway. Vietnam, and the horrors of losing his best friend, he hoped, were but a feint memory.

# PART III

# The Long Road Home

# CHAPTER 11

## The Long Wait

A S THE 70s rolled around, the Vietnam war had become a political hot potato. The politicians were dead set on not giving in to the threat of communism, nor staining the country's reputation as having 'never lost a war.' The protests and the political winds against the war, however, were growing. Now, people all over the country, from business leaders to housewives, were speaking out in opposition to the conflict that was now nearly ten-years old. Unsuspecting mainstream Americans were speaking out.

One of those unsuspecting Americans was Katie Wrann. She was now a mother who could not tell her son if his father was dead or alive. There were several other mothers and wives around the country in the same predicament. And, like Katie, they were becoming more politically active to find out the fate of their husbands and sons.

The prisoners of war, or POW movement was gaining steam throughout the country and Katie was right in the thick of it. From attending meetings to organizing rallies to marching in the streets, she had become a full-fledged activist in hopes of learning the fate of her husband. Was he dead or was he alive? Was he taken captive by the North Vietnamese? If so, where was he being held? And what was our government doing to bring our POW's home?

One evening while watching the news on television, Bobby, who was now living and working as a teacher in the complete opposite end of the state, spotted Katie on a newscast about the issue. She was standing in the front row of a raucous crowd of women demanding the return of POW's at a rally being held in Chicago. The newscast didn't identify her by name, but there was no question it was Katie. She was chanting the same way she used to chant at their high school football and basketball games.

That sickening pit in his stomach, that he had worked so hard over the years to eliminate, was back. If Katie couldn't let go, he knew he would not be able to let go. That tragic and fateful day that he had worked so hard to file away into his distant memory, was back, front and center.

He knew Katie had been interested in the return of POW's for obvious reasons, but he did not know she was active in the movement as the video footage seemed to indicate. If she was this adamant about the issue, he thought, the question of Jimmy's fate was not going away. His efforts to put the issue aside and move on with his life, would have to wait.

As the mid-Seventies approached, the news was less about the war itself, and more about the peace talks that were underway between the U.S. and the North Vietnamese. One of the major sticking points of those talks was the fate of POW's. It was known that the North Vietnamese had captured U.S. servicemen and were holding them as prisoners of war. Just how many, who they were, and where they were being held, were the big unknowns and major sticking points. For the country, most Americans were just ready to move on. For Katie, it was highly personal.

The U.S. had reported thousands of servicemen as missing-in-action (MIA's), and thousands more as MIA-presumed dead, of which Jimmy was one. Despite Bobby's strong beliefs about Jimmy's fate, the military counted Jimmy as one of those. The fact is, nobody knew for sure, and the Vietnamese were not being forthcoming about the issue. Withholding information about the American POW's had become a bargaining chip in the negotiations. The life and deaths of thousands of American G.I.'s had now become a political pawn.

Bobby had lived with his beliefs and uncertainties for years and was hoping the issue would just go away. But the emerging news about POW's and Katie's activism would not let it. She was determined to get to the truth about her husband's fate, and as Bobby knew all too well, when she set her mind to something, she wouldn't let go.


All throughout the first half of the decade, she never gave up hope. She was convinced that Jimmy would somehow, someway make it back home to her and his son. As the war was nearing an end, a major break-thru was announced . . . American prisoners of war were being released from captivity. It was a big spectacle across the country and the news tracked the process every step of the way. Katie was happy the POW's were coming home but her interest was focused on just one POW which she hoped would be among them.

When the first and only flight of live POW's came home in 1975, Jimmy was not among them. The Vietnamese declared they had released all POW's and the remaining G.I.'s that were unaccounted for were declared missing in action and presumed dead.

Bitterly disappointed and heartbroken, Katie finally accepted the fact that Jimmy was probably dead. For days, she was inconsolable. Though he had been missing for years, the news brought it all back again. It was if he had just died yesterday.

She now began to look at her son, Little Jim, differently. She studied his features more closely, seeing the strong similarities to his father. She began to talk of her husband in the past tense. Her mother noted that she began to describe herself as a 'widow.' The news of the POW's was hard to take, but it was the beginning of the healing process for Katie.

For Bobby, it was not quite as easy. Even though the rest of the country, including Katie, was beginning to put this painful chapter in our history in the past, he was still tormented by the sights and sounds of that tragic day. Even though years had passed, there were not many days that the flashback of Jimmy lying on the ground as their helicopter flew away, didn't haunt him. And the release of the POW's, without Jimmy being among them, brought it all back.


A year after the government had declared Jimmy dead, a military funeral was scheduled. The town was gearing up to pay tribute to their favorite son, and Katie and her parents were determined that Bobby be there to join them. She had stayed in touch with her childhood friend, but Katie had the feeling that Bobby was trying to escape the memories of that horrible time in his life. She didn't realize just how horrible it really was.

Katie contacted Bobby with the plans for the funeral and begged him to return home to attend. Knowing the trip would bring up old ghosts and knowing the relentless questions he would be asked, especially from Katie, he also knew it would be wrong not to be there. Bobby reluctantly agreed to attend

The funeral was regal. It portrayed the military and Jimmy in their finest light, and actually made Bobby proud. He was glad to see his family, friends and former classmates, and the interrogations weren't as severe as he had thought they would be. He was especially glad to see Katie, and spend time with her and his godson, Little Jim.

His homecoming was more enjoyable than he had anticipated. He enjoyed it so much, in fact, that he decided to extend his stay with his family for a while. His old bedroom still displayed the photos and pennants and trophies that were there when he was in high school. He studied an old picture of him, Jimmy and Katie together and actually smiled at the memories. Previously, since his return from Vietnam, any such thoughts or reminders would provoke that pit in his stomach. Perhaps the healing process was beginning for Bobby, as well.

One of the visits he made while home was to see his old high school principal. Having gotten his degree and now teaching, Bobby enthusiastically shared stories about his teaching experiences. He said he now understood why the principal was so hard on him and Jimmy and others. They were no longer principal and student, but now fellow educators. Eventually, the conversation got around to the prospects of Bobby coming home and teaching at his alma mater.

Initially, Bobby politely dismissed the idea, but the more they talked and the more he thought about it, the more he warmed up to the thoughts of teaching in his hometown. He even agreed to meet with the school superintendent, the principal's boss. That meeting resulted in Bobby agreeing to apply for a potential teaching position in his hometown.

In a matter of weeks, he had provided his college transcripts, completed the application process, and gotten references from his current employers. The school offered him a teaching position and by fall, he was teaching in one of the very classrooms where he, Jimmy and Katie had sat as students just years earlier. Bobby was back home.

As the school year progressed, Bobby began seeing Katie and Little Jim more and more frequently. In Jimmy's absence, Bobby took his responsibilities as Little Jimmy's godfather seriously. He babysat, took Little Jimmy for walks in the park, and anything else that would give him time with his god son, and give Katie a break as a single mom. Though the war and the POW issue had died down, Katie was still active and full of life, and Bobby's presence offered Little Jim the father figure he so desperately needed, and her the next best thing to Jimmy himself.

Their time together quickly grew to become more than mere convenience. Midway through the school year Bobby and Katie began spending time not just as friends, but as potential partners. They had loved each other since childhood and all who knew their history, viewed them as the perfect solution to all they had been through. Their budding relationship was welcomed by all three families and everyone who knew them. Jimmy Wrann was a local hero and it was only fitting that his son be raised by his God Father and his father's and Mom's best friend.

The following spring, Katie Wrann and Bobby Bowers were married. They had a son whom Bobby loved as his own and the two began to shape their lives together as the hometown's favorite young couple.

In his solitude, Bobby reflected on the amazing circle of events that had been completed. He left with his best friend to join the army. Before going off to fight a war together, he watched his best friend marry the girl who was the centerpiece in both of their lives. He returns from that war alone, to move away in an effort to escape a secret that nearly shattered him. He reluctantly returns home for his best friend's funeral. He decides to stay and winds up marrying the wife of that best friend.

He reflected on how that series of events changed him. He had gone from happy-go-lucky kid, to bitter, reclusive war veteran, back to being happy-go-lucky . . . this time as a happily married man and father.

He and Katie could now look forward to a future together, with the horrific past they both had experienced, finally behind them.

Or, so they thought.

# CHAPTER 12
## The Family

BOBBY AND KATIE were now settled in to a comfortable and happy routine. In the early days of their marriage, Bobby seemed self-conscious and awkward when he talked of being married to 'Jimmy's wife,' or being a father to 'Jimmy's son.' Over time, that began to change. When he spoke of his new family, he began referring to Katie as *my* wife, and Little Jim as *my* son. After months of feeling like he was a caretaker for his best friend's family, they were now *his* family. The change became evident in his conversations and in his general attitude. He, Katie and Little Jim were a happy family . . . *his* family.

The dark days of the war and that tragic day in Dak Seang was now becoming a distant memory for Bobby, as was the grueling eighteen-month-long rehabilitation period he endured. Those were undoubtedly the darkest, most sinister days of his life. From thoughts of moving to Canada or Australia, to thoughts of suicide, he marveled at how far he had come. He was once again living.

Occasionally, friends would ask him about his time in Vietnam, or students or sometimes complete strangers would ask how he lost his arm. Now, on those occasions, the knot that he used to feel in his stomach when those subjects came up, was not quite as gut-wrenching as it once was. He would casually dismiss the issue by saying, "Life throws us curve balls, and it's not what happens to us. It's how we deal with it. This was my curve ball." That part of his life was now a thing of the distant past, and he had every intention of keeping it that way. He was now back in the heartland, a husband, father, teacher and citizen. Life was good.

When little Jim was old enough for little league, Bobby and Katie were out there with him, just the way they were with Jimmy years ago. With Bobby now having the loss of his left arm below the elbow, they had to do some innovating for him to participate in Little Jim's backyard practices. Little Jim would throw the ball to Katie, who would catch it and give to Bobby, to throw it back to Jimmy. Those times were also fun for Katie, who was still an excellent athlete herself and always jumped at the chance to participate in Little Jim's practices. The best-friends-forever threesome that was formed over twenty years ago, was still intact. Only now, it was little Jim who was the third leg of the triangle.

Life for the Bowers family was trending in a good direction and was about to get even better. One Friday evening, Bobby returned from a long day at school and was looking forward to relaxing on the sofa with a beer in his hand, Little Jim on one side of him and Katie on the other. He had been in a teacher's meeting all afternoon where the discussion centered around the upcoming mid-terms. He had his examinations ready to go, but some of his fellow teachers did not. He was forced to listen to a prolonged discussion about the testing standards and the bureaucracy of the state's education department. A discussion he could have done without.

When he finally arrived home, Katie was there to greet him, with his favorite beer and a devilish grin on her face. Little Jim was playing in the back yard.

Bobby knew something was up just from the look on Katie's face, but he didn't want to overanalyze the situation. "What are you grinning about" he asked innocently. "This usually means you bought something, or you did something" he continued as he cracked open the beer. "Which is it?"

"It's neither Mr. Smarty pants. You think you know everything" she replied with that same grin. "But we *are* getting something."

"What's that" Bobby responded?

"A little brother or sister for Jimmy!"

With a confused look on his face, Bobby put the beer down. And with a delayed reaction, his eyes lit up, "Are you telling me your PREGNANT?"

"I am, Mr. Bowers. We're having a *baby!*"

"Holy mackerel" Bobby screamed, in the same tone of voice as if Jimmy had just struck out the last batter so many years ago. "Who knows? We've got to tell your folks. And my folks. And Jimmy's folks.

How far along? When's it due?" In his excitement, he was blurting out questions faster than Katie could answer them.

Bobby loved being a father to Little Jim. He loved honoring his best friend and Katie in that role, and he loved Little Jim for who he was. Now, he was going to have a child of his own. Be it a boy or girl, it didn't matter. This would be the icing on a cake that was already sweeter than he could have ever imagined back in those dark days in the rehabilitation unit. By the end of the school year, Little Jimmy had a baby sister and Bobby and Katie had a child of their own. She was named Kim.

Little Jim, who looked just like is Dad, was loved and spoiled by all three sets of grandparents. They, and Bobby and Katie saw in him the same rambunctious kid they all missed terribly. He now had a baby sister that brought the three families together even more.

Jimmy's parents were reliving their memories of their son through Little Jim. Katie's parents were thankful that she had endured the heartbreak of losing her husband the way she had and married his best friend. And Bobby's parents were so thankful to have their son back after all he had gone through and becoming the husband and father he had become.

In addition to the successful husband and father he had become, Bobby was also enjoying similar success as an educator. His school principal would be retiring at the end of the year and Bobby had been urged to apply for the job.

He was somewhat conflicted about the potential promotion. On one hand, he certainly welcomed the opportunity to advance. But on the other, he loved being in the classroom and the freedom that provided to spend time with his growing family. A principal's job, he thought, was a full-time, year-round commitment. He was unsure he was ready to make the jump, but Katie being Katie, convinced him it would be a good opportunity.

He went for it. He was the favorite by many members of the school board, but there was stiff competition, both within the community and from the outside. He learned he was one of eight candidates for the position, and later narrowed down to three. Of the final three, he was the only remaining candidate that was local to the community, and there were growing feelings that the job may be given to an outsider.

In the end, he was the unanimous choice and was later told by one of the board members that his selection was not even close. Beginning in the fall, he was out of the classroom and was in the principal's office. He couldn't help but remind Katie of the irony of his new position and office. There was an occasion when the two of them and Jimmy had sat in that same office as students, having to explain why they toilet papered the football field one time after beating their bitter rival in a big game.

Teacher Bowers was now Principal Bowers. And if that weren't enough, the retiring principal was also on the city council, and Bobby was asked to assume that role as well on a temporary basis until the next election. He was slowly drifting into the realm of being Principal Bowers *and* Councilman Bowers.

His days were now a mixture of budget meetings and teacher's meetings, and many of his nights consisted of PTA and school board meetings, and meetings with the City Council. Through it all however, he made it a point to be home with his family for dinner each night and back in time to tuck his two children into bed. His journey from childhood to fatherhood had taken him into some unexpected and, at times, haunting detours. But he was now living the life he would have never imagined.

Of the many unexpected joys Bobby was now experiencing, none were as joyful as his time with Katie. He had loved her since childhood, but that love was that of the best man, not the groom. He was the first to know that Katie and Jimmy were made for each other and the first on to say the two of them should be married. And through the strange and unexpected twists and turns that brought the two of them together as husband and wife, that love had grown even deeper.

He had always trusted Katie's judgement and especially liked the spunkiness in the way she expressed that judgement. But now, as his wife, he had come to rely on her as a partner, both as it relates to their family and his career. It was Katie that had urged him to pursue the opportunity to become the principal of his school. It was Katie that counseled him and soothed him when he was having a bad day at work. And it was Katie that kept them connected to all three sets of grandparents and the family roots that were so important.

He never felt like the two of them had enough time together as a couple, and once again, it was Katie that found ways to carve out time just for the two of them. He readily admitted to anyone that would listen, that Katie was the glue to their family and was primarily responsible for whatever success and happiness they enjoyed. He once confided to a colleague that he would not be where he was if it were not for his wife, and that he would be lost if he ever were without her.

Life was full of richness and happiness for the Bowers family. Bobby had gone from the American nightmare to the American dream. But that nightmare he had longed to escape was never far from his thoughts. As a City Councilman, school principal and veteran, Bobby was asked to speak about his Vietnam experience at the local Rotary Club. He had told his story before, so was practiced at speaking to generalities of his service and the war without getting into any graphic details, so the talk was pretty routine.

At the end, however, during the Q&A that followed his talk, the knot in his stomach returned. A member of the audience innocently asked, "What was your scariest moment during your time in Vietnam?" The sights, sounds and smells of that day in Dak Seang suddenly came rushing back. The image of Jimmy attempting to crawl as the helicopter began to depart flashed crystal clear in his mind.

Surprised by the question and his reaction to the question, he was silent for 10 or 15 seconds, as he attempted to regain his composure and answer the question. He wanted to give an honest answer but had no intentions of spilling his guts about that day, especially in a public setting. He searched for his words.

"I think" he said in a hesitating and somber voice, "it would have to be when I was wounded and lost part of my arm. We were engaged in a firefight in an area of the country known as the Central Highlands." He didn't dare utter the words 'Dak Seang' or make reference to Jimmy for fear of coming apart in front of the entire audience. "We were getting overrun by enemy forces and had to be rescued by helicopter. That would probably be the scariest moment for me."

Sensing Bobby's obvious discomfort, the moderator ended the Q&A, thanked Bobby for coming and adjourned the meeting. Bobby headed straight to the men's room in a cold sweat and sat in a stall in silence for fifteen minutes before going back to his office. He was enjoying his new life, but the occasion served as a stark reminder that the secret and the nightmares of his past life were constantly there, lurking in the shadows of his mind.

Fortunately, those moments were few and far between, and usually late at night when he had trouble sleeping. Katie had grown accustomed to his occasional nightmares, and even those when he would jump up from bed, screaming. One night, she listened to him talking in his sleep, having a conversation with someone about looking forward to taking a shower. She dismissed that as being a normal reaction by anyone who had been in Vietnam.

Overall, considering all he had been through, Katie felt that Bobby's adjustment back to civilian life from his war days had gone well. The two of them were happily married. They had two beautiful children, Little Jim, who was the spitting image of his father, and Kim, who looked like Katie. They had three sets of parents that loved them and their children only as grandparents can. Bobby was a successful educator and city councilman.

Considering the road they had traveled since graduating from high school, they had it pretty good.

# CHAPTER 13

## The Nightmare Begins

B OBBY WAS ENJOYING his work as a school principal, and as a city councilman. He was with a woman he loved, raising a family that he loved, serving the community that he loved. They worked hard and had developed routines as a family. He was home every night for dinner. Saturday nights were reserved for movie nights, either on TV or at the local theater. Sundays were reserved for church and family time with the kids in the afternoon. Whether it be a picnic at Griffin Park, a visit with the in-laws, or a drive through the countryside, Sundays were reserved for family.

One of Katie's regular rituals was a girl's night out with her girlfriends. Usually, one of the friends would run their husband off for the evening, while they hosted the event, or they would all meet for pizza or dinner together at their favorite restaurant.

On one of those occasions, the event took place at the home of one of their friends. Everyone brought a dish and the hostess provided the wine, and the conversations ranged from the challenges of raising their children, to managing their husbands, to local gossip, to politics.

With the TV blaring in the background, the girls had gotten into a discussion about how they had virtually given up most of their favorite personal activities since they had become mothers. As they were dining on the various dishes that had been brought and enjoying the wine, a news bulletin came on the television set that no one was watching. With her back to the set Katie heard these horrifying words,

*"An American P.O.W. has escaped from Vietnam and is now home on American soil. More on this late breaking story at 10."*

With that brief announcement, the television went back to its original program and the conversation about the trials of motherhood continued. But Katie was suddenly less interested and less involved in the discussion. She tried to continue engaging with her friends and act as nothing had happened. But her body had given her away.

Her face had become flushed, her hands trembled, and she began to perspire. Noticing Katie's change in her demeanor and her physical reaction, one of her friends asked what was wrong. "Oh, it's nothing," Katie replied. "It must have been something I ate" she said.

She tried her best to get re-engaged into the discussion, but her mind was on the announcement she had just heard. Her fears were immediate. Every emotion she had felt and every question she had asked during all those times she waited for Jimmy all came rushing back. Was he dead? Was he alive? Was he captured? Was he being tortured? Was he being held prisoner? Could the escaped P.O.W. possibly be Jimmy?

She could not engage in the conversation with her friends any longer. She was literally feeling as if she had been told of a death in the family. Complaining of an upset stomach, she excused herself from the gathering to return home. She left, insisting she would host the next one.

The drive home was no better. At one point, she stopped the car fearing she was going to throw up. All her fears and anxiety about Jimmy's fate had come rushing back. Plus, she was feeling the added guilt and anxiety of the possibility of Jimmy being alive and coming home . . . and she had married his best friend! She remained stopped on the side of the road, simultaneously sobbing and convulsing. Her thoughts were racing.

There was a real possibility the announcement was not about Jimmy, but about another soldier that had been held captive by the Vietnamese. There's no telling how many soldiers were unaccounted for, she thought. She began to rationalize the situation. What were the odds it could be Jimmy? And what are the odds he could have survived all this time? One in a hundred? One in a thousand? The chances were remote. She's just getting anxious and crazy over nothing, she thought. Bobby would know. He was there. She would try not to get ahead of herself, and just take this one step at a time. No need to get crazy over nothing.

She had regained her composure enough to navigate her way home, but her mind was still racing out of control.

She safely managed the remainder of the drive home, but once she walked in the door, she was nearly insane. She hurriedly went in to kiss the kids goodnight, attempting to remain as calm as she could be, then rushed to Bobby and began sobbing uncontrollably in his arms.

"What's up" Bobby asked? "What's wrong?"

"Did you watch TV tonight. Did you see the news bulletin" Katie asked her husband?

"No, I've been studying up on the bond issue for the new gymnasium at school. That comes up for a vote next week. Why? What did it say" he asked?

When she told Bobby about the news bulletin, they both began to cry. They both immediately grasped the implications. Did Bobby marry a woman that was still married to her best friend? Was she Katie Wrann? or Katherine Bowers? Why didn't they wait? What would they tell him? Would he insist on Katie honoring their marriage? What would they do? Who was Little Jim's father? He never knew Jimmy and only knew Bobby as his dad. What about Kim, their daughter?

The questions were endless, and all impossible to answer. Katie and Bobby were overwhelmed by the possibilities, and they didn't know if the P.O.W. that was announced was even Jimmy. And even if it was, could he possibly be the same Jimmy Wrann after spending so many years in a prison camp?

There were questions they could discuss openly with each other. But there were other questions they could only ponder alone, not daring to express their deepest thoughts about the possibilities to one another for fear of destroying their faith in each other, and their marriage.

Katie was racked with guilt. Had she given up on her husband too soon? Did the words, 'Til death due us part' not mean anything to her? A vow is a vow, but evidently, she thought, not to her. She felt so ashamed. She was punishing herself mercilessly and needed time to process this. Would she want Jimmy back? Does she hope it isn't him, or is that wishing him dead? The mere thought of wishing her son's father dead only caused the anguish of her guilt to be that much greater. . . . but oh my God, what if it *is* Jimmy?

The multitude of feelings Katie was experiencing paled in comparison to the emotions Bobby was feeling. He knew the truth. He saw Jimmy alive in Vietnam, and in that chaotic, desperate moment of life and death, he left him on the ground to die. He pleaded with the pilot to remain and allow them to try and rescue Jimmy. He fought as hard as he could. But would any of that matter? If Jimmy was alive today, would he understand? Would Katie understand? How could anyone understand?

It was, by any measure, the worst day of his life which he had hoped was in his past. Now, once again, he was being tormented by the possibility that Jimmy was alive. And further complicated by the fact that, assuming he was not, he had married his wife. He was raising his child. He was occupying the position that Jimmy had pledged to occupy when he and Katie were married.

Those vows Bobby made to Jimmy and Katie on their wedding day were coming back to haunt him once more . . . For better or worse, for richer or poorer in sickness and in health . . . and then those final words, "till death due us part." Just repeating those words caused that knot in his gut that he thought was gone was back.

Just the mere possibility that Jimmy was alive caused Bobby to reconsider what he had failed to tell Katie about that fateful day. Would he finally tell her, and when? How would she take it? What if he tells her what happened and then they discover the P.O.W. who was coming home was not even Jimmy? How would that affect their marriage? Could she forgive him? And would she forgive him for withholding that information? Is withholding information the same as a lie? If so, does that mean his entire marriage was based on a lie?

The torment was greater for Bobby than it had ever been since that day. During his rehabilitation, his struggle was what he did and didn't do for Jimmy. Now, his conflict included the impact of having moved on . . . with Jimmy's wife. What to do? What to do? The only way his torment would go away was if Jimmy was dead. Think about it, he thought to himself. The best solution is for your best friend to be dead!!!

There was no escape. He went back and forth. He begged and pleaded with God, 'Please dear God, please, don't let this P.O.W. be Jimmy. Please Lord, Please . . . I hope you took Jimmy in Vietnam.'

Then he caught himself, 'No I can't say that I can't wish him dead . . . but somehow I do.'

Would the only way to rid himself of this torment be to come clean? Does he tell Katie once and for all, even if the returning P.O.W. is not Jimmy? Does he run the risk of seriously jeopardizing his relationship with his wife, for nothing? Does he tell Katie the truth now, or does he wait? If he waited, the secret he had been keeping would continue to hang over his head like a dark cloud. If he told her, would it be for nothing? And would she understand?

The two of them were doing their best to keep everything together . . . their work, their marriage, their parenting of their two small children, their social lives . . . but it had grown increasingly difficult. During the first years of their marriage, Katie was open with Bobby, telling him anything and everything that was on her mind. Bobby was just as open with his wife, with the exception of the secret he had been harboring about that day in Dak Seang. They had typically shared their innermost thoughts since they days of their childhood.

But now, they both had a secret. They both had private thoughts and questions they could not share with one another. Katie's secret were her private thoughts about Jimmy that she could not possibly share with Bobby. Bobby's secret was about that day. They had become more reserved with one another. They had become more private in their thoughts about the returning P.O.W. and the possibilities of that being Jimmy. The long walks they normally took together, were now by themselves. They both needed time alone.

Katie was conflicted about her feelings. Did she want the P.O.W. to be Jimmy? Or does she hope it is not. Bobby was also conflicted over the same issue, but also how and when would he tell Katie the truth about that day.

Bobby decided to wait to find out the name of the P.O.W. before telling Katie the truth. But even if it wasn't Jimmy, he would tell Katie and hope that she would understand and somehow find a way to forgive him.

The very core of their lives, both individually and as a couple, now hinged on finding out who was the P.O.W. Katie had heard about in that television news bulletin.

# CHAPTER 14

## Bobby's Confession

AFTER A SLEEPLESS night of tears and turmoil and what if's, Bobby went to work determined to maintain his focus, despite the cloud that was hanging over him. Katie was home tending to her daily routine as best she could when she received a phone call. "Mrs. Katherine Wrann" the official sounding voice asked?

"Mrs. Katherine Wrann Bowers" she corrected the caller, emphasizing the Bowers.

"My name is Lt. Colonel Aranho from the U.S. Army, and I have some rather urgent business I need to discuss with you. Is it possible to meet with you and your husband later this morning or early afternoon?"

Katie already knew what would follow. She had even anticipated the call. "Yes. My husband is at work, but I'll call him. 2:00 o'clock this afternoon" she asked?

After confirming the address, the Lt. Colonel agreed to the time.

Katie, who was standing when she received the call, was now sitting and shivering. She immediately called Bobby. When his secretary put him through, she screamed, "Bobby, it's *HIM*. It's Jimmy."

"How do you know" Bobby asked?

"I just got the call. They are coming here at 2:00 o'clock today. Can you get home?"

"I'll be right there." With that, he hung up the phone and told his secretary to cancel his appointments. "Something rather urgent has come up" he told her.

When he arrived, Katie was lying on the bed sobbing. "It will be OK" he told her. "We'll get through this."

When Lt. Colonel Aranho arrived, he had a second officer with him whom he introduced as Captain McMahon, a military chaplain. Katie wasted no time. "It's Jimmy, isn't it?"

"Yes, it is. He had been held captive by the North Vietnamese all these years and managed to escape his captors. We don't have all the details as of yet, but it appears to be a rather miraculous story of what happened. The news media already has the story, so we felt you needed to hear it from us right away. There will be a series of debriefings and out-processing before he is released, but he's determined to come home."

The Lt. Colonel was as official as the situation required, but he and the chaplain were sensitive to the emotional nature of the news and what Katie and her husband were going through.

"We don't have all the information yet, and I know the two of you have a thousand questions" he continued. "All we can tell you now is that your former husband is alive, evidently in fairly good condition, and on American soil. We will keep you updated as we learn more details."

Throughout the brief meeting, Bobby remained in stunned silence, flooded with the same questions and emotions they had been through the previous night. He was in shock, as if he had been jolted by a stun gun. In a barely audible tone, he thanked the two officers and escorted them to the door. The couple was now left in their solitude to ponder what awaited them. They both were staring out the window in silence, deep in thought.

The news cut through the two of them like a knife. Jimmy Wrann was alive and wants to come home . . . to a son he's never met and a wife that had given him up for dead and married his best friend.

Their deafening silence continued.

The next day, the anticipated homecoming had made the front page of every major newspaper in the country, "Vietnam P.O.W. Escapes Captivity." The local paper, however, had a very different slant on the story. The entire town had watched Jimmy grow up and fall in love with Katie. Based on the government's declaration of his death, the town similarly embraced the marriage of Bobby and Katie. The local paper's headline, knowing the story behind the story, was more to the point. It read, "Jimmy is Coming Home. What Now?"

It was the topic of every coffee and donut shop and breakfast nook in town. What would you do? That was the question of the day in the coffee shops and between husbands and wives all over town. The government declared him dead . . . how long do you wait before you try and put your life back together? Who could blame Katie or Bobby?

Was it Katie's fault? She held out hope as a P.O.W. activist longer than anybody? Was it Jimmy's fault for surviving and wanting his life back? What about Bobby? Who could blame any of them? The debate raged all over town.

Katie couldn't leave the house without thousands of questions and constant tears. She and Bobby tried to explain the situation as best they could to Little Jim and Kim. But their children remained confused? Who is this guy? I thought Bobby was my father? And, why is this guy turning our world upside down? Katie and Bobby were being pulled in a dozen different directions.

The media wanted interviews, their children wanted explanations, and the townsfolks were offering commentary of sympathy and condolences for their dilemma. All the two of them wanted was some quiet time to sort through their emotions and the inner turmoil they were feeling.

And no one was feeling that inner turmoil more than Bobby. He had never told Katie about what really happened that day in Dak Seang. And now, he had no choice. His anguish was unbearable. He had to tell her, but when? Would she understand? Could she possibly forgive him? In the midst of everything else that was going on, he had to tell her. The events of the last 24 hours gave him no choice.

Katie had decided to go over to her parents' house to escape the bedlam that was going on around them and get their advice on the matter. As she was leaving, Bobby asked her to wait. He had something he needed to tell her. Sensing the seriousness and the agony in her husband's eyes, she sat down on the sofa. As he sat next to her, he grabbed both of her hands and began to cry.

In a tearful confession of the truth, he began to describe the sequence of events of that day in Dak Seang. Through the tears and the emotions, he was barely audible. Katie was attentive to every detail and had to ask him to repeat different aspects of the battle that had taken place. Bobby described Jimmy's heroic actions and how he had fought as hard as he could to save Jimmy. He desperately needed Katie to understand. He desperately needed Katie to know that everything that could have been done that day was done. He desperately needed his wife to hold him and to say it's okay.

But that's not the reaction he received.

Other than asking him for clarification of certain details, Katie remained silent, looking only at the floor. She failed to give Bobby the reassurance he so desperately needed. She never said the words," It's alright. You tried as hard as you could." Or, "I understand." Or, "I forgive you." She didn't give him the verbal reassurances or the hug he was so desperately craving from her.

He was in complete agony. He knew he had been wrong to withhold the truth from her about what happened that day. He knew Katie should have known the whole truth before she agreed to marry him. He felt like his marriage and his entire life was based on a lie. Or at least, deception.

In reality, Katie did understand. She didn't blame Bobby. She knew the burden he had been carrying. As she thought about it, she reflected on how difficult it must have been to live with the anguish of that terrible day for so many years. At that moment, she was just too emotional herself to comfort her husband. She simply didn't have the strength.

Bobby told Katie everything about that day. He answered her every question when she asked for clarification or more detail. His secret was out . . . finally. He felt awful, yet he felt liberated. He was finally free of the nightmare he had been living with for years.

Whatever Katie chose to do with this new reality, he thought, was up to her. He had visions of her saying she wanted a divorce, saying she could no longer trust him. He had visions of her asking him to leave. He could see her asking for time alone to sort through all she had endured over the last two days. He was imagining the worse. And her prolonged silence only re-enforced his fears.

Without uttering a word, Katie slowly stood up and went to their bedroom. Bobby remained on the sofa, thinking through every possible scenario of what his future might be. Would he lose his wife? Would he lose his children? Could he lose his job over this? His imagination was on overload. And the longer Katie was alone in their bedroom, the more he envisioned the worse.

Finally, after what seemed like an eternity, but in reality, was about fifteen minutes, Katie reemerged from the bedroom. She walked over to the sofa and Bobby rose to his feet as she approached. Expecting her to tell him she wanted him to leave, she instead embraced Bobby tighter than perhaps she ever had before. Saying nothing she held on to him and refused to let go. Throughout the prolonged embrace, they never made eye contact, only speaking into each other's ear.

"You are my husband, Bobby Bowers," Katie said. "And, if we're going to get through this, it's going to have to be together. I don't think I can survive this alone."

Bobby's eyes were closed and filling with tears as he listened to the happiest sounds he had ever heard. "I love you so much Katie, and I can't imagine living through this or anything else without you. We're going to get through this . . . together!"

After 48 hours of the loneliest, most desolate times they had ever known since they were married, Bobby and Katie were once again husband and wife, devoted to each other and committed to dealing with whatever they were about to face, together.

# PART IV

# The Reunion

# CHAPTER15
## The Reunion

A FTER MORE THAN two centuries of warfare, the U.S. Army had developed regulations and procedures for every situation imaginable. There were S.O.P.'s (standard operating procedures) for how to disassemble a weapon, how to clean a latrine, what to say and not to say if you are captured by enemy forces, and how you display the medals on your chest and the chevrons on your sleeve. But there were no S.O.P.'s for this situation. On this one, they were going to have to improvise.

Jimmy had a massive debriefing procedure to undergo upon his return to the U.S., which normally would have been the first order of business before anything else (that's S.O.P.). But the military knew something Jimmy didn't know. They knew that when he returned home, he was going to discover that his wife had remarried his best friend. And that would be a fiasco.

Knowing the embarrassment to the government from the media circus that was now following Jimmy, they offered him another option . . . a new identity, in a new town, with a fresh start to the rest of his life. They felt this would be better for all concerned. The military was still trying to escape the indignities of the Vietnam war, and this situation would not help. To the military, this was a matter of saving face. But to Jimmy, this was the highly emotional issue of getting back to see his wife and son.

Jimmy flatly refused the idea. He had one goal and one goal only . . . which was to get home to see Katie, Little Jim and Bobby.

The government had disclosed to Jimmy that Katie and Little Jim were fine and that Bobby had lost his arm and underwent months and months of therapy just to walk again. Though they strongly hinted that it was possible that Katie might have started a new life, they did not tell him that Bobby and Katie were now married. The relocation option, they felt, would be best for everyone.

But that was not an option for Jimmy. He wasn't going anywhere without seeing his wife and son.

As the Army is very accustomed to dealing with contingency plans, and given that Jimmy was adamant about reuniting with his wife and family, the government was forced to formulate a Plan 'B.'

The plan was to escort Jimmy to his hometown for a brief, private visit with his wife where they hoped she would inform him of the realities of the situation. That realization, the military hoped, would persuade him to move elsewhere. They would take him to a private location at a nearby military facility where Katie would meet him alone and out of the glare of the media circus that the situation had created.

That would afford the two of them the opportunity to address the delicate matter in private and provide Jimmy the dignity to come to grips with this new reality out of the media spotlight. He could then return to complete his military debriefing, hopefully convinced that the option to relocate and begin his life elsewhere would be best.

Jimmy was to receive a military escort that would take him to the meeting location. There were townspeople and media at the airport to greet his flight. Katie would be there as well and would be escorted separately to the meeting location.

The debriefing would take place after his visit with Katie. Bobby, Little Jim and Kim would not be a part of this initial meeting. This was for Jimmy to see Katie only, and only for a brief period of time. Enough time for Katie to disclose to Jimmy that she had begun a new life. To tell him she was now Mrs. Katherine Bowers. That was the plan.

But nothing went according to plan.

During the flight, Jimmy was as excited as he had ever been. For the first time since he and Bobby left to go to Vietnam, he would be seeing the woman he married almost a decade ago. The thought of seeing Katie and holding her again was the only thing he could think of. She was the driving force that had kept him alive in Vietnam, and now it was finally going to happen. This was going to be the best moment in his life.

Little did he know the secret that awaited him and the uproar it would cause. For Katie, the shear thought of seeing Jimmy again caused her heart to race out of control. She was so frightened and so ashamed she didn't know if she could go through with this reunion. She never wanted to see Jimmy again . . . or did she?

On the day of his arrival, the entire town was there to celebrate. The stores were closed along with the schools, the high school band was there to welcome home their hometown hero. The celebration, however, would be tainted with deception. What appeared to be was not. Jimmy Wrann, the All-American hero, was now an awkward embarrassment. He was an embarrassment to the government who declared him dead. And he was an embarrassment to the town he grew up in, to his wife, to his best friend and even to his son that he had never seen. Everyone there knew the real truth and wanted to witness this historic, if not awkward, reunion.

Jimmy was the only person not in on the secret.

Katie knew the actual meeting with Jimmy was to take place in a separate facility, but she could not resist being in the crowd at the airport to watch him as he arrived. Her plan was simply to be a face in the crowd to get a glimpse of her long-lost husband whom she had not seen for years. So far, so good.

As the plane taxied to its position and the whirring of the engines came to a stop, the anticipation grew. The crowd drew closer as the stairs were rolled up to the door of the aircraft. When the door opened and Jimmy approached the doorway, the crowd erupted in cheers. Katie, however, was overcome with emotion. She began to feel faint. Her heart was beating out of control. Jimmy was told Katie would be meeting them in a military facility, so he was not expecting to see his wife at the airport. The crowd of people, however, was unaware that the planned meeting was to take place in private. As Jimmy started down the small set of stairs, as if on cue, the crowd began to part, creating a direct path to Katie. It was too late for her to hide.

The military's Plan 'B' had fallen apart before it began.

Seeing Katie, Jimmy was overtaken by his emotions. He instinctively began running toward his wife, giggling uncontrollably. The first thing she detected was that sheepish, shy Jimmy Wrann grin that she had fallen in love with. But as he drew closer, she could see the deep and ugly scars of war that had ravaged his face. She had heard of the pain and torture he had endured and could now see its evidence.

The closer Jimmy got, the more emotional they both became. Jimmy's giggles turned to tears and Katie became increasingly weak. The moment was more than she could endure. When they finally touched Katie was too weak to talk, her eyes full of tears, she collapsed.

Jimmy immediately grabbed her and gently guided her to the ground, rocking her back and forth and sobbing. They were both crying, and he was feverishly trying to kiss away the tears on her face. Whether they were his tears from the joy and love he was feeling or her tears from the guilt and shame she was feeling, nobody knew. He just kept kissing her face.

When Katie collapsed, the crowd, including Bobby and their parents surged forward to help her, but were stopped by security. Even though the military officials had already realized this was not going to happen according to their plan, this was not the time or place for a town reunion. This was for Jimmy to see Katie, and for only a moment, and no more.

As explosive as the crowd had been when Jimmy departed the plane, they were now just that quiet when Katie fainted. Like being in the eye of a storm the whole town knew it wasn't over. They knew Jimmy's war had just begun.

Jimmy was as emotional as Katie. He was overcome with a combination of joy, relief, anguish and grief. He was holding the woman he had envisioned holding for all those years of captivity, but it was all those years that came flooding back in his mind. He was sobbing and repeatedly whispering to Katie, "It will be alright now. I'm home now. The war is finally over. I will take care of everything. It will be just like it was before. Where is little Jim? Oh God I love you, I love you Katie, I love you Katie." That is all Jimmy could say as tears were running down his scarred face. He was repeating himself as the flood of ten years of pent-up memories and emotions came pouring out.

As Jimmy continued to squeeze Katie close to him, still pledging himself to her in an almost incoherent manner, he was scanning the crowd. He was not looking for the familiar faces of his friends or family. He was suddenly taken back to Vietnam, looking for his buddies. His emotions were running rampant. He began hallucinating. He could hear the war again, he could smell it, and he could even taste it. He was suddenly reliving a terrible moment when he was screaming those same reassurances to a dying friend . . . "It's going to be alright. I'll take care of you. Just hang in there."

Jimmy knew his friend would not hold on. He knew he would not make it. He was holding his friend until death arrived. Now, his fellow prisoners were chanting reassurances, 'Lord give him the strength to survive . . . .no Lord no . . . Don't take him now . . . fight Jimmy fight . . . Lord, help him survive.'

In an instant, he was brought back to the moment. But now, this is Katie. She couldn't die! He was home now, and everything was going to be alright. He was reminding himself he was now home. Everything would be alright. He was holding Katie and scanning the crowd of well-wishers. But instead of seeing his family and friends he had grown up with, all he could see in the crowd were the seven of his fellow prisoners back in the jungles of Vietnam. They were all there with him, kneeling, praying, and chanting those very words that kept him alive in Vietnam.

He knew he was seeing things that weren't there. He knew he was having flashbacks. He tried to bring himself back to the moment, back to the woman that he was holding in his arms. He yearned to tell her everything . . . what he had been through, how he had suffered, how he escaped. But that was all now in the past. He was home where he knew he was loved and wanted. All of the pain and horrific suffering he endured was worth it. In his arms was Katie, the woman he loved. In his arms was the only reason he survived Vietnam. In his arms was the mother of his son, Little Jim.

In his arms, was . . . . Mrs. Katherine Bowers.

The military officials had seen enough. Their Plan 'B' had flopped and was not going to provide that private moment that would allow Katie to tell Jimmy the truth. They abruptly decided to end the unplanned reunion and return Jimmy to proceed with his debriefing. They would come up with a Plan 'C.'

When they stepped in to separate Jimmy and Katie, it was as if a gun had gone off. "No! No!" Jimmy screamed. "You can't take me. She is my wife and I need to be with her." His screams were echoing throughout the crowd who was in stunned silence, witnessing the anguish and the heartbreak that was taking place, all while knowing the truth that would not be disclosed to Jimmy. It was if they were watching a small child being taken from his mother.

The soldiers that were originally to act as an Honor Guard, were now escorting Jimmy to a military vehicle. He continued to sob uncontrollably as he protested being taken away. The officer in charge continued to assure him it would only be a matter of time before he could see his wife and family after the debriefing is completed.

Jimmy responded repeatedly through his sobs, "Thank you Lord. Praise the Lord."

Once inside the military facility, the officer reminded Jimmy that it was just 'too soon' and that he and the family would need a little time. Katie would be alright, they assured him, and he could return home for this long-awaited reunion after completing the debriefing. That could all be wrapped up, they said, in roughly 60 days.

Jimmy was attempting to regain his composure.

"60 Days?" he responded philosophically, "Hell after 9 years in a P.O.W. camp I can do 60 days standing on my head." But he kept coming back to the same questions. "But why do I have to wait to talk with my family?" "What about little Jim . . . and Bobby? Why can't I call them and talk to them now?"

As he pondered, he looked out the window, staring at the American flag that was flying on the flagpole. Between his sniffles, he began to reflect, "Hell, I'm just happy to be home." His eyes once again filled with tears. "Thank You Lord . . . Thank You Lord" he repeated. "Thank you, Lord for Katie, and Little Jim. Thank you, Lord, for saving Bobby's life. Thank you for everyone in this town that loves me and prayed for me. Thank you, Lord, for everything you've done for me."

Little did he realize just how cruel his eventual discovery would be. The same Lord he was thanking now, he would be cursing soon with hatred and anger.

Meanwhile, back on the tarmac, after being separated from Jimmy, Katie was guided back to her waiting family. Bobby stepped in to take his wife by the arm. He embraced her warmly and whispered to her. "We'll get through this and we'll do it together."

Through the entire ordeal he had just witnessed, he had stayed in the background, allowing his wife to have the moment they both knew would eventually come. He knew she would have to endure this one moment without him. But now that it was over, he was determined to be by her side every step of the way from this point forward. He was actually relieved the military's original plan fell through. He couldn't bare the notion of Katie having to face Jimmy for the first time, alone and in private.

Bobby was now the emotional rock Katie and the kids had learned to count on. And knowing there would be more encounters to come, perhaps even more emotional than this one had been, he knew he would have to be.

The episode had frightened Little Jim and Kim. They had never seen their mother so emotional and were distraught. They were afraid for her and for themselves. Through it all, they were wondering who is this guy and what did he do to their mother? It was Bobby who was there to support and whisper them the reassurances that it would all be alright.

After the terrifying and emotionally draining ordeal, Katie was back with Bobby and her family. She was back in the safety, security and love of her husband, children and parents and the most stable and fulfilling life she had known. But she couldn't help being haunted by the love she once knew and was reintroduced to in such dramatic fashion on that airport tarmac.

As the emotional episode mercifully came to an end and the crowd of onlookers began to disperse, the murmuring commentary immediately began . . .

"How can this be happening", one person asked? "How long can they keep Jimmy in the dark", another responded? "This is the most gut-wrenching thing I've ever witnessed," another said. The hometown hero was now the subject of sympathy and gossip varying from remorse to passionately felt opinions.

Jimmy, Katie and Bobby, who were once the town's sweethearts were now the town's soap opera . . . one that had only just begun.

# CHAPTER 16
## The Debriefing

JIMMY WAS SAFELY back on American soil from his almost decade-long ordeal, and back in the army facility from his all-too-brief encounter with Katie. But before he could be permanently released to go home to his family, he would have to complete his debriefing, which could take upwards of two months.

First, the government wanted him to retrace his every move during his time in captivity. This was standard operating procedure, both for intelligence and political reasons. They wanted to know what more Vietnam may have done that they failed to disclose during the infamous peace talks and release of P.O.W.'s? What other war crimes or atrocities may they have committed? That meant subjecting Jimmy to a series of extensive interviews in which he would be forced to relive the most harrowing moments of his life.

And one interview was never enough.

In an effort to flush out every last detail in his account of events, military protocol required multiple interviewers to cover the same ground and ask the same questions he had already answered. Though the military apologized and explained their reasoning for why they had to conduct multiple interviews, to Jimmy, having to relive the same events multiple times felt like another form of torture.

The military also had to sort through the medical and psychological trauma of his ordeal. Jimmy had endured multiple injuries from his time in captivity. Further, he was malnourished and would need time to regain his strength and his health. Then there were the psychological issues. His psychological treatment would be as extensive as his medical treatment, consisting of daily sessions with a psychologist to help him make the adjustment back into society.

Finally, there were the many administrative details to be addressed. There was the issue of re-activating a dead man back to active military status over a period of almost ten years. There were recalculations of years of service, paygrade issues, backpay, hazardous duty pay and ultimately, how they would treat his discharge from the military. How would all that be handled? The military had questions galore, and they and Jimmy would have to undergo a rigorous process to answer every one of them.

Then, there was the delicate situation of what he would face when he returned home. His family had moved on, based on the assumption he had been killed in the war. Knowing Jimmy's wife had remarried and had begun a new life, the military had to verify that he was psychologically prepared to endure the news that awaited him at home. That, doctors feared, could potentially be as traumatic as his experience as a P.O.W.

The process began with Jimmy being asked to provide a detailed accounting of his entire experience in captivity, beginning when he was first captured. He was forced to relive the most painful ordeal of his life which had occurred almost a decade earlier. In Jimmy's mind, however, it was if it were yesterday.

In a series of classified interviews, he detailed the events of his entire ordeal, beginning with that day in Dak Seang and what happened on April 21$^{st}$ of 1970. He described his position as a door gunner on a UH-1H Army helicopter and the types of situations he and his crew typically encountered. He then proceeded to tell them the harrowing details of how the combat assault mission they were responding to in the Central Highlands region of South Vietnam, turned into an emergency rescue attempt.

After landing, Jimmy told them, we immediately came under heavy enemy fire. Jimmy said he left the helicopter to retrieve and return soldiers back to the relative safety of the helicopter. As he approached the first soldier he came to, he began to lift him in an effort to get him to the helicopter. There was something vaguely familiar, and in the hail of gunfire, he heard the soldier say, "Jimmy it's me, Bobby."

Jimmy realized in the chaos, he had just retrieved his best friend, and gotten him safely onto the helicopter. Though seconds were ticking away, and the gunfire was getting closer, Jimmy once again tried to rescue other soldiers. In his attempt, however, he was blown unconscious by an incoming mortar round. He was barely able to move or get back to his ship as the artillery fire from the enemy had become increasingly intense. He was pinned down some twenty-five yards from the helicopter, and the artillery fire continued to get closer. His crew, Jimmy told his interviewers, had no choice but to evacuate the area.

He described how, being barely able to move and in a state of shock, he watched the helicopter leave without him. That moment, he told his interviewers, was the first time he had actually come face-to-face with the harsh reality of death.

"Everything was out of focus and happening in slow motion" he said. "The gunfire and artillery explosions were happening all around me, but I couldn't hear them. It was if I was watching a horror movie with no sound. But the reality was, I was *in* that movie."

He described being in tortuous pain and barely conscious. "I remember thinking that was it for me. I remember saying my goodbyes to Katie, Little Jim, Bobby and my family, and asking the Lord to look after them. He described being blind folded and continuously moved from location to location every other night for the next 30 days or so. He said he never knew where he was or where was going next. Eventually he was moved to a prison camp on the banks of a river where he was united with seven other prisoners. He did not know the location of the camp.

On the second night at the camp, he was finally able to speak with the other prisoners. As they shared their stories and discussed their situation, Jimmy was the most passionate and most determined of the group to survive and escape. His voice, his demeanor and his determination were immediately evident to the other prisoners and they quickly began to look to him for guidance. He gave his fellow prisoners encouragement and offered them hope and faith that they could endure their ordeal. They immediately began to gravitate toward his leadership.

Their first objective, he told the other prisoners, was to survive. To do so, he said, "We must always believe in three things . . . We must never lose faith in God, our Country, or our family. If those beliefs remain strong, we will be able to survive this and return home to our families."

Those words, he told his interviewers, became our credo, our battle cry of survival. That battle cry would become critical, as the interrogations and the beatings by the enemies began almost immediately.

He described how they were deprived of food and sleep, and often dragged from their cages in the middle of the night to endure beatings and other forms of torture. The nights, he told the interviewers, were the worst. That is when the torture was most severe.

"The most horrible sounds I'll ever remember" he told his interviewers, "are the sounds of the jungle night air, being shattered by a man's screams for mercy."

Jimmy agonized over what he and his fellow prisoners were being subjected to. But his faith in the Lord was strong, and he instilled that faith in his fellow prisoners. He told them he knew the Lord was watching over them and was hearing their prayers, and that above all, they must believe.

Their faith was tested nightly.

One of the prisoners, who was not as religious nor as emotionally strong as Jimmy, was on the verge of breaking. He told Jimmy and the other prisoners, he was not so sure there even *WAS* a God, much less one that would watch over them. "If there was a God" he told them, "we wouldn't be in this fucking hellhole in the first place."

Jimmy gently placed his hand on the fellow prisoner's shoulder. "We've got two choices . . . believe, or be left here to die. These men and your family back home are counting on you to make the right choice. Our faith is all we have."

Their time in captivity, Jimmy told the investigators, became a constant routine of heavy labor and abuse by day; and brutal torture by night. And with each passing day, it seemed to get worse.

"It became so severe" Jimmy told his interviewers, "that we soon developed a pact with God. When any of the men were being tortured, we would pray to the Lord to give the prisoner the strength to endure the punishment and survive. If at any time, however, any one of us felt the torture was so severe that we could not endure any more, we would pray to the Lord to take us and give our body and soul the peace we all deserved."

When it became unanimous that death was the only remaining option for any one of us, he told his interviewers, we counted on a merciful God to grant our prayers . . . but only when it was unanimous.

Jimmy continued the blow-by-blow account of his experience in captivity. He described a common tactic his captors would use to demoralize the prisoners. "They would line us up" he said, "and select the person they believed was the leader or the strongest prisoner. Then they would inflict the greatest amount of torture on that individual while the other prisoners watched. Their objective was two things . . . (1) destroy any possible leadership that might come from within the group, and (2) strike fear into the rest of the group."

'Once you cut the head off the snake', their tormenters believed, 'the rest of the snake can't hurt you', Jimmy said. And in this case, the North Vietnamese quickly determined, Jimmy was the 'head of the snake.'

He was the spirit of the group, and he was the one they needed to break. They would interrogate him, torture him and inflict pain that no human being could endure. They thought, eventually, he would either denounce his country and his fellow prisoners and beg for his life; or he would die.

In their determination to break him, he told his interviewers, they tied him to two small trees about five yards apart, each arm to a separate tree. Then, they would tighten the ropes until his shoulders would separate.

"I was screaming in pain" he said, "but as the ropes were tightening, I would visualize Katie and my new born son the whole time. I could also hear my fellow prisoners praying to the Lord to give me the strength to survive. I was determined not to let those brutal bastards win. I resisted until I passed out from the pain."

The Viet Cong were determined to bring Jimmy to the breaking point. And if that meant death, as far as they were concerned, so be it. They preferred that he survive so they could continue to make him the example to the other prisoners. But if he died, they would just choose the next strongest prisoner. They were determined to break us . . . break our will, he told his interviewers.

Jimmy described how the V.C. would leave him tied to the trees for days, throwing river water in his face to wake him up. He told of how they would loosen the ropes and then tighten them again to increase the level of pain. "In addition, when they didn't get the reaction they were hoping to get" he said, "they twisted my feet and dislocating my knees, making it impossible to stand or walk."

"All the while" he said, "I could hear the men praying for me to survive. They knew that if and when they finally killed me, one of them would be next."

Jimmy's interviewers knew he had gone through a terrible ordeal and could not understand how he could have escaped certain death. How was it, they wondered, that he was captured, tortured and presumed dead, and then escape? They were anxious to know more about that final night in captivity. "Tell us about that night" the lead interviewer said, "when the North Vietnamese captors thought they had killed you and yet, you were able to survive."

Jimmy took a sip from the glass of water that had been placed on the table for him, then took a deep breath. Just talking about the ordeal was as if he were back in captivity. He was getting emotional and trying to remain composed as he spoke. The interviewers knew he was re-living a horrible time and asked if he needed a break. "No" he said. "Let's keep going." He took another drink of water and proceeded to describe that final night.

"After a week of non-stop torture, I think they expected me to be dead by then, yet I was still alive. I think they had begun to lose their patience with me and wanted me dead and done with."

He told of how, on that night, after the V.C. had inflicted their usual means of torture, the camp commander instructed his soldiers to hold each of his hands to a tree. He then began to smash each of Jimmy's fingers with the butt of his AK-47 until all of his fingernails were bleeding, broken and beginning to turn black. As Jimmy screamed in agony, the commander then, slowly and methodically, would tear each his nails off of his fingers, one at a time. "The sadistic bastard took delight in seeing me in agony as he ripped off each nail, before proceeding to the next one" Jimmy told his interviewers.

As he recounted his ordeal to the interviewers, he began to shake visibly and look down at his fingers as he spoke. It was as if he were reliving the entire experience.

Before continuing, Jimmy took a long deep breath. He was not looking at his interviewers, but down at the glass of water on the table . . . and at his mangled fingers that still bore the scars of that night.

He slowly continued . . .

"Here's the strange thing. As the torture got worse, somehow, I got stronger. It was if the abuse and the pain being inflicted on me was making me stronger, not weaker."

When asked by his investigators how that could be, he told them, "I don't know. I just kept thinking about Katie and Little Jim. If they wanted to keep me from seeing my wife and newborn son, they were going to have to kill me. And I was damned determined not to die in Vietnam."

He continued, "The more I resisted death, the more frustrated and angry they became. It was driving them crazy. They were determined to make an example out of me, and I was just as determined to make it as hard as I possibly could. It was pretty obvious they wanted to either break me or kill me that night. And I think even my fellow prisoners were convinced I was a goner" Jimmy continued.

"In all the previous nights I had been tortured, I could hear my fellow prisoners praying for my survival. But on this night, as the beatings became more severe and my strength continued to weaken, the prayers changed. Instead of praying for my survival, they began to pray for my soul and a peaceful passing. Even they were convinced I would die that night.

I had gone through this before. And every time I felt myself letting go, I would think of Katie and Little Jim, and that would give me a little surge of hope, a surge of strength to continue the fight. But this time it was different. They were angry and wanted to make me the example. This would be their day. This would be the day they cut off the head of the snake, one way or the other."

Jimmy described those final moments. "After hours of torture I was left tied up. The pain being excruciating. But they weren't finished with me. And the camp commander seemed the angriest and most sadistic of them all. He approached me and took the butt of his weapon and forcefully began striking me in the face. He was smiling fiendishly as he hit me. I can remember him just glaring at me. His first blow struck me in the right side of his face, which I later learned, shattered my nose, upper jaw and right cheek bone.

He then ordered me held up so he could hit me again. This time, he backed up several feet before delivering what I was hoping would be his last, fatal act of a torturous execution. This time, he shattered my pallet and knock out several teeth. I was near unconscious now and probably in severe shock.

I was barely conscious, but I still wouldn't give him the satisfaction of giving in. 'Fuck him' I thought, 'I wasn't done yet'.

This was not the reaction this sadistic bastard was expecting. So, he hit me, yet, again. This blow drove my teeth through my sinus cavity and lodged them in the lower orbit of my right eye.

I don't remember much after that. I was totally limp and covered in blood. I could barely breathe.

With my feet dragging behind me, I remember them parading me in front of the other prisoners, as if they were reminding them of what awaited them next. As I was dragged in front of them, each one said their goodbyes and begged the Lord to take me home. Their prayers were unanimous now. They were convinced that my time in Vietnam had mercifully come to an end.

My shoulders were pulled back, with my arms tied behind me. I was on my knees, bent forward at the waist. The tendons and ligaments in my knees were torn apart, inflicting even more pain. Previously, when they were doing this to me, I would scream out in anguish. But on this night, I could only whimper. I had nothing left. I was fading fast. In their final sadistic act, I was thrown to the ground in the middle of the compound in front of all my fellow prisoners.

I was their prized trophy.

Then unbelievably, in the weakest I have ever felt in my life, I instinctively tried to stand up. This infuriated the prick that had been torturing me, who was already mad that I was even still alive at that point. He was holding the same rifle he had used to destroy my face.

Determined to finish me off once and for all, he took the bayonet end of his rifle and thrust its bayonet into my face. He was finally convinced that he had killed me. He brutally stabbed me one more time in my stomach for good measure.

He then ordered the guards to throw me into the river. My fight, I thought to myself, was finally over."

As Jimmy spoke those last words to his interviewers, there was a prolonged silence. After what seemed like minutes, the lead interviewer finally broke the silence, and said, "I think this is a good time to take a break."

In the latrine, Jimmy could hear members of the debriefing team talking. They had known of situations of torture and abuse, but they were not prepared for the graphic details they heard from Jimmy that morning.

Jimmy's fight was over. He had fought a hell of a fight. He never gave in to the torture and abuse he had received from his captors. He never gave them the satisfaction of breaking him down. He never let his fellow prisoners down. He had withstood everything his captors could throw at him until his last breath. He was now free.

He was with the Lord now in blissful peace forever . . . or was he?

# CHAPTER 17

# The Long Road Home

WHEN JIMMY WAS thrown into the river, the shock of hitting the cold water jarred his consciousness. He was weak and near death from the torture and loss of blood. He was barely conscious, but he could feel the chill of the river. Its invisible currents were taking him into places of unknown darkness, as he struggled to keep his head above water. Each time he felt his body submerge, his efforts to come back to the surface for air became more and more difficult.

Jimmy was already convinced this would be the night he would die. Now he assumed it would be the river, not the Viet Cong, that would ultimately take him. He simply assumed that, at some point, he would just drift below the surface and not come back up. His final thoughts were of Katie and Little Jim. It was their images that accompanied him as he struggled to stay afloat, drifting to wherever the Lord and the currents of the river chose to take him.

Just as he was sinking and being lulled into what he thought were his final moments on this earth, Jimmy was suddenly awakened. The currents had slammed his body into a fallen tree which was extended out some fifteen or twenty feet from the river bank. When his body was pushed up against the tree, he instinctively grabbed onto one of its branches. As he did, the currents continued to tug at his weakened lower body. The current was pulling him under. To keep from drowning, he would have to either let go of the tree or muster the strength to fight the river's currents. His survival instincts were awakened. He had survived the torture of the Viet Cong, and now he was fighting against nature.

He managed to withstand the currents and hold on to the tree and inch his way toward the river bank. The same hands and fingers which had been beaten and blackened only hours ago, were now the key to his survival. His enemy was previously the Viet Cong. Now, it was the currents of a river.

Feeling the painful effects of his torture with every move, he struggled but eventually made it to the river bank. With the lower half of his body still submerged in the flowing river, he held on to anything he could find on the riverbank. He was lying on his back in sheer exhaustion, with the blood from his wounds still pouring from his face.

He was to the point of wanting nothing but to sleep, but in his state of exhaustion, his survival instincts were still intact. He had survived a potential drowning from the river, but if he were to pass out lying on his back, he could potentially drown in his own blood. While his body wanted nothing but rest, his survival instincts prevailed.

After multiple failed attempts, he was able to roll over onto his stomach to prevent himself from choking to death from his own bleeding. There was no part of his body that was not in pain and screaming for relief. Now lying face down, he watched the blood from his injuries flow slowly down the bank and into the river.

His face was badly swollen. He was near-blind from the numerous blows he had taken to the face. His body was no longer able to move. And his mind was barely functioning. But in his exhausted state of near death, he was able to muster one thought . . . "I'm alive and I'm free . . . If I can get out of this damn river, I've got a chance to actually survive this fucking ordeal."

It was then that his body and his mind finally gave in to the sleep he could no longer avoid.

Throughout the night, his mind had taken him on many contrasting trips. In one moment, he was being nudged by one of his fellow prisoners during his captivity. And in another moment, he was being nudged by Katie, reminding him to be careful during his next mission.

He was awakened to realize it was neither of those things.

It was now daybreak and he could see through the glare of the sunlight, two figures standing over him. Jimmy's immediate thought was that the two were Viet Cong, or at least VC sympathizers and immediately cringed, thinking he had been recaptured and his nightmare would continue. He instinctively tried to react, but his body betrayed him. He was unable to move.

As he attempted to react against the two villagers, they instinctively jumped back further from the American and began speaking frantically in Vietnamese that they were not the enemy. They knew enough broken English to tell him repeatedly, "No V.C. No VC."

He was being nudged by two villagers who had been fishing nearby in the river. They had seen traces of blood in the water and thought it may be an animal that could serve as the villager's next meal. As they followed the flow of blood, however, to their surprise and disappointment, they discovered the blood was not that of an animal, but from a human.

Though Jimmy was barely clothed at the time, the remaining remnants of army fatigues on his body told the villagers he was a U.S. soldier whom they initially assumed was dead. After seeing he was breathing and still alive, the two villagers talked among themselves and pondered what to do in this situation.

The two fishermen were teenagers and totally naïve to the potential danger of their situation. Their inclination was to help the injured soldier, but in doing so, the consequences could be severe, both to them and their villagers. The Viet Cong were known to torture or kill any Vietnamese that were caught helping Americans. Naively, the two teenage fishermen believed their village leaders would welcome the dying G.I.

Jimmy could not speak or even move. His body and his mind were virtually lifeless. But he gradually began to regain his senses about him, and began to sense that the young fishermen wanted to help him. He could only watch helplessly as the two began to gather limbs and strappings from the trees of the surrounding jungle, to prepare a makeshift carrier. He was still veering in and out of consciousness.

Taking great care not to further injure the American, the two young fishermen gently placed the makeshift carrier under Jimmy's body. Through their Vietnamese language, their broken English and their hand gestures, they asked if he was able to hold on to the bamboo slats of the carrier in preparation to transport him through the jungle? When it was evident that Jimmy did not have strength to do so, they took strips of tree bark that served as makeshift ropes to tie his hands to the structure. All the while, they continued to reassure him, "No V.C. No V.C."

Jimmy had no idea who these two teenagers were, nor did he have any idea where they were taking him. He did not know if they were genuinely American sympathizers, or if they were doing the deeds of the V.C. But his instincts and his hopes were that their efforts were to genuinely help.

As they navigated through the jungle, each step sent a ripping pain through his body. Jimmy was still feeling the pain from the previous night, plus the terrain of the jungle itself torturous. The vegetation was thick and the tree limbs and leaves continually scratched his body as they navigated the jungle. Under different circumstances, Jimmy could have been a king being transported by two servants. But these were not different circumstances.

He was an American prisoner of war who had been tortured and given up for dead by the Viet Cong, and now being taken to destinations unknown by two Vietnamese teenagers that seemed sympathetic to his plight. He was grateful for what he hoped might be a potential rescue. His broken body and the overall state of his health, as well as the ultimate intentions of his rescuers, however, remained in question.

As they continued, however, with each ribbon of jungle brush that sliced his depleted body, Jimmy was becoming more optimistic that he was in the hands of people that were not his enemy. And that wherever they were taking him, might offer him a source of refuge. He could only hope he was right. Every ten minutes during the tortuous journey, his rescuers continued to ask him in their limited broken English repeating, "OK? OK?"

Jimmy's body was broken badly. He could barely nod his head in response.

After more than an hour of being carried on a make shift bamboo configuration by two men he did not know, the threesome eventually arrived at an opening in the jungle and a series of thatched huts. As they arrived, the villagers began to scurry around the two fishermen and their visitor, chattering and gesturing frantically at the two teenagers.

Jimmy was barely conscious, but he could tell immediately that his presence had created an uproar in the village. Contrary to the earlier beliefs of the two fishermen, the other villagers were not pleased at the prospects of having an American P.O.W. in their village. That could mean the immediate death of them all if the Viet Cong knew, or even suspected they were harboring the enemy.

The chatter became heated. Jimmy's body was broken and battered, but he could clearly detect the concern, apprehension and even anger among the villagers. Though he could not understand any of the conversation that was taking place, it was clear the villagers were discussing the potential dangers of having the American in their village. The Viet Cong were brutal towards Americans. They were even more brutal towards Vietnamese that sympathized with Americans.

The villagers were screaming at the two teenagers who had created this dangerous situation. They began making gestures suggesting they must kill the prisoner before the V.C. discovered his presence and killed all of them.

Jimmy knew that after all he had gone through and escaped, his fate was now in the hands of these villagers, and knew the outcome of his fate was being decided right there in his presence. It was if he were inside the jury room listening to the deliberations of a jury that was deciding his fate, but in another language he could not understand.

All the while, as the village leaders were discussing Jimmy's fate, the remaining villagers stood by in silence, never taking their eyes off of the strange foreigner that had been brought into their village. He realized he was a novelty to peasants that had perhaps never seen an American. He was no different than the circus animals he used to stare at as a child back in Indiana. He was a novelty whose very presence represented a threat to the entire village. But the inhabitants could not keep their eyes off of him.

Meanwhile, the discussion among their leaders grew more animated and more heated. After a prolonged debate, it appeared that the jury had made their decision. And it didn't look good for the American. To preserve their own survival from the Viet Cong, the villagers believed the prisoner must be killed. The most vocal of the group was gathering other villagers to take the American into the jungle to be killed, when one of the villager elders stepped in to halt the proceedings.

A man began speaking to his fellow villagers in an authoritative voice. With what appeared to be his family standing behind him, he spoke passionately of keeping the prisoner alive. He clearly had the respect of the other villagers. With his family nodding in agreement, he appeared to be telling the other villagers that he and his family would hide the prisoner, and take care of him.

In a more muted tone, the other villagers listened and finally agreed. The elder prevailed. The decision was made that his family would take responsibility for the American. It was also decided, however, that he could not be housed in the village. The Viet Cong were in and out of the village continuously, and his discovery would mean certain death for all of them. His presence must be kept a secret.

This village, like all villages in south Vietnam, had been subject to the war and the intrusions of the Viet Cong for years. And they were accustomed to protecting their families and their resources in places where they could not be harmed or stolen. From hidden areas of the jungle, to secret tunnels and caves that had been dug for their protection, every village had their secret hiding places. And this village was no different.

The elder villager's family gathered to carry Jimmy into a tunnel that led to an underground cave. As they gently lowered him to the ground, one of the family members, presumably a daughter, said in the same broken English as the two teenagers who discovered him, 'V.C. no find you here.'

The tunnel and cave dwelling was crude in its structure, but it was relatively safe. That crude dwelling would be Jimmy's home for the next eighteen months.

# CHAPTER 18
## The Healing Begins

THE FAMILY THAT had taken Jimmy in consisted of a father, his wife and young daughter. The father was well respected in and around the village, and was considered wise and influential. He was clearly not supportive of the Viet Cong, and seemed determined to help the American regain his health.

The Viet Cong were disrespectful to the villagers and threatened them with mutilation or death if they were ever caught aiding the Americans. Though the villagers were Vietnamese, the difference between them and the V.C. were like the Hatfield's and the McCoys. There was deep bitterness between the two. The V.C.'s tactics made the divide between the two even deeper. This was a country in the midst of a civil war, and that war was playing out right here in this village.

Now, at the risk of losing his own life and that of his family, the farmer had saved Jimmy from certain death. Jimmy was unable to speak or move, but he was deeply moved by the farmer's actions. He was like a prisoner trapped in his own body, but he hoped he would be able to repay the man at some point, assuming he survived.

However, at that point, Jimmy's survival was far from certain.

His wounds were so bad, the father decided he would have to risk bringing in an outsider in a last-ditch effort to save the American. He knew of a woman in the adjacent village that had some medical training. She was someone whose family was indebted to him from previous favors, and someone he felt he could trust. He traveled to her village to meet with her and her family and explain the situation.

At first, the woman was very reluctant because of the potential dangers of being discovered by the VC for helping an American. Secondly, she told the father, if his condition is as bad as he says, she would be foolish to put herself in danger, given his remote chance of surviving. The father pleaded with her and she finally agreed, saying she would make one visit and one visit only.

If he dies, he dies, she told the farmer. The father agreed and proceeded back to his village with her agreement that she would come the following day to examine the POW.

The next day when she arrived, she took one look at Jimmy and was convinced even more that the American's time was limited. The right side of his face was so swollen and twisted that he could see the left side of his face with his right eye. His teeth were ripped through his palate, his nose, his tear duct and the sinus cavity on the right side of his face. The lower orbit of his right eye was shattered. And he had double vision because of the swelling in his face.

In less than fifteen minutes, the woman was convinced Jimmy would be lucky to survive his wounds another day. The severity of his wounds, combined with his weakness and his inability to breathe, she told the father, meant certain death for the American. But, at the family's pleas for mercy on the young American, she agreed to give him a chance to live . . . if only a chance.

She gave him a crude, homespun sedative, and began working on Jimmy's face and mouth. She removed several bone fragments from his severely broken jaw, as well as several teeth that had penetrated his jaw from the many blows he had suffered. She then set his jaws and secured them together with a leather strap. Because of the swelling she cut open a small hole in his throat and installed a primitive device to act as a temporary trachea which would allow him to breathe.

After working on him for more than an hour, she then stitched him up the best she could and told the father not to count on him surviving the next 48 hours. It would be a miracle, she said, if he survived. She told the elder his family should begin making plans to dispose of the American's body without the V.C. knowing of his presence. She then reminded him that she would never return, and that he must give his word to never disclose to anyone that she had been there.

Meanwhile, Jimmy was left unconscious, to recover from the woman's many medical procedures. His head and the upper portions of his body were tightly wrapped in cloth. His eyes were covered, and his mouth was barely visible. The homemade trachea device in his neck were exposed just enough to allow him to breathe.

The next 24-48 hours for the American would be the most crucial.

He would either die, as the woman had predicted, or begin his long road back to some form of recovery. Amazingly, Jimmy survived.

For the next 4 to 6 weeks, Jimmy's motionless body was adjusted to where he would lie on his stomach, sipping juices and soup from the family that saved his life. His movements were restricted to being turned over each day and changing the tightly wrapped bandages that covered his face and upper body. He was conscious but was barely able to see or speak.

When the man's wife and young daughter would help him with his dressings, Jimmy would look at the family members, but could only see blurred figures. His eyesight was virtually non-existent, compounded by the swelling in his face and a blurred double-vision. He attempted to utter a Vietnamese phrase to them he had learned previously back at his crew's base in Pleiku, but his mouth and body refused him.

"Com-on," he would try to say to them, which he was told was Vietnamese for 'Thank you.' He could not speak clearly enough for them to understand him because of his tightly wrapped jaws, but he continued to try. Whatever the family members did during that time, he would mumble, 'Com-on,' trying his best to show his appreciation for the family who had saved his life. He could not speak, and the family could not understand him, but that didn't keep him from trying.

The recovery was grueling, but, contrary to the woman's grim assessment, Jimmy was still alive and slowly re-gaining his strength. It was months before he could lift himself from the makeshift cot that had been his home during the entire time. He had lost considerable weight and his complexion was ghost-like from having been confined to a tunnel. The last time he had seen the sunlight was the morning he had been rescued from the river by the two teenage fishermen. He had the appearance of a holocaust survivor.

Jimmy lost all sense of time. On several occasions, he had wanted to mark the days on the walls of the tunnel to keep track of time, but that, too, was more than his body would allow. He tried to count the days in his head, but there were many nights when he would wake up in a cold sweat, not knowing if it was the same day or the next one. Time, like the control of his body, was something he had long lost track of.

Not knowing if it had been three months, six months or nine months since the family had taken him in, Jimmy finally regained the strength to stand. Initially, he would hold on to the walls of the tunnel to maintain his balance. On multiple occasions, his knees would buckle, causing him to fall to the floor. He would have to crawl to his cot to get back to his feet. He was reminded of his days in boot camp, where the recruits were required to crawl under ropes for an extended period of time.

Boot camp, he thought to himself. This was his new boot camp that would prepare him to eventually go home. Talking to no one but the walls of the cave, and through the jaws that could not move, he muzzled the thoughts, 'I'm coming, Katie and Little Jim. I'm coming.' Even then, Jimmy was smart enough to keep his jaws bound by the straps that had been placed there. He knew the less he moved his mouth, the better chance it would have to heal. His jaws remained frozen, as did the disfigurement of his face and the double vision that accompanied his injuries.

But the swelling was beginning to lessen.

It seemed as though when one part of his body was beginning to heal, however, he experienced strange new sensations he had never known before in other parts of his body. Strangely, small pieces of bone were beginning to come to the surface of his face like pimples. He didn't know it at the time, but his body was beginning to reject the shattered bone fragments that had been lodged in his body and face from the torture he had endured months earlier. Because of his condition, they easily found their way to the surface of his skin, and began breaking through.

His recovery was for the most part, a lonely vigil. The only human beings he came in contact with were the three family members that had taken him in. The other villagers knew he was there, but that day he had been brought into the village by the two teenage fishermen, had all but been forgotten. They knew they had a captured American POW in their village, but kept his presence a closely guarded secret, given the risks the Viet Cong know might find out.

Of the three family members, the father and mother seemed to spend most of their time working the fields of their small farm, and the day-to-day care of their secret guest fell to their young daughter. As Jimmy began to regain his senses, he could not yet move or speak, but the young girl could. She was able to introduce herself by pointing to her chest, and repeatedly saying, "Leen. Leen." Jimmy would soon learn the young girls name was Lin.

Though Jimmy was too focused on his own recovery to notice, Lin was fascinated by the American. On several occasions, she sat on the stool where Jimmy was being kept, watching him, even as he slept. She studied his scars and his many broken features and imagined what he must have looked like before being beaten by the VC. When Jimmy would wake up and discover her presence, she would look at him, embarrassed by the discovery, and look down. It was clear she was captivated by his presence and would do anything to help him.

As the time passed, and Jimmy was still unable to speak or barely move, he and 'Lin' developed a warm, caring relationship. He relied on her heavily throughout his rehabilitation, and though Lin was much younger, she welcomed any opportunity she could find to help the patient. Jimmy was appreciative. Through some of the darkest and most difficult days of his recovery, Lin became his lifeline.

Jimmy continued to defy the odds and expectations for his recovery. From the torture at the hands of his Viet Cong, to his survival in the river, to the low expectations of the woman who treated him, Jimmy Wrann was like a cat with nine lives. With images of a wife he had not seen in years, and an image of a son he had never seen, and his never-ending faith in the Lord, it seemed he was destined to survive and someday return home. He just did not know when, nor how.

He was also beginning to feel the sensations of the healing process his body was going through. As his jaws and the roof of his mouth had begun to heal, the leather strap that he had kept in place for months, had begun to loosen. One night as he slept, he awakened to find the strap lying on his bed. For the first time since he had been treated by the woman who had predicted his death, he could move his mouth. Just to test his newfound capability, he verbalized the word, 'Hello.' Then he mouthed the word, 'Katie.' It was a weak sounding voice and when he said his wife's name, it sounded more like 'Kah-te.' But that was progress. He could actually move his mouth and speak.

There were times when he wondered if he would ever speak again. He had forgotten what his voice sounded like and wondered if others had too. He was like a child with a new toy.

In a matter of days after regaining his ability to speak, he awoke one morning and realized that his double-vision had also disappeared. His body, that had been shattered from the prolonged torture at the hands of the V.C., was beginning to heal. Realizing he could once again move on his own power, move his jaws and speak with a little more clarity, and see without the blurred clouds or double-vision, he began to weep openly.

Looking up at the roof of the tunnel where he had been confined for months, Jimmy began to thank the Lord repeatedly and say, over and over, "Katie and Little Jim, I'm coming home. Somehow, some way, I'm coming home!" He then repeated his thanks to the Lord, "Thank you, thank you, Lord."

Hearing his cries, Lin came rushing in, thinking he was in more pain, only to see him rejoicing. "Com-on. Come-on", he said repeatedly to the startled young girl. In a gesture of joyful innocence, he actually tried to embrace the shy, young Vietnamese girl. His enthusiasm had gotten the best of him and made him forget the limitations of his body. He attempted to swing her around the way he had swung Katie on their wedding night.

For the first time in months, he was beginning see glimpses of his former self. The old Jimmy, he thought, was slowly returning. He could barely move, but was feeling joyful about his progress and the prospects of eventually returning home to Katie and Little Jim. Speaking to himself as if he was talking to his young son, whom he had never seen, "Your Dad's coming home son. He's coming home. I don't know when and I don't know how, but he's coming home. You tell your Mom to have faith and just hold on."

Though his body was healing, Jimmy was far from being able to move around freely. He was still a mere shadow of his former self, plus, there were still Viet Cong roaming the area. V.C. soldiers regularly came through the village, either in search of Americans or to pillage supplies from the villagers. The villagers simply wanted peace and were caught up in the war between the VC and the U.S. The V.C. were notorious for taking their food and even taking up camp in the villages where they could live off the farmers while fighting the Americans.

So far, Jimmy's presence in the village appeared to remain a secret. He was safe as long as he remained completely out of sight. He was able to get out into the sunlight only early in the mornings or late in the afternoons when the villagers were assured there were no Viet Cong in the area.

All the while, the Vietnamese family that took Jimmy in, continued to take care of their guest. Their young daughter, Lin, especially. She continued to delight in nursing the young American back to health.

Jimmy was being held captive by his own body, but being cared for by a family he hoped to repay someday.

Someday . . . .

# CHAPTER 19

## The VC Return

As days turned to weeks and weeks to months in the Vietnamese village that was now Jimmy's home, he continued his rehabilitation under the care of the family that vowed to save him, especially their young daughter, Lin. She was becoming infatuated with the American and was devoting every spare moment she had to his care. When she was not cooking for the family or taking care of chores, or working in the fields, she was taking care of Jimmy.

Jimmy, likewise, appreciated Lin, not just as a caregiver, but as a trusted friend. He was living in a very dangerous situation. He was a stranger in a strange land, and virtually disabled physically. Lin had become his lifeline, both physically and emotionally.

As he began to regain his strength, their time together became more than her just helping him turn over, or holding him up as he attempted to walk. She taught him Vietnamese words and phrases and he taught her English. He drew male and female stick figures in the ground and taught her to say 'man' and 'woman'. He would point to the male figure and then to himself, and say 'man'. He would then point to the female figure and then to Lin, and say 'woman.'

Lin very proudly responded by pointing to Jimmy and saying, 'man;' then to herself saying, 'woman.'

As their lessons continued, Jimmy tried to explain the words, 'husband' and 'wife.' Redrawing the same male and female stick figures in the ground, he would point to the male drawing, and say, 'Man ... Husband.' He would then point to the female and say, 'Woman ... wife.' Initially, this confused Lin. In his further effort to explain, he hugged Lin, while pointing to her, he repeated the words 'wife, wife.' And then to himself, 'Husband, husband.'

Eventually, their lessons progressed to the point where Jimmy would point to the female figure and say 'wife', then point to himself and say 'Katie.' Through continued efforts to demonstrate affection, he eventually explained that Katie was his wife. To test her understanding, Lin pointed to Jimmy and said, "Husband, Jeem; Wife . . . Kah-tee."

Yes, he nodded enthusiastically as he clutched Lin's hand to his heart.

Though their language barrier limited them in what they could say to each other, it was obvious that their fondness for each other was growing. Especially for Lin. She seemed to understand that Jimmy had a 'wife' that he was clearly devoted to. And her shy, almost childlike demeanor would never allow her to act on her true feelings. But her devotion to the American was evident.

She would even demonstrate her respect for Jimmy's love for his wife. On one occasion when Jimmy had made some reference to 'Katie,' Lin began hugging herself with her hands across her arms in a swaying motion, and said "Kah-tee, wife."

Though he was fiercely loyal to his wife and child, and still hopeful he would one day see them again, he was developing a deep appreciation for the young Vietnamese woman. She was perhaps sixteen years of age, perhaps twenty. Jimmy couldn't tell. But her Asian beauty was clear, and her heartfelt gestures toward Jimmy were genuine and very much appreciated.

The two clearly enjoyed spending time with each other. The fact that Lin spoke and understood very little English did not deter Jimmy from talking with her for hours about Katie and Little Jim. She was constantly busy doing her chores and cooking for her family, but she always made time for 'Jeem.'

She saw him through his worse days when he could barely hold his head up. She listened, knowing little of what he was saying, as he decried the brutality of the Viet Cong and his P.O.W. experience, and wondering what had happened to his fellow captives in the prison camp. Many nights, she would hold him as he cried, and lay with him to comfort him and even sleep with him during his frequent nightmares.

Their relationship was separated by language, but bound by a sense of love and caring for one another. In so many ways, he leaned on Lin the way he would lean on Katie. If he were to ever survive this ordeal, he thought, much of the credit would have to go to Lin. The time they shared together had all the ingredients of becoming sexual. But Jimmy would not cross that line. He was married to the love of his life and there was no way in hell he was going to be unfaithful to her.

As Jimmy was slowly becoming stronger and more mobile, the presence of Viet Cong soldiers roaming through the village had begun to subside. This allowed him to mingle more with other families in the village. He was still a novelty to the villagers and was the center of attraction when he was around, especially with little children and young girls.

His face was still badly scarred, and he walked very gently and with a limp. But below his imperfections, he was the embodiment of the myth and image that the villagers had in their minds of Americans. He was a broken shell of the man he once was. But to them, he was everything they envisioned to be *American.*

He soon began making walks around the village as part of his daily routine. He still had difficulty speaking, and between his limited ability to form words and the language barrier that existed, he tried to engage the villagers. Much the way he tried to teach Lin various words and phrases in English, he made similar efforts with the villagers. He would point to himself and say, 'Jim.' He followed that by waving and saying, 'Hi.' He then tried to combine the lessons by waving and saying, 'Hi, Jim.' The villagers would respond by saying, 'Hi Jeem.'

Seeing the confusion in the villagers' faces, he would try to explain the difference between the greeting, and his name, but determined it would be too much, too soon. It was from that point that he became known throughout the village as, 'Hi, Jeem.' As he limped through the village, he could hear them all, from young boys to old ladies, calling out, 'Hi Jeem. Hi Jeem', accompanied by an enthusiastic wave.

'Hi Jeem' was becoming a local hero of sort. His scars and broken body were evident to all, and the stories of how he had escaped from the Viet Cong were becoming legendary, as each version seemed to become more dramatic than the last. But still no-one other than the family that took him in was willing to get too close to the American. No one dared risk their lives in the event that word got back to the V.C. That would mean certain death.

Jimmy was just trying to get out and regain his strength. He even tried to show his gratitude and repay the family by doing menial chores, or even working in the fields with them. The family would gesture their appreciation for his efforts, but would wave off his attempts. They, as did the other villagers, remained ever fearful of the Viet Cong. If it were ever discovered that they were harboring an American, they feared, the V.C. would kill everyone in the village.

The Viet Cong were notorious for taking extreme measures to intimidate the villagers to send a message. They made it clear to every village in South Vietnam . . . if you hide or take care of an American, every man, woman and child in the village would be killed.

That fear became a reality one afternoon.

As Jimmy was slowly making one of his daily rounds to greet the various villagers, he stopped to engage an old villager that he had become friendly with. Every day when he saw the old man, Jimmy would try to teach him one English word. A 'word a day', he reasoned, would eventually allow the two to communicate with each other. On this occasion, he was explaining, or attempting to explain, the English word, 'buffalo.' Water buffalo were prevalent in Vietnam, and were essential to their crude method of farming. Jimmy made it a habit of taking objects that were common to the villagers, and teaching them the English word or phrase.

Pointing to one of the buffalo in the field, Jimmy was saying to the villager, 'buffalo.' The villager was attempting to repeat the word, when they were interrupted by a young boy who came running through the jungle and up to the man. He was almost out of breath and speaking frantically. Jimmy could not understand what the boy was saying, but did hear the phrase, 'VC' and then 'Hi Jeem.'

As they talked, the man pointed toward Jimmy and excitedly directed the boy to go and retrieve the family that had been caring for Jimmy. He then looked at Jimmy and said, 'VC . . . no Hi Jeem . . . no Hi Jeem.'

Jimmy was quickly beginning to grasp the message. His head was buzzing with questions . . . Had he been careless? Had he become too complacent in his growing comfort of the village? Had the woman who had helped him with his wounds revealed his presence? Had one of the villagers? Were there VC sympathizers in the village that told of his presence?

On more than one occasion, Jimmy had reconciled himself to the thought of dying. But now, he was subjecting an entire village to being wiped out. His thought went to the family that had cared for him for so long and their whereabouts. And what about Lin? What had his careless actions done to them?

The answer to the many questions swirling around in his head would have to wait. Most immediately, he had to get back to the tunnel that had been his hiding place these many months, and as quickly as his broken body would carry him.

However they had learned about his presence, a small band of VC had heard rumors about an American working in one of the villages and apparently were on their way to the village to find him.

As Jimmy approached the tunnel, he could already hear the Viet Cong interrogating the villagers. The threatening language was unmistakable. He knew the VC were there for him. He could run from them and perhaps even escape. But by saving himself he knew he would be bringing certain death to much of the village, including the family that had taken him in, and including Lin.

He was halfway down the tunnel when he stopped. He had been running from those VC bastards for years, he thought to himself. "And I'm not running anymore" he said out loud, "especially if it will save the villagers. Maybe if I give myself up, the VC will be satisfied with that and not hurt the villagers." His thoughts were with the family that had done so much for him, and the young Lin, who had nursed him back to health and loved him. Could he possibly save them, he wondered?

As his thoughts became clearer, he turned and started walking back toward the entrance of the tunnel. As he approached the entrance, the commotion that was taking place with the Viet Cong was getting louder. Villagers were already being lined up and threatened with execution if they did not reveal the whereabouts of the American. As Jimmy came to the opening of the tunnel, he paused momentarily, bracing himself for whatever awaited him. As he stepped into the open, he did so with a sense of purpose he had not felt in months. With his arms raised as high as his body would allow, he surrendered to the VC..

The scene was already chaotic. Villagers were already being lined up by soldiers with rifles and bayonets and being interrogated. It was clear they wanted the American and the family that had been hiding him. The fellow villagers had already pointed out the Vietnamese family who were being rounded up. When the VC spotted Jimmy, their focus immediately shifted from the villagers to the American they had come for.

Two soldiers immediately ran over and grabbed him and shoved him into the center of the village grounds where they had already gathered and placed the three family members.

As the other villagers looked on, the leader of the VC squad approached the father of the family and began screaming insults at him. The soldier was mere inches from his face and shouting at him, but the father continued to look straight ahead and showed no emotion as he listened. The leader then shouted orders to a member of his patrol. The soldier came up to the father and knocked him to the ground with the butt of his rifle. He then proceeded to brutally beat and kick the father into a state of unconsciousness, as his wife and daughter and Jim helplessly watched.

The VC leader then looked at the man's wife and mumbled in Vietnamese, as if to say, "This is what happens when you help the Americans." He then coldly shot her husband in the back of the head.

As she watched her husband being shot, the wife began screaming hysterically and pleading for her life and that of her daughter. Her husband was lying dead and she wanted to kneel down and cradle him in her arms, but her focus was now saving her daughter and herself.

Blood was already running down her face from wounds inflicted by the soldiers when they retrieved her. She was screaming in anguish at the sight of her dead husband and fell to her knees. The commander watched her as she lay on the ground, clinging to her dead husband and pleading for her life. As she began to grasp at his trousers, begging for mercy, he calmly took the pistol out of his holster, and shot her in the back of the head.

With the bodies of the husband and wife lying on the ground in a pool of blood, the VC leader then turned his attention to Jimmy. He once again summoned the soldier who was carrying out his orders, who then proceeded to strike Jimmy with the butt of his AK 47. The first blow was to his rib cage, causing Jimmy to double over in pain. A second blow was aimed at his face. Jimmy could see the next blow coming and was able to partially deflect it, but it still connected, knocking him to the ground. He was now on the ground next to the bodies of the husband and wife that had saved him. He was still alive, but unable to move.

The VC then turned to Lin.

Having just witnessed the brutal murder of her parents and the attack on Jimmy, she bravely tried to stand erect to face her tormenters, but she was trembling.

Jimmy was crumpled up in pain on the ground and barely able to see, but he wanted desperately to protect Lin from the V.C. He watched helplessly as they approached her. She was the woman that had taken care of him and nursed him back to health. She was the woman that had consoled him those many nights as he talked and cried about Katie and Little Jim. Jimmy loved Lin, not in a romantic sense, but in the way a brother loves his sister, or a father loves his daughter. And now, he was powerless to help her against the Viet Cong he had come to hate.

The leader of the V.C. approached Lin with a cruel and sadistic grin on his face. He began speaking to her in an insulting tone. He then knocked her to the ground, prompting Jimmy to instinctively crawl to his knees in an effort to defend the young woman. He was promptly knocked back down to the ground by the leader's hit man.

Seeing Jimmy's protective reaction, the VC leader assumed the two were lovers, or clearly had some affection towards each other. The Vietnamese hated their women being with American GI's. If a Vietnamese woman showed any type of affection toward an American, she was regarded as nothing more than a prostitute. The VC leader believed Lin was Jimmy's prostitute, which gave him even more reason to exact his cruelty on the pair.

With the two on the ground where Lin's parents lay dead, the leader grabbed Lin by the hair and dragged her to within inches of Jimmy's face. He was laughing as he moved the two toward each other, mocking the sounds and the motions of two lovers. He forced the two even closer, simulating a mock kiss. As he was enjoying his sadistic cruelty, he laughingly looked at his soldiers, as if he were entertaining them with his cruel playfulness.

He then looked at Lin, no longer grinning, but with a face filled with anger and hatred. Suddenly exploding in a state of rage, he began shouting at her. He then became quiet and grabbed her by the hair and forced her to look at him. As she looked up, he calmly removed the pistol from his holster, and shot her with a single bullet through her head.

As the bullet went through her head, Lin's brain matter and blood had exploded all over Jimmy's face. He had witnessed the execution of the family that had saved him, including the young woman that had cared for him and nursed him back to health. He assumed he would be the next to be executed as the soldier began to taunt Jimmy with his pistol.

He first put the barrel of his pistol next to Jimmy's temple. Jimmy had his eyes closed, assuming certain death. As he waited for his execution, he heard a loud cry, 'BLAM.' Jimmy was so keyed up, he flinched at the sound. It was the soldier simulating a gunshot to scare the American. He then looked back at his group of soldiers, laughingly conversing with them in Vietnamese, as if to say to them, 'This big, brave American is scared shitless. Shall I do some more?' He then placed the gun under Jimmy's chin, cruelly rubbing it back and forth while he continued laughing with his fellow soldiers, as Jimmy awaited his execution.

Ignoring the soldiers' playful taunts, Jimmy began speaking to the Lord. He was not pleading for his life, but begging forgiveness for what he had caused. "Oh Lord, what have I done?" "How could I have done this to this family?" "God please forgive me . . . please forgive me".

Feeling as though he deserved being executed for what he had done, Jimmy was surprised when, rather than shoot him, he was stood up by the soldiers and tied up. His arms, which were still not healed, were tightly bound behind him. As he winced in pain, the leader of the VC smiled, clearly enjoying his taunting of the prisoner.

The VC enjoyed nothing more than killing American soldiers, whether in combat or as prisoners of war. The Americans were their enemy and they wanted them dead. The Viet Cong, however, were supported and funded by Communist China, who needed man power. The Chinese had instructed the Viet Cong not to kill any American prisoners that could be used as slave labor, but to capture them. They paid the VC a bounty for prisoners. Jimmy became a bounty.

Rather than be killed, he was taken from the Vietnamese village and transported to China where he would be put to work in a slave labor camp.

That long-awaited reunion with Katie and Little Jim seemed to be drifting further and further away from his grasp. It would be nine grueling years and a daring escape before he would ultimately get home.

# CHAPTER 20

## The Great Escape

J IMMY'S JOURNEY FROM Vietnam to China was long and grueling. The first leg consisted of him being forced to march with the VC squad through the jungle to their base camp. There he was held in captivity in a bamboo cage for three days awaiting pick up by the Chinese.

During his captivity there, however, he was thankfully not tortured, but he was treated with disgust and cruelty by the Viet Cong soldiers. It was evident that they hated Americans, as the guards would often spit at him from outside his cage. He was given water twice a day and a bowl of maggot-filled rice in the evening. He was completely unaware of where he was or how long he would remain.

Days later, two guards approached and pulled him out of his cage. He was then tied to the bed of an old military vehicle that appeared to be from World War II. The two new guards were in different uniforms, so he assumed they were Chinese. It was then that Jimmy thought he was being turned over to the Chinese, either to endure more torture or as slave labor.

He learned it would be the latter. The Chinese were not above torturing their prisoners, but they needed healthy manpower. They wanted Jimmy healthy so they could put him to work.

China supported North Vietnam with weapons and equipment, and in some cases, manpower. In exchange, among other things, the Viet Cong agreed to provide them with P.O.W.'s that could be used as slave labor.

It was because so many American P.O.W.'s were given over to China to work as slaves and unaccounted for by the North Vietnamese, that the P.O.W. issue was such a hot button topic during the peace negotiations, and later with the American people.

The second leg of Jimmy's journey from Vietnam to China was not much better than the first. He was riding in the back of a military vehicle and not forced to march, but the roads were little more than muddy, backwoods trails and the jungle terrain was hilly and bumpy. He was tied up and being bounced around mercilessly in the back of the truck as the soldiers made their way to their destination.

Jimmy was once again in the dark as to where he was being taken or how long it would take. After more than 48 hours of nonstop travel, the vehicle pulled into what appeared to be a military camp. He had not eaten since the beginning of the trip, and was only given water on two occasions. Upon their arrival at the camp, Jimmy was given a bowl of rice and immediately put to work.

He was given a pair of old, worn pajamas, sandals, and a sunshine hat which he recognized as a 'coolie' from his days in Vietnam. He was given a broken-down wheelbarrow, with a metal wheel and handles made of bamboo, and a shovel that appeared to be US Army issue.

He was directed to a mountainous pile of sand and then to a contraption some 40 yards away that he assumed was a cement mixer. The Chinese soldier that was directing Jimmy was frail and wrinkled. Jimmy could not tell if the man was 30 years old, or 50. The man simply pointed first, to the pile of sand, then the wheelbarrow and shovel, and then the large cement mixing contraption that was 40 or 50 yards away, and simply said what sounded like, 'Gong zo.' The soldier kept repeating the phrase until Jimmy seemed to get the message. The phrase apparently meant something like, 'Get to work', because when Jimmy began moving, the soldier stopped repeating it.

With an orientation session that lasted less than five minutes, Jimmy began what would become his full-time job in a Chinese slave labor camp. He would fill the wheelbarrow with sand and transport it to what he had thought was a cement mixer, and then go back for another load of sand, and perform the task all over again, repeatedly every day.

One thing he was not issued when he arrived, was a pair of gloves. By the end of the first day, his hands were blistered and bleeding. On one occasion, because of the pain from the blisters, Jimmy only loaded the wheelbarrow with less than half a load of sand. He was then introduced to another Chinese phrase.

'M'yong da, M'yong da', the Chinese soldier yelled at him while wagging his finger disapprovingly. 'M'yong da', Jimmy quickly determined, meant, 'No, that's not good' or some variation. With blistered and bleeding hands, which were still healing from the torture he had received, Jimmy filled the wheelbarrow and continued working.

About the best thing Jimmy could conclude from his current circumstances, is that he was not being tortured. For the first few months of his captivity as a slave laborer, he just continued to keep his head down and do his job, all while thinking of getting home to Katie and Little Jim.

Jimmy had no idea where he was in China. He frequently heard the word, 'Shanghai', and was near a large body of water, so he guessed he was in the vicinity of that Chinese city.

Surprisingly, he saw no other American prisoners in the camp. He did meet some Canadians and New Zealanders, but most of the workforce consisted of Chinese, Vietnamese, Filipinos, and Laotian's.

One of the laborers was a thirty-something year-old Chinese dissident who spoke very good English and appeared well educated. Jimmy learned the man was a physician and political activist, and well-informed regarding world events, including the war in Vietnam. He had been a vocal critic of the Communist Chinese government, and was jailed for 'crimes against the people.' There were no doctors employed by the camp officials, so having a doctor as a prisoner was a bonus in the camp. The doctor's name was 'Hai Non', which Jimmy translated to 'Hey Now'. That is what Jimmy would call the doctor for the duration of their time together.

The laborers were housed in small, mud-hut type buildings that housed 40-50 laborers in each. The huts contained no furniture and small rugs on the floor that served as cots. 'Hey Now's' cot was in the same corner of the hut as Jimmy's, which allowed the two to frequently communicate at night.

'Hey Now' had been in the camp for over three years. He had a wife and son at home, which provided him and Jimmy an instant connection. Jimmy frequently talked to the doctor about how much he missed Katie and Little Jim and his desire and determination to escape and get back home. 'Hey Now' gave Jimmy the lay of the land and what he would be up against in his efforts to escape.

"First", the doctor told Jimmy, "we are in an ocean inlet but the waters are too shallow to allow freighters and heavy barges to get into the inlet. So, the Chinese must dredge the inlet and build larger docks to accommodate the larger ships. That's why we're here."

He went on to explain how the Chinese economy was heavily dependent on selling products and produce to other countries, but were restricted by their ability to get those products to the large ships. With minimal heavy equipment for their large construction projects, the Chinese relied heavily on manpower . . . both their own and prisoners from China and other countries. That included American P.O.W.'s imported from Viet Cong prisons.

His only realistic chance to escape, the doctor told Jimmy, was to get to the freighter that comes in each month. That ship, he continued, is not a Chinese ship, but an international container. The closest they get, however, was five to six miles out to sea.

"How good a swimmer are you" the doctor joked?

As time went on, Jimmy and 'Hey Now' became friends and talked frequently. It was with the help of the Chinese physician that Jimmy began to devise his escape plan. The doctor continued to warn Jimmy of the extraordinary risks of his plan. "First", he said, "you have to navigate over five miles of ocean just to get to the ship. Then, you have to hope they will accept you and not turn you back over to the Chinese government."

Despite the risks, the doctor could see the determination in Jimmy's eyes. He knew he was going to try to escape, no matter the odds or the potential repercussions from the Chinese.

"Failure", he told Jimmy, "is a death sentence!" That was a risk Jimmy was willing to take. "If I can't get back to Katie and Little Jim," he told the doctor, "I'd just as soon be dead."

There was one thing working in Jimmy's favor. This particular labor camp was the Chinese version of Alcatraz. They were remote and bound by the open sea, and had never had a successful escape. From the Chinese vantage point, no one was ever going to escape the camp, so the need for 24- hour armed guards didn't seem necessary. As a result, the security at the slave camp had become somewhat relaxed.

That, however, did not negate the many other questions that would need to be successfully addressed.

Would the ship arrive at the same time each month? Could Jimmy slip out of the labor camp unnoticed? Could he safely navigate the waters to get to the ship? Would the ship's captain and crew allow him to board? Was the ship of Chinese origin, or from another country? Was it a country that was friendly to Americans? Was it being monitored by Chinese patrol boats? Jimmy was flooded with questions and would literally spend years trying to answer them.

All the while, "Hey now' warned him, he must do his work at the camp and give the Chinese no reason to be suspicious of the American. After all, the doctor reminded him, America and the Chinese communist government were on opposite sides of the Vietnam War. You don't want to become a political pawn in the middle of a cold war, he told Jimmy.

After years of monitoring and calculations, the two co-conspirators learned that the ship was consistent in its arrival out at sea. Jimmy and 'Hey Now' calculated that every 29-31 days, its lights appeared and remained there for a twenty-four to thirty-six hour period, just long enough to load its cargo from the Chinese.

They also calculated that the Chinese guards during the midnight shift at the camp were extremely lax. On more than one occasion, Jimmy left his hut at night to go to his work area where he found the guard asleep at his post. On another occasion, during the winter, the same guard stayed inside the guard shack during his entire midnight shift to remain warm, leaving the area completely unguarded.

Jimmy's work area led directly to the water and to his preferred path of escape, which seemed to be a favorable situation, given the lax security.

His biggest hurdle was his ability to navigate five-plus miles out to the freighter. Small boats traveled back and forth to the large container vessel, carrying produce and other products. But those boats provided no reasonable chance of stow-away potential. First, they made their trips during daylight hours when the camp was buzzing with activity. Second, those were the most heavily guarded vessels by Chinese soldiers. As tempting as it was to simply take a boat out to the large ship, to do so undetected was impossible.

The only remaining option was to build a small raft or flotation device that would support the American as he swam the distance to the ship. Jimmy and 'Hey Now' calculated that, with the aid of a flotation device, the American could navigate roughly one mile-per-hour. Assuming six miles in distance, that gave them a window of six hours.

Jimmy was not a particularly good swimmer, but his body had been pushed to the limits before. He believed that with the aid of some type of flotation device he could make it to the barge. It would be, he thought, more of a mental challenge than a physical one.

They further determined that, while the container ship was anchored at sea, the small Chinese delivery boats loaded their first cargo shipment of the day at 8:00 AM. That gave them an additional two hours.

So, based on their calculations, he had a timespan from midnight to 8:00 AM to execute his daring escape. And that assumed he could construct a workable flotation device *AND* the ship's captain and crew would take him. The two continued to work on and refine his plan.

One evening during their late-night conversations, Jimmy asked 'Hey now' if he had ever considered escaping or would he be interested in joining Jimmy in his quest. The Chinese physician told Jimmy, "When I was convicted of what the government considered 'crimes against the country', I received a sentence of twelve years at hard labor. I have completed almost ten of those years. I will soon be allowed to rejoin my family, and would not do anything to put that at risk. I will always help you plan what you have to do, but I will never actively participate in a way that jeopardizes my situation."

Jimmy began to have a sense of déjà vu when 'Hey Now' told him his story. One family that tried to help him was already put at risk and ultimately killed for doing so. He did not want to subject yet another family to the same torment. He pleaded with the Chinese doctor not to do anything more that could jeopardize his situation. Jimmy told him what had happened to Lin and her family, and could not live with the guilt of having someone else suffer by helping him. 'Hey Now' appreciated Jimmy's concerns, but was determined to help his friend get back to his family. He would be careful, he told Jimmy.

Just as he said he would, 'Hey Now' continued to help his American friend. Given that he was Chinese, he could eavesdrop on the discussions when he was in earshot of the camp officials. He learned that the Chinese used two different container companies to transport their products. One was Dutch and the other was Russian. With Russia's political ties to Communist China, they would surely return the American P.O.W. back over to the Chinese if he approached their ship. So, he would have to wait for his opportunity to escape only when the Dutch container was present. 'Hey Now' learned that the Dutch vessel only came through every four months.

The Chinese doctor also discovered how Jimmy might be able to construct a potential flotation device to aid his swim. A collection of bamboo stalks had been tied together to serve as pallets for heavy materials. From his life in China, he knew that bamboo was used for building rafts, and the stalks tied together, the doctor told Jimmy, could serve as his swimming aid.

Slowly, Jimmy's plan for his 'Great Escape' was beginning to come together.

Much of the final preparations took place at night, under the cover of darkness. Jimmy confiscated the bamboo stalks and managed to hide them under heavy brush close to the water.

He now had to wait until he knew it was the Dutch container ship that had arrived for its cargo. When the large vessels came in, they were five or 6 miles out to sea and barely visible. The only distinction that could be made was their lights. Fortunately, the Dutch vessel had a different lighting configuration than the Russian ship. Jimmy could always tell the Dutch container ship by three mast lights at the bow of the vessel.

According to their calculations, and other information obtained by 'Hey now,' the Dutch container ship was scheduled to arrive in the early part of June. That was a perfect time. The evenings were warm, and the water temperature would be good for the long swim that awaited Jimmy.

As the time drew near, Jimmy planned his escape for the following evening. All throughout that day, he worked hard so as not to create any suspicion. That evening, just after midnight, Jimmy quietly made his way over to his Chinese friend's mat where he was sleeping. He gently shook his friend to say his goodbyes.

When 'Hey now' awoke, he looked at his friend and said something in Chinese that sounded like *Zu ni how yun*, followed by, 'Good luck, my American friend, and God speed.'

Jimmy hugged his Chinese friend and said, "God bless you, 'Hey now.' I couldn't have done this without you, and I'll never forget you."

With that, he quietly made his way out of the hut and down to the water where his bamboo stalks were hidden. He made his way to the water's edge and began to swim out into the bay. He headed toward the lights of the ship he hoped would get him back home. As he kicked his feet quietly, he looked up at the starry night and said, "Thank you, God. You have given me the strength and the endurance to make it this far. Please help me make it the rest of the way back to Katie and Little Jim."

The water was cold when he first entered, but it warmed up as his movement increased. Jimmy had mentally and physically prepared for an all- night swim, and now, all he had been planning over the past nine years was now happening. From the years of torture in Vietnam and his years as a slave laborer in China, could it be? Was he finally free of abuse and captivity? Could he really be on his way to freedom and back to his wife and son? Could it possibly be?

Just as his body was swimming, so was his mind. His thoughts were swirling between the euphoria of his possible freedom and return to Katie and little Jim, and the fear of being recaptured or even killed if his plan did not work. According to his calculations, he could get to the container ship by sunrise. He had the next 4-5 hours to swim and let his mind wonder about the range of possible outcomes. He was apprehensive, but his faith was strong.

As the hours passed and the dark of night was beginning to disappear, Jimmy was exhausted but estimated he was within a mile of the vessel.

As he continued to kick towards the ship, he began to see two workers out on the deck preparing for the day's deliveries from shore. So far, it appeared he had been undetected, though this was also about the time the officials back in the labor camp would detect his absence. It is possible they would alert the ship to be on the lookout for an escapee.

Minutes later, with the help of tidal waves, Jimmy's body began to crash up against the hull of the vessel. One of the workers had spotted Jimmy in the sea and alerted the ship's captain. As he continuously bounced against the hull of the ship, Jimmy then saw a large rope with a type of harness on the end of it being lowered toward him. The ship's worker was literally offering him a lifeline. When the harness was within arm's reach, Jimmy grabbed the rope and, at the same time, let go of the bamboo that had kept him afloat all night. In doing so, he was bidding farewell to a life of slavery and abuse, and hopefully, saying hello to his return to freedom and his family.

He pulled the harness around his exhausted body, and began being pulled up by the unknown sailors. He grew anxious as he was drawn closer to the deck of the large flat-bottomed barge, wondering who was rescuing him, and what would be his fate.

As he was pulled onto the deck by the sailors, Jimmy was near exhaustion and prune-like from his night in the water. The flimsy pajamas he was wearing when he began his escape were almost all gone. His skeleton-like body was exposed from the waist up and he flopped onto his back, on the warm deck of the vessel.

Squinting through the bright glare of the morning sun, Jimmy could see that the sailors looked Scandinavian in appearance, but that could mean they could be Russians or Dutch. He was anxious to verify he had not been rescued by Russians. That anxiety left him when he heard one of the sailors speak. "American?" he asked Jimmy in a foreign accent. "We are from Holland." Jimmy faintly smiled when he heard that.

Though he spoke with a European accent, the sailor spoke fluent English. He explained that the ship comes to China every four months, and from there, travels to Bangkok, Singapore and then to South Africa.

He asked Jimmy if his boat had capsized, but Jimmy remained silent. He did not want to divulge that he was an escaped P.O.W.

As the sailor spoke, a man Jimmy assumed was the ship's captain approached. He did not acknowledge Jimmy, but instructed the two sailors to take him down to a secure room in the ship's bulkhead, and get him clothes, food and water. And, the captain emphasized to the two sailors, 'You are to tell no one about our 'visitor.'

The captain didn't know if Jimmy was a stranded sailor, an escapee or what, but was not going to take any chances until he found out.

Jimmy was immediately given water and a fresh set of clothes to wear. He was then confined to a small room in the bulkhead of the ship to await questioning by the ship's captain. There he was given his first meal consisting of something other than poorly prepared rice or fish, in more than a decade. He was given eggs and toast.

Fortunately, at this time of the morning, very few of the sailors were up and working and were unaware of their visitor. The captain wanted to keep it that way. He told the only two crew members that knew of Jimmy's presence, 'We could have a very sensitive situation on our hands.'

Once in the small room, Jimmy immediately began to doze off. He was still recovering from his all-night swim. About 45 minutes later, his sleep was interrupted by the arrival of the ship's captain, who was immediately startled by the appearance of the stowaway. Jimmy's body was gaunt and full of scars. Before saying a word, the captain knew Jimmy had endured abuse of some sort and was most likely an escaped prisoner.

'But, how could an American be a prisoner in China', the captain wondered to himself? The war in Vietnam had been ended years ago and the political climate between the U.S. and China had begun to improve.

"Are you able to speak," the captain asked Jimmy in a thick European accent? "I know you escaped from somewhere, and my responsibility as Captain is to return you to your captors, and I assume that is China. Is that correct?"

The captain continued, "I, and all of the men who work on this ship could lose their lives if it is discovered that we are harboring a stowaway, and worse, and escaped prisoner. We have a very delicate situation here, and I need you to tell me how you got here."

Jimmy proceeded to tell his story. He told of his time fighting in Vietnam and being captured by the Viet Cong. He told of the nine years he spent as a slave laborer in China. He told of the long and painful saga he has endured in his efforts to get back home to Katie and Little Jim, and of how many have risked their lives in their efforts to help him, and how some have been killed. He told of how he wanted no one else, especially the captain or his crew to risk their lives for him, but how he was desperate to once again see his wife and child. He told the captain that his escape from the labor camp was his final hope.

The captain was visibly moved as he listened to Jimmy for more than an hour detail his saga of the last decade. He knew Jimmy was exhausted and told him to get some sleep, and talk again later in the day.

Over the course of the day, the captain's primary objective was to get the Chinese produce and products loaded on his ship. His second objective was to determine what to do with his new American visitor. He had received alerts about an escaped laborer from the Chinese government, and was instructed to turn him in or notify them if he was spotted. He was also told by his lieutenant that the few crewmembers who knew he was aboard expressed strong sentiments that the man should be turned over to the Chinese. They wanted nothing to do with the escaped prisoner. The American, they told the lieutenant, was a risk to the lives and livelihoods of the crew, and should be disposed of.

After hearing from all concerned, and listening to Jimmy's story, by the end of the day, the captain had come to a decision.

He proceeded down to the cabin where Jimmy was being held. When he arrived, he sat down at the edge of the cot where Jimmy had been recovering. The exhausted American was peering out through a tiny porthole at the open sea. He grew anxious as he waited for the Captain's verdict. The captain began to speak slowly.

"You have caused quite a stir, young man. The Chinese government is looking for you. You have put my crew at risk. The one's that know you are on board want you gone. My shipping company could lose its contract if you're discovered. And you have put me in a position where I could lose my job."

Jimmy began to grow more anxious as the captain spoke. His mind was racing. Was he being turned over to the Chinese? Would he ever see Katie and little Jim again? He strained to listen to the captain's words as he spoke in his heavy Danish accent, as he silently began to pray. 'Please no, Oh God. Please don't send me back there. Please let me get home to see Katie and Little Jim.'

The captain continued. "You have been through a lot . . . a lot more than most men could have endured. So, I'm going to make you a proposition." Jimmy's hopes began to surge. "If you can abide by the following conditions, I will agree to help you" the captain continued. At this point, Jimmy was sitting up right, hanging on to the captain's every word, waiting to hear his conditions. His heart was beating out of his chest.

The captain began to outline the conditions Jimmy must swear to adhere to. "I will agree to take you to the next stop on our itinerary, which is Thailand, which is friendly to the U.S. I have contacts there that may be able to help you. I will turn you into them. For your own safety and for the safety of my crew, I will keep you here in the bulkhead, in solitary confinement until we get there. But, you must agree to the following . . . ."

The captain continued in a very stern voice. "You must not speak with anyone on this ship, not even the crew members that bring you meals. You must never mention that you were an American P.O.W. until your feet touch American soil." The captain was aware of P.O.W.'s in Communist countries and he also knew of the embarrassment it would cause all America if one would return home after the United States had declared them all dead.

"You tell no-one . . . you trust no-one. This world has been cruel to you, young man, and you deserve the opportunity to return home to your wife and child. All you have to offer me is your integrity and your honor. Do I have your word? "

Jimmy was waiting and listening intently for more conditions. There were no more. He was now as excited as he was the day he married Katie, but tried to restrain his joy. "Yes sir! Yes sir!" Jimmy repeated excitedly. "You have my word. Thank you, Captain. Thank you, Captain." When the captain left, Jimmy bounced around on his cot like a little boy. He was going home!!! Just as he had thanked the captain repeatedly, he began thanking the Lord, "Thank you, God. Thank you. Thank you. Thank you."

The freighter departed China and slowly made its way to Bangkok where the ship captain's friend had been notified and was waiting. Jimmy was desperately hoping he was on his way to freedom, and into the arms of Katie and Little Jim.

It was nearly midnight when the ship pulled into the Bangkok harbor, where the captain's friend was waiting. The captain introduced Jimmy to his friend, calling him, 'Johnny G.' Jimmy shook Johnny G.'s hand and then turned back to the captain, "Thank you so much for your help, Captain. You have given me my life back. And I don't know if you will ever know how grateful I am. Thank you. Thank you.."

"Just get back to your wife and son, young man. That will be all the thanks I need. Good luck to you. Johnny will help you get home" the captain responded. With those words, he turned to go back to his ship, and Jimmy and Johnny G. headed to the parking lot.

As Jimmy remained silent, Johnny G. directed him to a covered three-wheel vehicle that would serve as their transportation to Johnny G.'s quarters, a small dingy room in the shipyard. Along the way, they passed several other 'Tuk tuks.' Jimmy quickly learned that the three-wheel motorcycle-type devices were the common means of transportation in Thailand, and far less expensive than cars. They were the vehicle of choice for the Thai working man. And Johnny G. was just that.

"What does the G. stand for" Jimmy innocently asked Johnny G. when they arrived at his quarters? The cramped room looked to be part-office and part bedroom.

"'G.' not important," Johnny replied. "What is important is getting you on a plane going back to America."

That was his way, Jimmy assumed, of telling him don't ask personal questions.

"You will sleep here." Johnny continued. "The captain has asked me to help you get American passport and plane ticket to the U.S. Where you go?" he continued in his broken English.

"As close to Chicago as I can get. How do you do this?" Jimmy asked, puzzled as to the 'how' and the 'why' of Johnny G.'s willingness to help him.

"No questions, please!" Johnny replied sternly. "Captain is good friend. He do me many favors. I do him favors. No more questions, please. Just wait here. Don't leave."

Johnny G. departed, and soon returned with a bunch of bananas and jug of water, and just as quickly, departed again, leaving Jimmy alone in his new quarters.

Within an hour, the door to the room opened again. But this time, it was not Johnny G. It was a small framed Thai woman with a camera. She evidently spoke little or no English, but motioned for Jimmy to stand for a photograph. She said repeatedly, 'passpote', 'passpote.' She took three pictures of the gaunt American stranger and left.

Once again alone, he eventually fell asleep on the small cot in the room.

For the next few days, Jimmy's only visitors were delivery boys who periodically arrived with a variety of fruit and containers of water. He had not seen or heard from Johnny G., but assumed he had not forgotten the American. On occasion, he would wander outside the small room to stretch and look around the shipyard. But, he stayed close, as Johnny G. had instructed. He felt relatively safe being in Thailand, but invariably had flashes of anxiety given his close proximity to Vietnam.

On the sixth day in the confined shipyards of Bangkok, Johnny G. returned. He had clothing for the American, consisting of a shirt, suit jacket, pants, shoes, socks and underwear; a U.S. passport with the new photograph of Jimmy taken by the woman photographer, but in a different name; and a plane ticket under that same name that would take him to San Francisco, and onto Chicago's O'Hare airport..

Jimmy was dumfounded. 'How could this be?' he thought. He wanted to know more about how this man could have done all this?

And why *would* he do all this for him? But once again he was reminded by Johnny G. in his limited English, "No questions! Your friend asked me do favor. I do favor!"

Jimmy thought back to the ship captain that delivered him to Thailand. He thought of his promise to tell no one of his circumstance and his experience as a P.O.W. He silently thanked him again, and gave thanks to the Lord, "Thank you, God. You really did deliver me. Thank You."

The next day, he was on an international flight headed to San Francisco. With visions of Katie and little Jim in his head, he marveled at how this flight was a considerable upgrade to the last time he had been on a plane. That was over a decade ago when he was on his way to Vietnam on a plane loaded with other GIs. He was returning home just as he had planned to do. It was only 10 years later than he had planned.

He soon dozed off and did not wake up until he heard the captain giving instructions to the flight attendants to prepare the passengers for landing.

The connection from San Francisco to Chicago was tight. He barely had time to make to his departure gate before the attendant began boarding passengers. Fortunately, he had no baggage to contend with. He was now on American soil. As he boarded the flight, he was thinking of how he would make it known that, despite what his passport and ticket said, he was in reality, Jimmy Wrann, escaped P.O.W.

Compared to his previous flight from Bangkok to San Francisco, the flight to Chicago seemed short. He was trying to remain calm, but his emotions were getting away from him. He ordered a drink to hopefully steady his nerves. His first taste of alcohol since his days in Pleiku tasted strong but sweet. His emotions, however, remained on the edge.

When the flight landed at O'Hare airport, Jimmy had kept his word to the ship's captain. He was now ready to tell the world. As the plane was taxiing to the gate, he called a flight attendant over and calmly said, in the presence of all his fellow passengers, "I am Jimmy Wrann, I am an American soldier that has made it home from a P.O.W. camp in

Communist China!" He was almost screaming with excitement as he spoke.

The flight attendant didn't know if he was joking or was drunk. The Vietnam war had become a fading memory to people in the U.S. How could that be? After a moment's hesitation, she shook her head and nervously proceeded to the front of the plane. She entered the cockpit and told the pilot what she had just been told. He looked at her with a puzzled look and she repeated, "I'm serious. He told me he was a P.O.W. who had escaped from China."

The airline captain alerted security, who agreed to meet the flight at the gate.

When the plane arrived at the gate, the other passengers were asked to remain in their seats as Jimmy was escorted off the plane. Having heard him tell the stewardess he was an escape POW, the word had quickly spread among the passengers.

As Jimmy was escorted to the gate, as promised, airport security staff, who had also notified the Army, was waiting for him. Their intent was to take Jimmy to their private offices where he would be turned over to the military, but circumstances quickly got out of hand.

Jimmy was like a drunken sailor, talking with everyone and jumping and shouting "I'm home . . . I'm home." A crowd quickly formed around Jimmy and some of the crowd took pictures of him. A local news crew was at the airport to cover a political event, but quickly caught wind of the Army P.O.W., and began to converge on Jimmy, shouting questions.

"What's your name?" "Where are you from?" "Where were you being held in China?" "How does it feel to be home?" The questions came fast and furious and Jimmy was all too willing to tell his story. The security officers that had detained him were beginning to lose control.

Then the national media arrived, and the questions continued. In the midst of the media frenzy, an army contingent consisting of three officers and four military policemen approached the scene and assumed control from the security officers.

No interviews were allowed by the military officials who answered each question that was being shouted out by the media with a terse,

"No comment." The video footage they did get, however, was enough to turn the media buzz into a media wildfire. The footage showed the returned P.O.W. being escorted out of the terminal by the military police, with the caption reading, "Local Vietnam era P.O.W. escapes China after a decade of captivity.

Jimmy Wrann was home, on American soil, and anxiously awaiting the dream that had lingered in his imagination for over a decade.

That dream would soon become a nightmare.

# CHAPTER 21

# Hell No I Won't Go

JIMMY, NOW BACK in the hands of the U.S. Army and in the midst of what was supposed to be a 60-day debriefing, was experiencing a variety of emotions. He was back on American soil and happy to be home. He was excited about the prospects of being reunited with Katie and Little Jim. But he was frustrated at why the debriefing was not going at a faster pace.

His initial visit with Katie was aborted before it even began. With her in his arms on the airport tarmac, he was whisked away before he could even talk to her. Just when he could smell the scent of her body that he had been imagining all these years, she was separated from him. Just as he could feel her body as he had in his dreams all those years, she was gone.

In a matter of minutes, he had gone from the ecstasy of feeling Katie rocking back and forth in his arms, to the sheer agony of being separated from her. All the pain he had suffered from his years of torture by the Viet Cong could not compare to the sheer anguish and emotions of that moment. He was determined not to have a repeat of that horrible episode.

He knew her life must be different now, but instead of helping him adjust to the new realities, the government seemed to be holding him back. It was if they were telling him, 'Just forget you ever had a wife and child, and move on with your life.' How could he just forget the very thing that had kept him alive all these years.

From the beginning of the debriefing process, Jimmy had regularly scheduled visits with a psychologist. The sessions began innocently enough, having him talk through his experiences in Vietnam and in China. About the fourth week into the sessions, however, the psychologist seemed to shift directions. Rather than listening and allowing Jimmy to process all he had been thru, the psychologist seemed to begin 'guiding' the discussions toward the ex-P.O.W. simply letting go of his past and beginning a new life elsewhere.

Eventually, the sessions began to reveal what the government was suggesting, and why. The topic of Katie and Little Jim began to creep into the discussions more and more, and how the two had moved on to start a new life. The discussions seemed to shift towards vague and elusive 'what if' scenarios, all designed to ease him toward understanding that Katie's life was different now.

'What if', they posed, Katie had remarried? 'What if' she had a new family? It was typical 'shrink talk,' offering no specifics, but throwing out possibilities for Jimmy to consider. Nothing was concrete. That is, until one day when the head of the debriefing team requested a meeting with Jimmy.

After sharing pleasantries and small talk about how good it must feel to finally be home, the officer began to ease his way to the point. "Your wife has endured a lot from this ordeal. She spent years as a POW/MIA activist fighting for your return and waiting for you. When she was told that all POW's were returned and you were not among them, she had to confront the most difficult situation of her life . . . that you were dead. She and the entire town said their goodbye's to you. And reluctantly, she had to begin the process of starting her life over. Jimmy, your wife remarried."

The officer gave Jimmy time to digest this new reality. Jimmy was devastated. He had often thought of that possibility, but the harshness of the reality jolted him. Hiding his head, he began to cry, but was determined to keep his pain hidden from the officer. After moments of tears that he tried so desperately to hold back, he braced himself and looked at the officer. In his best attempt to remain calm, he said, "OK, now what?"

The officer responded as if he had anticipated the question, "Jimmy, your wife has gotten on with her new life, and we think it's time for you to do the same. We believe you should relocate to another city, which would allow both of you to begin new lives."

Even before the officer finished his sentence, Jimmy immediately came out of his chair.

"Not no, but HELL no" he responded. He was tired of this 'pussy footing' debriefing process, and was now in the same defiant mode as he was with his Viet Cong torturers. He continued, "There is no fucking way I'm going to simply walk away from my wife and son, and relocate to another town. I've come too damn far. Do you think I would go through everything I've gone through for as long as I have, when those two were the only thing that kept me alive? And get this far and simply say, 'Never mind, I'll just go to a new city? *FUCK* you and your relocation package. I really don't give a shit what you think is best for everyone . . . this is my life . . . and my wife and son . . . and you just want me to walk away from them . . . go fuck yourself. I'm not going anywhere, but home!"

Jimmy had one more thing to say to the officer, with the same defiant tone, "I refuse to believe any of this until I hear it come out of Katie's mouth. I refuse to leave my wife, my son, my family and my best friend or the town I grew up in until I know the truth!"

Jimmy was seething with anger and was displaying a side of himself the debriefing team had not seen. And the debriefing team had not even told him the worse part . . . that it was Bobby, his best friend, that Katie had married. Or, that the two had conceived a new daughter.

With Jimmy standing and visibly shaking, the officer offered the soldier some time alone to process what he had just heard. As the officer closed the door behind him, Jimmy began openly sobbing, saying repeatedly, "No! No! No! "As he gradually came to grips with the situation, he then looked to the Lord and said, "God . . . you have brought me this far . . . please don't leave me now . . . Please help me make this right again . . . Please God please help me."

Once back in his office, the officer went to work considering his next steps. He decided to call Katie to share the exchange that had just taken place with her, and to ask her willingness to meet to Jimmy. After an extended discussion, she told the officer she was not ready to put herself in that situation. "I am scared," she told him. After they hung up, the officer convened his team to discuss what had happened and what to do next.

Jimmy had flatly refused the relocation option and was as emotionally charged as I've ever seen him, the officer told his team. "He's not mentally prepared to do anything right now," he told them.

"And his wife is refusing to speak with him. Meanwhile," he continued, "based on the media coverage that has made him a national story, the whole damn country is waiting to hear the next chapter of the Jimmy Wrann saga."

The team met for over an hour, debating options of what to do next. The alternatives varied from releasing him, 'cold turkey,' to confront the whole story, to having him committed to a military mental institution. Every option had pitfalls. The military was simply not prepared to deal with what the officer referred to as the 'Jimmy Wrann' saga.

In the end, they decided on a temporary solution. They decided to keep him confined in a controlled setting in a military mental institution until the right thing could be done . . . . but what was the right thing?

In his confinement, Jimmy could only watch restricted television and he couldn't read the paper or listen to the radio. His story was on the front page of every newspaper and all America awaited his release. But the military thought it best that Jimmy be reintroduced back into society slowly. Jimmy's debriefing continued be a steady, drip . . . drip . . . drip process of his re-indoctrination back to his new life . . . and to the truth.

After a few days, he had come to grips with the notion of Katie being remarried. He began to think through just what it would take to get him released from his confinement and get back home to confront the situation. He began to think about the whole psychology of the military and how he could best work the system. After all, it was his savvy that kept him alive in Vietnam and in China. He knew in order for him to gain his release, he would have to play the game.

During his continued psychological sessions, Jimmy began to sing a different tune . . . one that demonstrated an understanding and acceptance of the situation. He told the psychologist that he knew Katie had probably remarried and he understood. "After all, he told the psychologist, "how long could she wait? As far as she knew, I was a dead man," he continued. "What else would she be expected to do?"

He talked of how he was happy just to be home, and just wanted to start over again. "I accept that she is remarried," he said, "and I wish her nothing but happiness. I just want to be able to be around my son and be a part of his life. Is there anything wrong with that?" he asked.

Jimmy's pitch and desire was to present himself as accepting of the new reality, and willing to be supportive of the new situation of Katie's new life. His goal was to convince the military that he was a reasonable man and was prepared to move on with his life.

The stark reality, however, was twofold . . . first, he didn't know the extent of what Katie's new reality was; and secondly, he was in no way prepared to move on with his life. He still had dreams of once again, being with Katie and Little Jim. Deep down in his heart, he was still clinging to 'till death due us part.'

'I had her first, and by God, I'm not dead yet' he thought to himself 'I'll play their silly fucking game,' he continued. But I know one damn thing . . . I'm going to see my wife and child again.' Once again he had to caution himself to stay calm. He was getting emotional all over again.

Jimmy was living in a world of fantasies, truths and half-truths, but he became more and more convincing in his pitch to the psychologist and the rest of the debriefing team. The team began to see the changes in Jimmy and decided he was finally ready to be discharged. They began preparing for his discharge from the military and the prospects of him returning home.

But before they could do anything, they would have to convince Katie first. She would not only have to be prepared to co-exist with her former husband in the same community, but first, meet with him to tell him the rest of the story. Up to this point, not only had Katie refused to talk with Jimmy, but everyone in the community, including Jimmy's Mom and Dad, had grave concerns about how he would receive the brutal truth.

After an extended series of discussions with the commander of the debriefing team, and with Bobby, Katie agreed to once again, to meet with Jimmy and tell him the whole story . . . Bobby, Little Jim, Kim, everything! She asked for some time to brace herself for what would be there second reunion. Hopefully, this would go better than their first.

Their first meeting that occurred back on the airport tarmac that day was aborted quickly after the two saw each other. From the military's point of view, the meeting was a disaster. Nothing went according to plan. Katie was supposed to have a private meeting with Jimmy in a pre-arranged location. Instead she showed up at the airport to get a glimpse at her former husband. Once the two saw each other at the airport instead of the private room that had been arranged for them, as one Army official put it, 'things went to hell in a hand basket.'

Virtually the entire community of Black Oak was there to witness the highly emotional reunion. As one of the towns people recalled, it was like watching 'a bad soap opera.' Like everything else that occurred that day, that was not supposed to happen.

This meeting would have to be more tightly scripted than the last reunion. "Zero defects," the debriefing commander said.

Jimmy's official discharge from the Army and his long-awaited reunion with Katie was set to occur in ninety days. That gave the military a chance to plan and process Jimmy's discharge and reunion with his former wife and family. It gave Katie and Bobby a chance to prepare for what will possibly be the toughest moment of their marriage. And, it gave Jimmy a chance to begin mapping out his life as a civilian.

# CHAPTER 22
# The Transition

THE GOVERNMENT'S FIRST attempt to reintroduce Jimmy back into his family and community was a fiasco. They had arranged a private meeting between Jimmy and Katie that they hoped would begin the process of easing him into his new realities. Contrary to the plan, Katie showed up on the tarmac where the entire community witnessed their emotional reunion.

The reunion was quickly aborted.

This time it would be different. The Army mapped out a tightly scripted 90-day plan that would reveal to Jimmy all of the hidden truths that had been kept from him, and lead to his eventual discharge from the military. Jimmy could not be released from the military, they felt, until he knew and could accept the whole truth about Katie and Little Jim, their new life with Bobby, and the existence of Kim, their young daughter.

Given the highly charged atmosphere and Jimmy's emotional state, they planned to introduce this information to him gradually, bit by bit. They scheduled a series of meetings for Jimmy with Katie, Bobby and his family, each to be followed by meetings with the psychologist to monitor his progress and emotional reactions to each. The intent was to conclude this 90-day plan with Jimmy's eventual discharge from the Army. But, before they released him, they wanted to ensure that he knew everything, and was prepared to accept his new realities.

The plan also included pre-meetings with Katie and Bobby to brief them on what they could and could not discuss with Jimmy. This would be a series of what the military described as 'rolling disclosures.' They would share only what the psychologists determined Jimmy was prepared to hear. His first meeting, as per the plan, would be with Katie.

Katie was a basket case leading up to their first meeting. She was nervous about seeing Jimmy again and nervous about remembering the government's instructions about what she could and could not say.

When she arrived at the meeting room, Jimmy was seated at the table but immediately jumped up as she was escorted through the door. He approached her and instinctively held her. Jimmy could hardly control himself. He held her tightly for two or three minutes remembering everything about her . . . her touch, her feel, her smell, her hair, her very soul.

More than a decade of pent-up emotions came pouring out of his body. He was tearing up. He was trembling. He was finally experiencing the very moment that had kept him going for all those years and didn't want it to end. He couldn't let go.

Katie was feeling the same sensations and was holding him just as tightly. But as she held him, she was haunted by the guilt, fear, and shame that overshadowed her feelings. She too, began to whimper. Jimmy, feeling Katie's emotions and tears, held her face in his hands and gently wiped away her tears. He thought to himself, he had actually made it back home to his wife . . . she was finally back in his arms . . . there is indeed a God in Heaven, and Jimmy thanked him with every bone in his body.

Given that she was now married to Bobby, Katie was hoping she would not feel the same love for Jimmy as she had before, but that was not to be. Their love was still as strong as it ever was. It was obvious from the first time she saw him again that she still loved him, now in his arms there was no doubt. Her love made her feelings of guilt and shame even greater. But how could this be? How could she feel so strongly about someone only months before she had wished was dead.

After what must have been 5-10 minutes of the deeply emotional reunion, the two finally sat down at the table to begin talking. Jimmy was feeling the sheer ecstasy of being back with his wife. Katie, however, was feeling the emotional anguish of still loving this man that was once her husband, but now being married to his best friend. She felt terrible guilt for not disclosing this information to Jimmy, but had been given strict instructions not to.

Jimmy was not allowed to ask her about her new life. They could talk about little Jim and the life they had before. Katie couldn't talk about Bobby except for his injuries and that he had returned to become a teacher. Jimmy talked of how he was anxious to meet with Bobby, who he said was next on his calendar. He was eager, he said, to learn more about Bobby's new life and transition back into the real world. It was ironic, Jimmy said, that it was Bobby and not him that finished his college degree first.

With every mention of Bobby or Jimmy looking forward to getting back with his wife and best friend, Katie felt the twinge. She hated the deceiving the man she once loved and looked forward to the day when everything would be out in the open.

Their first meeting lasted less than an hour and ended with the same emotional hug it began with, and the pleasantries of looking forward to their next meeting. As much as she still loved Jimmy and was glad to see him, she felt ashamed that she had been superficial and dishonest with him. When she arrived back at her car, she was emotionally exhausted. She rested her head on her hands on the steering wheel and sobbed uncontrollably.

Jimmy, meanwhile, went back to his room, looking forward to his debriefing with the psychologist and his upcoming meeting with Bobby. He described the meeting with Katie as having gone 'very well', and he felt equally optimistic about his meeting with Bobby. After his meeting with Katie, Jimmy was on an emotional high he had not felt since his wedding night. He still knew very little about Katie's new life, but whatever it was, he felt it could be managed. He was convinced they were still in love with each other and that's all that mattered . . . or so he felt. No matter what her new life may be, he thought, I loved her first, and I know she still loves me.

He had three days to enjoy the emotional high he had gotten from his meeting with Katie before his next meeting. That would be his long-awaited reunion with his best friend since grade school.

Once Katie had returned home from her meeting, Bobby was anxious to hear all about it. Before she even had time to sit down, he was peppering her with questions. How was he? What did he ask? What did he tell him? Do you think he knows about us? Did she stick to the script? How do you think he will take it when he learns everything?

Katie was now feeling overwhelmed with guilt. She was not only holding back information from Jimmy, but was now doing the same with Bobby. She tried to answer his questions truthfully, but she could not tell her husband everything. She could not tell him about her feelings that remained for Jimmy. She could not tell him about how they held each other longingly and passionately. She could not tell him that, despite his deeply scarred body from the many injuries he had suffered, to her, he was the same old Jimmy and the passion was still there.

Citing exhaustion, Katie tried to gracefully remove herself from the constant questions from her husband. She truly was exhausted, but what she really wanted was time to think. She was more conflicted than ever before. She loved her husband and had no intentions other than to maintain her family. But she could not stop thinking about the passion she felt as she and Jimmy held each other.

Her world was spinning. She had a loving husband, two beautiful children, three wonderful families, and a community that truly loved and embraced her and Bobby. But the love of her life she had long ago given up for dead was suddenly back in her life. When could they tell him the truth? When could they end the deceptions and let Jimmy know the new realities? Katie's life had been turned upside down and was living in sheer agony.

Soon they would get closer to the truth, but not yet. It was now Bobby's turn to meet with Jimmy. He too, was under strict orders as to what he could and could not share during his visit with Jimmy. Any discussion about Katie was off limits, as was any discussion about Bobby's personal situation. Their first discussion, however, was about neither of those topics . . . it was about that day back in Dak Seang.

Bobby had agonized about that day ever since he saw Jimmy laying on the ground as the helicopter scrambled to get the hell out of there. He had his apology all planned and had emotionally prepared himself for the possibility that Jimmy would reject his apologies and never forgive him

To the contrary, when they met, Jimmy cut him off from his planned speech of apologies and instantly forgave Bobby. He told his best friend to forget about any guilt he may have felt. Jimmy knew he had fought with every ounce of strength in his body to save him that day in the jungles of Vietnam, but it just wasn't meant to be. "Forget it man" Jimmy told him, "this war is finally over for both of us. I know you did what you had to do, and I would have done the same thing."

The conversation immediately shifted to old times and their lifelong friendship. From Little League playoffs to high school football games, to the many times Bobby had been there for Jimmy, they reminisced and joked about those 'good old days.' From there, the conversation went into catch-up mode.

Bobby told Jimmy about attending college and how odd the experience was for him. "I was older than most of the other students and missing an arm. It was a strange experience but I'm glad I did it. It set me up to be a teacher and a school administrator. Imagine me . . . a teacher." They laughed about the irony of Bobby now being on the other side of the desk dealing with delinquent students.

Jimmy then asked about Little Jim. "Do you get to see him? Have you been to any of his games? Have you seen him pitch? What about his grades?" Jimmy was clearly anxious to talk about Little Jim and Katie, and each time the subject began to touch on either one, Bobby would just die inside and try to shift the conversation back to some old football and basketball games and all the fun they had in high school. He knew the truth would eventually come out, but not now . . . not from Bobby.

Throughout the conversation, Bobby tried to keep the conversation focused on the past, but all the while, he was thinking about the present, and more so, the immediate future. He agonized over how Jimmy would feel when he learned that he had married Katie. 'Would he be so quick to forgive him for that' he wondered?

His thoughts would then shift to his efforts to convince himself he was not a villain, as if he were having an argument with himself. 'It wasn't my fault . . . I didn't do anything wrong' he thought to himself. 'How was I supposed to know Jimmy would make it back alive?' he continued. As Jimmy was talking about how anxious he was to see

Katie and Little Jim, Bobby was continuing his imaginary argument with himself. 'Our government declared him dead, not me. No Hell No! I didn't do anything wrong. I'm not the bad guy here!'

As Jimmy was talking excitedly about his upcoming discharge and return home, Bobby was barely listening. He was more attuned to the conversation going on in his head. 'Ok, so I chose not to tell Katie the whole truth about that day in Dak Seang. But I did it because I was ashamed that I left Jimmy. I didn't do it to try to steal Katie from my best friend. We just fell in love . . . it wasn't anyone's fault . . . was it? Would Jimmy understand? How could he?'

Bobby eventually drifted from the conversation he was having in his head back to the conversation with Jimmy. "I know we're not supposed to talk about these things," Jimmy said, "but tell me about how Katie's doing. How do you think she's dealing with all this? How do you think Little Jim's doing? What can you tell me?"

Bobby shifted in his chair uncomfortably as Jimmy was asking the questions. "Come on Jim." Bobby responded, "You know we can't talk about that, so as your best friend, please stop asking me. OK?"

When he said those words, "as your best friend," Bobby felt like Peter in the Bible denouncing Jesus, he felt like a traitor and a liar. He was keeping something from Jimmy that was going to hurt him much more than the torture he suffered in Vietnam. He knew that the truth was coming soon, but he could not be the one to tell him, and he agonized over being deceptive to his best friend.

As the meeting ended, the two friends embraced one another and held the embrace patting each other on the back. Jimmy was elated to see his best friend and reiterated how much he looked forward to the 'three amigos' once again being back together. Bobby felt a twinge in his gut when Jimmy said that, knowing that may never happen once Jimmy discovers the truth.

Like Katie, Bobby left the meeting feeling emotionally drained from having to continue the deception that the Army had imposed, and the anguish of Jimmy's reaction once he discovers the truth. After several more visits from Katie and Bobby, however, that web of deception would soon come crashing down.

Some six weeks into Jimmy's 90-day transition plan the Army had created for him, he showed up for his weekly meeting with the head of the transition team. Feeling that the transition was going well, Jimmy was feeling upbeat when the two sat down.

"I understand your meetings have been going well" the Commander began, "and the psychological reports show you're making good progress toward being ready for discharge" he continued.

"Thank you, sir" Jimmy responded, "I'm feeling pretty good about the way things have progressed, and I'm definitely ready to go home."

"That's good" the Commander responded, "but there's some critical information you're going to need to know, and it may be the toughest issue yet in preparation for your eventual return home."

"Yes sir?" Jimmy sat up in his chair, as if preparing himself to hear whatever was to follow.

"As you know" the Commander began, "your wife has assumed for years that you were dead. And, as we told you, she had to start her life over." The commander continued, choosing his words very carefully. "Now, your ability to understand and accept that fact will be the ultimate determinant in you being discharged." The officer's tone was now sounding very formal, less like a friend and more like a bureaucrat.

"Yes sir. I understand" Jimmy said, waiting for the other shoe to drop.

The commander continued, again being careful with his words. "You need to understand the full extent of her new life, and it's not going to be easy."

Jimmy's mood had shifted from feeling upbeat to feeling anxious. 'What was he about to hear' he wondered anxiously? "Yes sir. I'm listening" he said.

"Jimmy" the officer said with more forcefulness, determined to finally lay out all the facts, once and for all. "Your wife has remarried. And she's married to your best friend, Mr. Robert Bowers! Your wife's name is now Katherine Bowers!"

Jimmy sat in his chair, looking at the officer with his mouth opened wide. He was stunned by what he just heard. After sitting in silence for almost a minute, he responded in a weak, hesitating voice, "Did I hear you correctly that my Katie is married to Bobby . . . Bowers?"

"That is correct soldier" said the commander, speaking in a firm and formal voice. "You heard correctly." And to get everything out on the table, he added, "And that's not all. "Bobby is Little Jim's father. He adopted him. And Bobby and Katie also have a little daughter, named Kim."

With that, the officer exhaled. The former POW who had fought for over a decade to get back to his wife and son finally received the whole story. How he deals with this shocking new information would be the final determining factor for the military's next steps, and Jimmy's future.

The officer continued, "Now, I know this is pretty surprising news, and I want to give you some time alone to absorb all you have been told. I'll leave you here to take it all in, and I'll check back in with you in a half hour or so." With that, the officer left Jimmy alone in the conference room.

"Pretty *surprising* news?" Jimmy said to himself as the officer walked out. "Pretty **surprising** news?" he repeated, this time with more emphasis. "Pretty surprising news? It's fucking DEVASTATING news! Are you fucking KIDDING me?" He was ranting in anger and at the same time sobbing.

The pain he was feeling was unlike any he had endured in Vietnam. He had never felt hurt like this before. As he sat there crying, with his head in his hands, he suddenly raises up. He begins to put the pieces together. 'The whole fucking town knew all along,' he thought to himself. 'They had all given up on me . . . even his Mom and Dad! Everyone quit on him. Maybe it would have been better if I never made it back' he thought. The chants of his fellow POW's began to play in his head . . .

*"No Lord No!" he heard. " Give him the strength to fight and survive."*

It was his friends from the P.O.W. camp urging him to fight . . . urging him to never give up. It was his *true* friends back with him from the jungles of Vietnam.

The more he thought, the angrier he became. He was angry with everyone . . . Bobby, the Army, his parents, the whole town of Black Oak. He was angry at everyone, except Katie. He still thought he could fix everything if only he was free. He knew his feelings for Katie, and better yet, he knew that she still had the same feelings for him. 'He loved her first' he reminded himself. If he could just get back home, he was convinced, he could change all this.

His thoughts immediately shifted to the government and what he would have to do to convince them that he could handle this news. If he ever wanted to be free again, he needed to convince them that he would be able to start his life over again without Katie. He knew he would have to project an indifferent, almost uncaring attitude about what he had just been told.

After 20 minutes or so, the commander reappeared to check on Jimmy. He was surprised by what he saw. By outward appearance, the officer thought, Jimmy seemed almost unfazed by the information he had shared with him. As he pulled up a chair, Jimmy spoke to him in a calm, deliberate manner.

"I know I may have overreacted a few minutes ago, and I'm sorry. But I'm really OK with this. I really am. I was a little surprised that Katie married Bobby, but the more I think about it, the more logical it would be. Bobby was our best friend and the person Katie would most logically turn to for comfort. I don't blame Bobby and I certainly don't blame Katie. It was impossible for them to know I would still be alive after all these years."

The officer was surprised, almost shocked by Jimmy's composed response. He commended him. "I'm very impressed and actually relieved that you are taking this as well as you are" he said to Jimmy.

"Please, sir" Jimmy replied, "all I want is to be able to start over again and let this God forsaken ordeal be over. I just want to be able to spend time with my son." He repeated his earlier statement that he was not willing to relocate for that reason, and only for that reason. He was hell bent on staying local to be around his son.

In the end how could our government deny him this? Convinced that Jimmy was sincere in his response to this news, the Army drew up the papers to finalize his discharge from the Army, which would only be weeks away.

There was one final twist for Jimmy prior to his discharge. It was a portfolio of photographs of Katie and Bobby's family the Army had prepared for Jimmy in an effort to assist him in his transition. There were pictures of Katie serving meals at a community gathering. There were pictures of Bobby dressed in his suit conducting a school board meeting. There were pictures of Little Jim in his Little League uniform. Finally, there were pictures of Katie and Bobby's daughter, Kim. Jimmy could not take his eyes off of the photos of Kim. She was a drop-dead ringer for Katie, and if you compared pictures of Jimmy Wrann and Katie with pictures of little Jim and Kim the resemblance was almost scary.

As the final weeks approached, Jimmy's heart was ripping inside, but he kept up his brave front. He continued to make it a point to state how happy he was for the Bowers family (he emphasized *Bowers*), and how much he looked forward to moving on with his life, and being able to spend time with Little Jim.

With agreements in place to attend counseling twice a week and also not to contact Katie or Bobby unless invited, Jimmy was finally discharged from the U.S. Army. His enlistment, which was originally to be for two years, was more than ten. He had endured the most hellish POW experience imaginable, and enslaved in a Chinese work camp. He endured beatings and tortuous treatment, and risked his life on multiple occasions, all to get back to the wife and son he loved more than life itself. Only to learn that his wife was now married to his best friend and raising the son he fathered.

And now, he had agreed to simply take it all in stride and co-exist in the same town that had long ago given him up for dead. He would move back to Black Oak, but he could never regain the prominence he once enjoyed in the community where he was once adored. He was no longer the hometown hero, but now a broken shell of the man he once was when he left so many years ago. In some ways, he preferred it that way.

He moved into a small house in the woods right outside of town. As he promised, he was determined to not do anything to upset Katie. If she wanted to be with Bobby and that made her happy, then that would make him happy as well. Though it was devastatingly painful, he loved Katie that much.

As he settled into his new home and new life, that love would be tested in unimaginable ways.

# CHAPTER 23
# The Final Reunion

THE FIRST FEW weeks of Jimmy's return to Black Oak, on the surface, seemed uneventful, but the undercurrents could be cut with a knife. He was spending the bulk of his time getting settled into his new home, which consumed him with projects. He needed to buy new furniture. He needed toiletries. He needed wall hangings and other decorations. Additionally, the electrical system needed to be upgraded. He was getting a lesson in the new appliances and home technologies that had come into existence over the past decade.

This was the first time in his life that he was creating a home of his own, and he wanted it to bear his personality. No frills, nothing fancy, just clean and neat and in the style of Jimmy Wrann.

Katie and Bobby spent their time trying to get back into their routines, but now they were doing so with a shadow hanging over their heads, and the seeds of doubt creeping into their marriage. For the first time since they had come together, they both sensed an element of secrecy in their interactions with one another.

Part of the major attraction they found in each other was the belief that they shared everything. Bobby knew what Katie was thinking, and vice versa. Their relationship was completely open. Now, it seemed different.

Had Katie told her husband everything about her meetings with Jimmy? Bobby knew and understood that Katie would still have strong feelings for Jimmy, but now he was 20 minutes away. Before, when Katie would tell Bobby she was going to the supermarket, he knew she was going to the supermarket. Now, when she said she was going to the supermarket, a seed of doubt would briefly creep into Bobby's mind.

When Katie was quiet, he could not help but wonder if she was thinking about Jimmy. Did she want to see him? Did she want to be with him? Was she still *in* love with him?

He was consumed with questions. Did staying away from Jimmy make Katie happy? Did staying with Bobby make Katie happy?

The tension that was growing between he and Katie was unspoken, but it was real. Their whole relationship was hanging by a thread.

Then there was the torment he continued to feel about his friend. Every day, he thought back to that day and those frantic moments when the helicopter pulled away, leaving Jimmy on the ground. He could not escape the thoughts about how much Jimmy had suffered, and how he was Katie's husband first.

How could he have done this to his very best friend. But Damn it! He fought as hard as he could . . . what more could he have done? He was terribly sorry about leaving Jimmy at Dak Seang. He was sorry that Jimmy had suffered some much physical pain. But could he possibly give up his family now? Where would Little Jim and Kim go? He could not allow himself to even think about life without them. He was truly sorry for what happened to Jimmy but now he was ready to fight like hell to keep what was rightfully his . . . even if it means fighting with his lifelong friend Jimmy Wrann.

Between his questions about Katie, being unable to escape the guilt of what Jimmy had endured, and his fears of losing the kids, the once tranquil life that Bobby enjoyed, was now on shaky ground.

Katie, in the meantime, was feeling the same. She, too, had questions. Did she love Jimmy? Of course not. She was married to Bobby . . . she didn't even know Jimmy Wrann anymore. Was it possible to love them both? Bobby was the only dad little Jim ever knew and he loved Bobby so very much. How could she even think that she could still love Jimmy after all this time. Her relationship with Bobby, however, was becoming strained. She had not slept with her husband since Jimmy's return. Even though she knew that would relieve the strain the two were experiencing, she could not bring herself to do it.

The questions persisted, and the more she tried to convince herself to the contrary, the more the answers were painfully obvious. She knew and could not escape the truth. She was beginning to feel like her life was spiraling out of control.

Maybe the three of them just needed more time to adjust to this awkward new reality. Maybe, as He had done so many times before, the Lord would step in and give them the answer.

In one of his prescribed therapy sessions which were part of his separation agreement with the Army, Jimmy continued to dwell on the same questions . . . How did we get into this mess? More importantly, how do we get *out* of it? Who is to blame for the situation we're caught up in? No one was at fault. There were no bad guys here. There was no greater love and togetherness than what the three of them shared for each other, he told his therapist, yet, when they needed that togetherness the most, no one seemed capable of giving it.

Ironically, in a separate part of town in different settings, Bobby and Katie were struggling with the same issues. While Jimmy was obsessing over Katie being married to his best friend, Bobby was wondering if he could now fully trust Katie. Katie's dilemma was even worse. She couldn't be completely honest with Bobby or Jimmy about how she really felt.

The 'three amigos' that once shared everything and were completely open with one another, were now spending little to no time with each other and being very guarded in their communications with one another. That togetherness and love they once shared together, they thought, would eventually return. But so far, it was coming apart at the seams. Bobby and Katie decided to sleep in separate bedrooms to allow each other the space to sort things through.

That fall, Jimmy started to college, hoping that would get his mind off the situation and on to something more constructive. He had always planned to go to college. In fact, that's exactly where he was headed, with a football scholarship in hand when Bobby got drafted and he agreed to go with his friend into the Army instead. 'Look how that turned out' he thought to himself.

Now, he was in no shape to play football. He was approaching his thirties and his body had been severely broken by years of torture and abuse. The truth is, he was not in shape emotionally to go to college, either. The constant reminders of his current situation was a recurring distraction. His thoughts were constantly with Katie and Little Jim. And, he was continually obsessing with the fact that Bobby was now married to *his* wife. 'He loved her first', he continued to remind himself.

His hope was that college would get his mind back on positive, more constructive topics, and away from the recurring nightmares of war, and Bobby, Katie, and Little Jim . . . but it didn't.

He couldn't concentrate. He had no real interest. He was self-conscious about his age and the physical reminders of war that everyone seemed to notice. And he had no one he could really talk to about what he was going through. The two people he had relied on since childhood, he felt, were now on opposite sides. And to make matters worse, the townspeople that once viewed him as their favorite son, seemed to be on opposite sides as well.

Everyone, he thought, sympathized with Bobby and Katie. He was convinced that everyone hoped he would just give in and everything would be like it was before he came home. The townspeople just wanted things to be like they were before. But that was not to be. Jimmy knew it. And Katie and Bobby knew it.

The ultimate blow to Jimmy's sense of isolation in his own hometown, was Little Jim.

Katie and Jimmy had arranged for him to have visitation rights to his son, as part of the discharge agreement. But Little Jim wanted nothing to do with his Dad. He had to literally be forced by Katie to even acknowledge him, and would only tolerate his Dad when Katie forced him to. To Little Jim, Jimmy was nothing but a stranger that had come into his life and made it miserable. He watched as his mother cried or was sad all the time, and he blamed Jimmy. He hated the fact that his life was turned upside down. Once he angrily shouted at his Dad, "I wish you were dead!" "Why didn't you die in Vietnam like you were supposed to?"

Jimmy could understand the situation with Katie and Bobby. He could understand the reactions of the townspeople. He could understand how he was such a disruption to the tranquil life that everyone once enjoyed. But the reactions from little Jim, who he wanted so desperately to spend time with, cut him like a knife.

Little Jim could never know how much his Dad had gone through just to see him again. He could never know how much his rejection hurt Jimmy. It took his pain and anguish to a new level. Jimmy was on the verge of being severely depressed.

The transition back to his hometown, which the Army had so carefully orchestrated, seemed to have reached a new depth and was spiraling further and further out of control. He had no solution to the saga that accompanied his wife and his best friend. His son totally rejected hm. And the townspeople seemed to reflect the same attitude of his son. 'Why didn't you just die in Vietnam the way you were supposed to?'

Those words echoed in his head. He had become an outsider in the town that once loved and adored him.

Jimmy's only source of solace was the heavily wooded area behind his house. He would go there to think and reflect. The area was desolate and full of wildlife. It was a place of nature and solitude, but it also reminded him of the jungles of Vietnam. He made a seat out of an old log and a firepit next to it. He would light a camp fire, and gaze into the flames for hours on end.

His time there was peaceful, but also eerie. Each time he would go, he would take an old revolver with him that was his grandfathers which was given to him by his Dad when Grandpa passed away. Whether it was a wolf, a coyote, a bear or a strange trespasser, he wanted it with him, just in case.

One night after class, with a beer in one hand, a picture of Katie and Little Jim in the other, and his trusty revolver in his hip pocket, that's where he went. He was thinking through all that had happened and the horrible state of affairs, and was determined to get a handle on things. The situation with Katie and Bobby was unchanged. The situation with little Jim was unchanged. The situation with the townspeople was unchanged. He sat on the ground next to his favorite tree to think.

As he pondered the situation, he found himself having a conversation with God, "Lord, we've got more issues here than I know how to solve. And I certainly can't solve all of them at once. I'm just going to pick one and leave the others with You, Lord."

He couldn't solve everything now, but if he had to focus on one thing, what would it be?

After more than an hour alone in the woods, he concluded the answer was . . . Little Jim. He began to think the challenge to win over his son was no different than the challenges he faced in Vietnam. He didn't quit then, and he would not quit now. He would endure Little Jim's reactions during their visits, and not react. He understood why Little Jim felt the way he did. The boy didn't even know his Dad. Jimmy decided he would give his son time to get acquainted with his dad, and hope he could eventually win him over.

And that's exactly what happened.

The strain with Katie and Bobby continued, as it did with many of the townspeople. But Little Jim began to come around. He began to pay more attention to the stories about his Dad; how special he was and how everyone in the town loved him. He asked his Grandma Hankins, whom he loved, to tell him more about his Dad.

Katie's mom was delighted to tell her grandson about the boy her daughter married years ago. She loved Bobby, but she had a special place in her heart for Jimmy Wrann. He was the boy that helped Katie adjust to her new hometown when they first moved to Black Oak, and she watched as their love for each other grew from those early childhood days. And given all the despair and heartbreak her grandson was in the midst of now, she was only too happy to tell him about those happier times.

She brought out the photo albums and began by saying, "You know, your Dad was Black Oak's all-time sports star." She showed him pictures of his Dad in his Little League uniform. She read to him press clippings of his high school football heroics. She showed him all the pictures of Jimmy and Katie's wedding.

"Mom was so *young*" Little Jim said to his grandmother. He then pointed to a picture of his Dad on the pitcher's mound, and asked her, "Is that why everybody says I look like him?" For the first time, Little Jim was beginning to see this man, not as some stranger that was making his Mom sad, but as his Dad. He seemed to no longer be angry at his Dad for disrupting his life, but now genuinely intrigued to learn more about 'Jimmy Wrann, the man that was adored in Black Oak.'

Soon the visits to his Dad's house became more frequent, and many times, Little Jim's ideas. Their visits were no longer awkward times spent on the sofa talking about meaningless subjects that Little Jim cared nothing about, but now were spent in the backyard, doing the things that fathers and sons do.

His Dad taught him the curve ball, and then got to watch him pitch a no-hitter that summer, doing just what his dad had taught him. The first time Little Jim threw that famous curve ball, there was a buzz in the stands amongst the old timers that had seen his Dad do the same thing. "I was sitting right here" one of them commented to his friend, "when his dad threw that same pitch to win that game against Junedale that time." Another one said, "Damn, this kid may be as good as his Dad was."

Katie and Bobby, who were also in the stands, heard every word, and were both getting choked up and holding back tears as they were taken back to those times.

Jimmy was not in the stands, but leaning against the backstop, beaming with pride as he watched his son. Wearing torn blue jeans, hands in his pockets, wearing a white tee shirt, and an old faded Cubs hat, he was grinning that same sheepish Jimmy Wrann grin that his son had on his face out on the pitcher's mound. When the game was over, as Katie and Bobby hugged Little Jim and left separately, Jimmy and his son walked off the field together arm in arm . . . father and son together again for ever and ever . . . or so it seemed.

As summer turned to fall, baseball season turned to football season. Little Jim, like his father those many years ago, was on the team and engaged in two-a-day practice sessions, preparing for the new year. Katie and Jimmy had worked out a schedule to get Little Jim to and from practice while, hopefully, minimizing their contact with one another. Katie wanted an arrangement where she didn't see Jimmy during the drop off's and pick up's. She knew that the more she saw of Jimmy, the more she would want to see him. She knew it. Jimmy knew it. And, Bobby knew it.

She would take Little Jim to the morning practice session. Jimmy would attend the morning session, and then take his son home with him afterwards. He would then take him to the afternoon session and Katie would pick him up after the afternoon session.

The arrangement was working. Little Jim was getting to and from his practices. Jimmy was enjoying watching his son. Katie was maintaining her distance from Jimmy. Bobby, who was generally uninvolved with the arrangement, was simply hoping to keep his family together.

All that changed when one fall day Katie called Jimmy's house after the morning practice to talk with Little Jim. She was calling to tell him that there had been a cancellation in the doctor's schedule, and he could come in between the morning practice and the afternoon session to get his football physical. So, she would come by to pick Little Jim up for the appointment.

Every time Katie had to call Jimmy, her pulse would race. She could virtually not breathe when she heard his voice. She had to emotionally brace herself just to say hello to him, much less carry on a conversation with him. There was no denying how Katie felt about Jimmy. As much as she tried to hide it, her voice and her body gave it away. As she was listening to the phone ring, she could feel her heart racing.

No answer. Phew! Now to be able to leave a message without sounding nervous. As the phone continued to ring, she remembered Jimmy saying that he and Little Jim often played catch or worked in the yard, but they rarely went anywhere. When she heard the answering machine, she calmly left a message that she was coming by to pick Jim up and take him to get his physical between practices.

After leaving the message, she held the phone in her hand before hanging up, pondering the prospects of seeing Jimmy. For reasons she could not even admit to herself, she decided to change clothes. She chose a thin white top. But before she changed tops, she decided to remove her bra. Katie was still very attractive with the body of a teenager. Not wearing a bra with her small, firm body was normally no big deal. But with the white top she had chosen, going braless would reveal her to be the woman she wanted Jimmy to notice . . . just in case. This was a woman only Jimmy would know . . . a woman even Bobby had never seen.

As she was removing her bra, she thought to herself, 'How foolish is this? He probably won't even come to the door. I'm acting like a damn schoolgirl.' Foolish or not, she let her unsnapped bra fall to the floor.

After continuously fussing with her hair in the mirror, she took a closer look to spot the slightest strand of premature grey beginning to emerge. 'Geez God', she said to herself. 'As if things aren't bad enough, now I have to worry about going grey!' She was getting flustered and nervously proceeded to Jimmy's house to pick up her son. This would mark the first time she had been to his house, and she was nervous, but excited. As she got closer, she was arguing back and forth with herself. A part of her felt what she was doing was wrong, but then, she would argue . . . was it really?

Jimmy was her husband and the father of her son, she rationalized. Little Jim would be there. What could possibly happen? And why was she so nervous? Parents who are separated or divorced do this with their children all the time. She steadied herself as she pulled into Jimmy's dirt driveway.

When she rang the doorbell her heart was pounding with anticipation, and that was just the beginning. Unbeknownst to her, on that particular day, Little Jim had stayed at school to go over some game films with the coaches and receivers.

With Little Jim still at practice, and not expecting anyone, Jimmy had been working on the deck in the back of the house. He was sweating from the autumn sun. He made his way to the front door. He was shirtless, wearing a baggy pair of jeans and had a carpenters belt hanging from his waist. Startled by his presence, much less his appearance, she stammered, "Where's Little Jim?"

"He's still at practice. They're going over game film and other stuff, so I came home." He had not heard Katie's phone message.

Secretly, that was just the answer she wanted. When Katie saw Jimmy's sweaty, shirtless body, her heart nearly jumped out of her chest as she tried to appear unfazed by the news. She was trying to maintain eye contact but could not resist glimpsing down at the half-naked body she had once made love to.

Her breathing became quicker. She could feel her breasts beginning to swell and her nipples hardening. Her body was revealing desires she was desperately hoping he wouldn't notice through her braless white top.

He noticed. Stumbling for words he quickly took off his work belt and grabbed a towel to wipe off some of the sweat from his body.

"Well come on in" Jimmy said. "Take a look around. This is my place." As he watched Katie enter, he was reminded of how she still had the fresh-faced beauty of a teenager. The only trace of wrinkles in her face appeared to be a slight trace of lines from her eyes down to her mouth. In reality, whatever lines she may have had in her face most likely were formed by the constant flow of tears of anguish she had endured over the years.

Katie tried her best to seem interested in Jimmy's new home, but that was not her focus at the moment. She was overwhelmed by the sensation of now being alone with Jimmy, and trying desperately to refrain from showing it.

"It's nice" she said politely, as she crossed her arms to hide what she feared her breasts were revealing. "It's classic you" she said. There was a single framed poster of a group of football players hanging over the fireplace which seemed to be his only decoration. "Who are those guys" she asked?

"Who are *those* guys" Jimmy repeated in mock astonishment? "*Those* are only the greatest players in the history of the Chicago Bears. That's Gayle Sayers. That's Walter Payton, the one they call 'Sweetness'. That's Dick Butkus, the greatest linebacker in the history of the game. That's George Halas. He was one of the co-founders of the NFL and owner of the Bears. They called him 'Papa Bear.' As Jimmy pointed to each figure in the poster, Katie could not avoid noticing his biceps flexing gently across his body. As he continued his commentary on the portrait, Katie was nodding politely, but she was not really that interested in the Chicago Bears.

"That's not my only wall decoration. I've got one that's even more special in my bedroom. Come see what's hanging over my bed"

Excitedly, he takes her hand and starts toward his bedroom. With the utter mention of his bedroom, Katie's nervousness intensifies. Her emotions are now out of control. As she is being tugged by Jimmy with one hand, she's wiping her tears with her other. Her head is telling her she shouldn't be going to the bedroom. But her heart is telling her that's exactly where she wants to go. He's pulling her, and she's not resisting.

As she goes into the bedroom, she immediately sees a collection of photographs, clustered together in a collage at the head of Jimmy's bed. As she gets closer, she can see the photographs are of Little Jim at various stages of his childhood. Jimmy, meanwhile, remains at the foot of the bed giving her time to reflect and reminisce. With the focus now on her son and not on obsessing about being alone with Jimmy, she begins to relax.

She walks to the side of the bed to get a closer look. She begins to reflect and offer commentary on each of the photos. "This was his first day at school. He was a nervous wreck", she says. She points to another and says, "This was him with his first trophy." Then, looking at another, she says, "I remember this day . . . .."

As she is about to continue, Jimmy approaches her from behind with another photograph, and interrupts. "Do you remember this day" he asks? He is holding their wedding picture, an 8 x 10 framed in an ornate gold leaf frame. Katie looks at the picture and stops in her tracks. Without saying a word, she takes it from Jimmy's hands and pulls it to her chest.. directly over her heart as if she could feel the picture. She then raised it to her lips and kisses it slowly. She responds softly, "Of course I do." Her voice quivers as she begins to weep. Jimmy then embraces her passionately to comfort her. The embrace leads to an equally passionate kiss as the two then fall into Jimmy's bed. Katie lets go of the photograph, allowing it to fall to the floor.

The tears, the pain, the torture, the sadness, the heartbreak, the roller coaster ride of not knowing, then assuming the worst, then finally re-discovering each other . . . they were all playing out in Jimmy's sparsely decorated bedroom. The intensity was beyond anything either of them had ever experienced. It was if they were finally exorcising the demons that had ripped their lives apart so many years ago. They worked themselves into a state of physical and emotional exhaustion, eventually fell asleep in each other's arms.

At some point, as Jimmy continued to sleep, Katie awoke and found herself face-to-face with the man she had loved and missed all of these years. As she stared at his face, being careful not to wake him, she began to softly trace the scars on his face with her finger. She imagined his physical scars mirrored the emotional scars she bore on her soul for what she had done to him, by not waiting for him to return. She then thought of how she, Jimmy, and Bobby, all three had born those emotional scars.

The physical scars, she thought to herself, would heal. But you can't put a band aid on the soul, she thought to herself. Still in Jimmy's arms, she dozed back off to sleep, wondering how the three of them could ever recover from the ordeal they were suffering.

After hours of making love and napping and catching up on a decade of lost time, they begin to get dressed. Katie looks down to realize she had dropped their wedding picture on the floor. She picks it up to discover the glass in the frame had cracked. In the ultimate of ironies, the glass was broken down the center of the photograph, separating Jimmy and Katie.

When Katie hadn't shown up for the doctor's appointment, the doctor's nurse called to make sure everything was alright. After being told that his wife had missed the appointment, Bobby knew exactly where his wife was. When he hung up the phone, he wasn't sure how he felt. Was he angry? Was he hurt? Was he even relieved, knowing that the two of them were bound to get together at some point?

As his wife was lying in bed with his best friend, Bobby was sorting through his emotions and what he should do next. Then he remembered, they have two children to think about. When it was time, he picked up Little Jim from practice as his mother usually does. Then he picked up Kim. But instead of bringing them home, he took them to his Dad's house. He explained to them that he had to pick up their mother, and it may take a while. He did not know what, but he knew something was about to happen that the kids need not witness.

He then returned home and waited for Katie to call.

By the time Jimmy and Katie had awoken and come to their senses about the situation, it was nearly dusk. Startled at the time, they looked at each other as if they had been busted. What now? How did little Jim get home? Where is Kim? What was she going to tell Bobby? They were scrambling to put their clothes on and straighten up the bed. As Katie was straightening the pillows, Katie thought to herself, 'In one form or another, the issue they had been dealing with for months, was about to come to a head. There was no avoiding the reality of what had just happened. There would be no lying, as if to cover up an illicit affair.'

She would not have any of that. All her life, Katie had been a straight shooter and had grown weary of all the dancing around the situation they had been doing since Jimmy returned home. It was virtually destroying them. Instead of loving each other as they had their entire lives, she thought, the three of them were growing apart. It was time to bring this situation to a head. She, as were Jimmy and Bobby, was convinced the lifelong love they had for one another was strong enough to fix this.

She decided to call Bobby and tell him where she was and ask him to come to Jimmy's house to join them. They would all be together . . . face to face. Surely, she thought, with the love they had for each other all these years, they could solve this monster of a problem. Nothing else was working. She was nervous as she dialed the phone, but determined.

When Bobby answered the phone, he showed no emotion. He did not hesitate. He said, "I'll be right there."

His cold, unemotional tone, made Katie even more nervous. She was visibly upset, shaking and once again began to cry. Bobby's tone reminded her she had hurt her husband and potentially destroyed their family and the lives they once enjoyed. She was becoming more emotional as they waited for Bobby's arrival, but she was determined to deal with the issue head-on.

She was in love with two men. This crazy war had turned three friends into virtual enemies. Two lifelong friends were now pitted against each other, and she was left to choose between them. How could she? She didn't create this problem, she thought. The military did. They first tried by having them go their separate ways. When that didn't work, they came up with this convoluted plan, full of stipulations and requirements, all designed to keep them apart. 'How was that working out?' she thought to herself sarcastically. The more she thought, the angrier and more determined she became.

The government created a problem none of them were responsible for, and if it were going be solved, it seemed, it would now be up to them to solve it. Up to now, the three had been grappling with the situation separately, and that had gotten them nowhere. Jimmy was in his own world with Little Jim; and Katie and Bobby were barely speaking to each other. To hell with the Army's well laid-out plan, Katie thought, we'll fix this ourselves.

When Bobby arrived at Jimmy's house, he came directly in. He didn't knock or wait for Jimmy to come to the door. He walked in the living room where he saw Katie sitting in a chair with her knee's pulled up to her chest and slowly rocking back and forth. This was the moment of truth and she had prepared herself the worst. Jimmy was standing, facing the fireplace with his back to Bobby as he entered the room.

When Bobby walked in, he seemed void of emotions. There was no anger, no accusations, no finger pointing or demands or ultimatums . . . only silence.

He went and sat on the couch directly across from Katie, looking at no one in particular. He was almost expressionless, acting as if he had simply dropped by to see old friends.

After about 3 or 4 minutes of deadly silence, each waiting for the other to speak and no one knowing what to say, Bobby got up and went to the kitchen and returned with a pitcher of water and three glasses. In an odd way, it was as if he were the host, and Jimmy and Katie were the guests. He offered each of them a glass of water.

He sat the glasses of water on the coffee table, then sat back and casually, almost nonchalantly, broke the silence. "Jimmy, do you remember that curve ball you threw that skinny little girl? You know, the one that wanted to be a boy back at the Black Oak Little League Field?" Looking at his glass of water, he smiled and continued, "Boy, that was a great pitch. She had no chance of hitting that one."

"That ball was outside" he heard Katie murmur in a low voice, as if she were talking to herself.

"Outside your ass! It was strike three and you know it" Bobby said back to his wife.

Jimmy turned slowly toward Bobby and Katie and said, "That was strike three, and you both know it."

Katie, determined to get in the final word, fired back "Your both full of shit. That ball was three inches outside!"

Something had just happened. What the Army was unable to do through a carefully orchestrated series of meetings, counseling sessions with psychologists, and debriefings, had just been accomplished in one two-minute exchange. A childhood memory, based on a curveball that may or may not have been 3 inches outside, finally broke the ice.

After months of mistrust, second-guessing, suppressed thoughts and passions, Katie, Bobby and Jimmy, were once again speaking to one another. Where it would go and how long it would last, no one knew. But for that one moment, they were what they had been to each other since childhood . . . three amigos. For the first time since Jimmy's return, they were speaking as friends. Their undying love for each other had once again, taken center stage.

The love that had been overshadowed by suspicion and second-guessing, had been re-born, almost with the flip of a switch. This is what they needed all along . . . to forget about the damn problem and be best of friends again. They all believed that somehow, someway their love would work it out. That night they became best friends again. Sitting on the floor together talking for hours and hours, the reminiscing continued well into the night.

From Little League, to high school football games, to the day Bobby received his notice for his military physical, to their memories of boot camp, they reflected on the times they had enjoyed as friends, and the times they had missed. They even talked about Bobby being the best man at Katie and Jimmy's wedding, and getting drunk at the reception.

What was *not* brought up during the marathon session, however, was anything about their time in Vietnam. Certain topics were still a little too recent and a little too raw. Especially that day in Dak Seang.

Finally, around 2am, Katie broke up the session. She said "We should probably get going. We've all got things to do tomorrow and we better get a little sleep before the sun comes up. They each stood and stretched from sitting on the floor for hours.

As they were saying their goodbyes, they each had smiles on their faces . . . smiles they had not seen for months. The tension and awkwardness that had dominated their existence since Jimmy returned home, was gone. Although nothing was solved and nothing was decided, all three felt it was a beginning. A beginning of what, no one knew, but it was a start.

Before leaving the three stood and faced one another. They stood as they had so many times and so many years ago. With glasses raised they said together, "For better or for worse, in sickness and in health, for richer or for poorer, "Till Death Due Us Part!"

# CHAPTER 24

## What Next?

As JIMMY BID Bobby and Katie a late good night, he sat alone on his sofa reflecting on the all-night session that had just taken place. He smiled as he thought about his afternoon session with Katie . . . feeling her kisses again, her body against his. *God,* she felt good, he thought to himself. She was as firm, trim and beautiful as ever. She still had that natural, fresh-faced beauty that seems to never change, he thought. He smiled at the thoughts of the three of them arguing the way they did about that last pitch to Katie. She knew it was a strike, he thought to himself. She just refused to admit it. Stubborn as ever, he chuckled.

He winced when he thought about Katie going home with Bobby when the night was over, after spending all afternoon in bed with him. Still having the love for each other they always had . . . 'she should have stayed here with *me!*'

Then he thought about the way they ended their evening. "Till death due us part." That was not some cute little saying they came up with those many years ago, he thought to himself. It was a lifetime commitment they made to one another. And despite all they had gone through and their current circumstances, Jimmy was convinced Bobby and Katie still felt the same way. Tonight proved that, he thought.

Jimmy was wired by the events of the day and evening. It was three in the morning, but he couldn't sleep. Instead of going to bed, he went outside. The early morning autumn air was still warm. It felt good on his body. He surveyed the back deck he had been working on. He then drifted out into the woods behind his house. That was his place to go to think. As he found his favorite tree, he rustled up leaves to create a soft spot on the ground, and sat down leaning back against the mighty oak.

The words, 'Til death due us part,' continued to echo in his head, accompanied by images of Katie's body pressed against his. 'Damn it, we can make this work' he thought, 'We've just got to.' His thoughts danced and darted in his head, from determination to doubts. The questions and the doubts soon began to take center stage in his mind. A new, darker image began to emerge. He saw his fellow POW's back in Vietnam.

"NO ! ... Lord ... No! Give him the strength to fight and survive," he heard them chanting. With visions of them vividly in his mind, he reminded himself, 'They're the only ones I can really trust.' He watched as they chanted to him, pleading with him to continue. They were in their bamboo cages, but present with him in the woods. He was no longer alone.

In Vietnam he was tortured for simply be an American soldier. Now, back home, he was being tortured for being a husband and a father. He raced to keep up with the zig zags of his mind ... from the three of them saying, "Till Death Due Us Part," to his fellow POW's screaming, "No Jimmy NO."

With his head leaning back against the tree, he was thinking to himself, 'Something, or somebody has to give.' He began to doze off.

After what little sleep they could muster from the long night and early morning of reminiscing, Katie and Bobby arose to take care of the day's routines. Little Jim was still involved in two-a-day football practice sessions, and Kim was attending a pre-school camp. Their first tasks were to get the children where they needed to be. Additionally, Katie called the doctor's office to apologize for missing Little Jim's appointment and to reschedule his football physical. After taking the children to their appointed designations, Bobby arranged to take the day off and came home to take a nap. He was exhausted, both physically and emotionally.

Though Katie and Bobby said nothing to each other about the previous evening's activities, it was weighing heavily on both of them. Katie did tell Bobby, "I can't apologize for what happened yesterday, but I do believe we need to get this issue resolved, once and for all." Bobby agreed when she proposed that they meet with a psychologist, and if Jimmy agreed, all three together.

Jimmy was sound asleep when Katie called him about the possibility of the three of them meeting with a psychologist together. He groggily agreed. "I'm up for anything that will stop this damn merry-go-round" he told her.

With that, Katie made the arrangements. The three of them would meet with a psychologist at Jimmy's house, twice a week. All three began the sessions believing their genuine love for each other would somehow solve the problem, and stated the same to each other and to the psychologist.

As the sessions started up and continued into the fall, the three continued to express the same sentiments, but after a few sessions, their emotions and their bodies began to betray them. Katie was losing weight and becoming increasingly distraught. Bobby was beginning to show signs of aging and fatigue. He was gaining more weight than his already large frame was accustomed to, and was visibly tired in many of the sessions. The creases in Jimmy's scar-torn face were deepening.

The sessions were becoming increasingly emotional, and at times, confrontational, mostly between Jimmy and Bobby. It was becoming apparent that the crux of the dilemma boiled down to the age-old dispute . . . two men wanting the same woman.

But this was not the typical age-old dispute. These were lifelong best friends. These were 'three amigos.' These were 'where two go, the third one is not far behind. These were 'til death due us part.' But these were also two men who wanted the same woman, and neither was willing to back down.

At one point, the psychologist told them, "There is no solution to this problem, unless somebody is willing to give in. If not", he continued," it was going to destroy the three of them". At the end of another of the sessions he told them, "When I met with you two months ago, I saw genuine love between the three of you, and really believed in your mantra, 'Til death due us part.' However, that's not what I see tonight."

The conflict and tension they were feeling in their sessions was also beginning to spill over into Bobby and Katie's relationship at home. Unless it pertained to the kids, they had little to say to one another. And Little Jim, who was feeling the stress between his parents, began to withdraw from his Dad. After picking up Little Jim from Jimmy's one day, Jimmy told Katie he was feeling a distance growing between him and his son. Katie tried to explain. "Little Jim is feeling, however right or wrong, that this is somehow your fault. This is tough for him just like it is for us."

Jimmy tried to remain calm as he listened to Katie, but after she and Little Jim left, he screamed to himself, "My fault??? It's my fault for serving my Country?? My fault for surviving? My fault for fighting like hell to come home??? Are you fucking kidding me!!!"

He begins to see the toll these sessions are having on Katies health and realizes that if they don't solve the problem soon this is going to kill her. He could not blame himself for doing all those things he did to survive and get home. But the harsh reality was, his son was right . . . if he had not come home none of this would have happened. Jimmy was beginning to feel it from all sides now. Maybe that is the only solution is, "Till death due us part"

The tension in the counseling sessions continued. Jimmy and Bobby continued lobbing accusations at one another. Bobby accused Jimmy of not being willing to accept the new realities after he had been gone and presumed dead. Jimmy accused Bobby of being all too willing to comfort and eventually marry his wife. Those accusations rose to a new level, however, when Bobby answered a question posed to him by the psychologist during one of the sessions.

Bobby was asked by the psychologist, "What's the biggest emotional strain you're dealing with in all of this?" Bobby paused and looked down at his feet for a moment, then raised his head and said, "Probably that I never got to fully explain to Katie about Jimmy struggling on the ground that day in Dak Seang when the helicopter pulled away."

With that comment, the room exploded with emotion. Whatever trust or consideration they were trying to show one another in the sessions, was now gone. All the pent-up frustration of having no solution to this problem exploded into outright anger. Even Katie reached her boiling point. But it began with Jimmy.

First, he thought to himself, 'That motherfucker! He knew Katie would have never married him if she thought there was even a glimmer of a chance I would still be alive. He knew and didn't tell her. That rotten, no good, *motherfucker!*' He then spoke.

"Hang on a second, Bobby." Jimmy began, sitting upright in his chair. "Did I hear you say you never told Katie that you saw me alive on the ground that day? Are you saying you let Katie believe I was dead this whole time? Listen Bobby, I don't give a rats ass about Vietnam anymore. There was nothing you could have done differently. All that's in the past. But you should have told her Bobby. You should have fucking told her!

"I TRIED to fucking tell her." Bobby interjected. "Two different times! She's sitting right here. Ask her. TWICE I sat her down and told her, 'There is something I need to tell you about Vietnam'. And both times she stopped me. She said, 'Bobby, I don't need to know anything else about Vietnam. It's me and you now. Jimmy is gone forever. He will always be a big part of our lives, but it's you and me now.' Katie, is that true, or not?" he asked Katie.

As she listened to the tense exchange between the two men she loved, Katie had her head buried in her hands. Slowly, she looked at Jimmy and said, "It's true, Jimmy. I didn't want to hear another word about Vietnam. Do you have any idea what it was like dealing with this nightmare day in and day out? Looking at your son and trying to explain that we don't know if his dad is coming home again? And dealing with the thought of losing you? Do you have any fucking idea what I was dealing with every day as I waited, Jimmy . . . do you?" She was crying as she spoke.

Her language was jarring, especially to the psychologist as he listened passively. Katie was not finished.

"Every day for years, I waited for you, Jimmy Wrann, agonizing over every news bulletin thinking it would be about you, only to be told by our government that you were dead! "How was I supposed to know what Bobby was going to tell me? I didn't really CARE! For all I knew, it could have been about another horrible war story about innocent people being killed, or babies being blown up, or something like that. I didn't want to hear any more about that God forsaken war. I just wanted to get on with my life. What else could have been so damned important about Vietnam? Our government told us you were DEAD! Do you hear me, Jimmy? DEAD!

Katie's outburst was met with complete silence, as both men kept their heads down.

Eventually, Jimmy responded in a near whispering tone, repeating his earlier point, "All I'm saying is you should have told her, Bobby. You know you should have told her I was alive."

Bobby interjected, again raising the volume level, "Jimmy, why the hell would I tell her and risk losing the only good thing left in my life? The government declared you dead, Jimmy. I came back to this town to bury my best friend . . . not to marry his wife! *Sure*, we found comfort in each other. We had both lost someone we both loved! *Sure*, we leaned on each other. And, yes, we fell in love. But it was the most natural thing in the world..

The more I saw Little Jim, the more I wanted him to know what his Dad was like. The more I wanted him to be raised the way his Dad would have wanted. Be honest Jimmy, who else would you have wanted to raise your son? The more Katie and I spent time together, the more we were doing to keep your memory alive . . . the more we became a family." Bobby too, was now sobbing, but he continued, perhaps more impassioned than he had ever been.

"Jimmy after having our lives shattered, we began to feel whole again. We began to heal! Can you understand that, Jimmy? For the first time, it seemed like this damn war could be put in the past and we could start looking toward the future. We could actually laugh and love again, Jimmy. And you wanted me to throw all of that away in hopes that the government was wrong . . . that you endured and survived years and years as a prisoner of war to the damn Viet Cong? Katie's right, Jimmy. We thought you were dead. What did you expect?"

"Not everyone thought I was dead!" Jimmy interrupted. Not everyone. YOU knew I was alive."

"I knew you were alive that day in Dak Seang" Bobby responded, "but what were the odds you would still be alive after all these years in a POW camp?"

"Jimmy, I'm sorry for leaving you in Vietnam" Bobby continued.

"I'm sorry I didn't tell Katie what I saw. But I'm not sorry for falling in love with Katie. And I'm not sorry I tried to raise your son exactly the way you would have."

Jimmy interrupted Bobby again. He was not buying Bobby's emotional argument. "Go ahead, Bobby. Go ahead and say what you're *really* sorry for . . . You're sorry you left me in Vietnam. And you're sorry I came home and upset your perfect little world with my wife and my son."

Concerned that the intensity of the exchange between the three was becoming too heated, the psychologist proposed that they end the session at that point. The three agreed, but barely acknowledged each other as they gathered their belongings to leave.

After Bobby, Katie and the psychologist left, Jimmy, as he usually did after each session, retreated to his favorite spot in the woods to reflect on what had just transpired. This is where he could hash out his thoughts. This is where he would share those thoughts with the many invisible faces in the woods that accompanied him. On this night, he needed that more than ever. Another ingredient had just been thrown into this nightmarish stew.

He took a beer from the refrigerator, grabbed his trusty pistol for protection, and out he went. Rehashing what he had learned in the counseling session, he reminded himself once again, 'There's no fucking way Katie would have married him if she thought there was any possibility I was still alive. This whole mess could have been avoided.'

Now what?

He came to the conclusion, 'If this nightmare is going to end, somebody must die. Death, he thought, was the only answer. If something or someone didn't give pretty soon, this was going to kill Katie, and she should not be the one who should have to suffer. None of this was her own doing, he thought. She simply acted on the information she was given. She loved them both. They are the fathers of her children. This was not Katie's battle, he thought . . . this was between Jimmy and Bobby.

Maybe Bobby should die? He's the one who left me in Vietnam to die. He's the one who lied to Katie when he told her he didn't know if I survived or not. He's the one who tricked her into marrying him. If she knew I was alive she would have never married Bobby. The more he thought, the more he became convinced. 'Yes! It was Bobby that must die', he thought. 'But how? And when?'

Though he still had questions, a sense of calm and clarity swept over Jimmy for the first time since he had been home. 'That's it,' he thought, 'somebody must die.'

That sense of clarity, however, was all too brief, as other images began to invade his thoughts . . . the Viet Cong, his fellow POW's, Little Jim, Katie, Bobby, they were all there, clamoring to get inside his head. His mind began dancing and darting from subject to subject. He was once again in Vietnam as a POW. With his eyes closed, his body began to twist and ache. He was reliving the pain from the torture he had suffered at the hands of the Viet Cong. His fellow POW's were there with him, watching and chanting. They were consoling him, urging him to fight.

From there, he listened to Little Jim, his own son, screaming, "I hate you, I wish you would have died in Vietnam."

From Little Jim, to Katie and Bobby, to images of having Katie in his bed, back to that POW camp and his fellow POW's, they were all there flooding his mind. The pace was speeding up. He couldn't keep up with his thoughts. He was hearing the chants. He was feeling the pain, just as he did those years ago. His mind was spinning.

As his thoughts returned to the POW camp, he could see his fellow POW's in their cages. He could see the sadistic smile of the Viet Cong officer. He could see the jungle terrain. As he surveyed the surroundings, he removed the pistol that he kept in his hip pocket and put it to his head. He then forced it inside his mouth, then under his chin. It wasn't him that was holding the gun, it was the Vietnamese officer . . . taunting him with execution, torturing him, intimidating him. He could feel the same ungodly pain he had endured at the hands of his captors. It was so intense, so real, so agonizing, he eventually passed out.

The morning sun began to reach through the autumn woods to

eventually find Jimmy's eyes and awaken him. His Grandpa's revolver was in his right hand. He assumed he had drawn it from his pocket to protect him from the night's critters. His legs resisted as he attempted to stand. The half-contorted position in which his body had ultimately come to rest, did not agree with him.

The last thing he could recall from the previous evening was his conclusion that 'somebody must die.' The flashbacks he experienced had evaporated into the air with the morning dew. The only other thing he remembered was the pain of the comment from Little Jim. 'Why didn't you just die in Vietnam like you were supposed to?' He slowly stood.

After stretching his aching body, he made his way back to his house to get some coffee and something to eat. He had planned to finish the work he was doing on his back deck on this day, and time was urging him forward.

As he approached his living room, he looked at the half-filled glasses that had been left from the previous evening's session. He once again thought of Bobby and his failure to tell Katie that he could still be alive. He shook his head in disgust and wondered how the next session would go.

Surprisingly, after the intensity of the previous session, the sessions, for Jimmy, became easier. He now had a clarity that he had not had before . . . someone must die. He seemed more at peace with himself, more subdued, and relaxed. The sessions were not as intense as they had been, not as confrontational. Even when Bobby again made reference back to the exchange from the previous session, "Who could have imagined Jimmy would have survived this long?", Jimmy passively agreed with him. Bobby and Katie both commented on how Jimmy's demeanor had changed. "Maybe he's finally beginning to accept the new reality" Bobby said to Katie.

"We'll see" Katie responded wistfully.

Then, in another of their follow-up sessions, Jimmy was even more unusually quiet. Halfway into the session, he asked for a short break. Everyone agreed to take 15 minutes. Katie, Bobby and the psychologist went to the kitchen for a drink. Jimmy walked back to his bedroom.

Without anyone noticing, he picked up his Grandpa's pistol and quietly slipped out the back door.

He proceeded into the woods to his favorite spot . . . the spot where his fellow POW's joined him . . . the spot where his tormentors waited to taunt him, to torture him. On this night, he would confront the monster that had inflicted the pain and abuse on him those many years ago.

As he got closer to his spot, he could feel his shoulders begin to separate. His face began to throb, and his double vision returned. Blood began to once again run down the open wounds on his face. He was back in Vietnam, ready to face his tormenter.

By the time he reached his spot, he could hardly walk. All the torture he had felt then, he was now feeling again. His knees were torn about . . . his hands were mangled, and his fingernails were half torn off. He fell to his knees. He bent forward at the waist and placed his hands behind his back as if they had been tied. This time, however, he was holding tightly to the revolver in his right hand.

The rain that had been a light mist throughout the day had now turned into a drizzle, which seemed to have intensified his flashbacks. The images were vivid. Everyone was there. He could see Katie. She was on her knees in front of him. Her cries, which were once screams for the former POW, were now only faint sobs.

Standing next to Katie, he could see Bobby, whose wounds were once again fresh, no longer healed. His left arm was shredded from the elbow down. His leg was mangled and bloody. As badly injured as he was, he stood strong and erect and said to Jimmy, "Till death due us Part. It's the only way!" Then there was Little Jim, standing by his sobbing mother, shouting "I hate you! I wish you were dead." They were all there. This was his welcome home . . . home to a place where he was once loved, but was now hated.

Then, almost as if they were trying to overrule the taunts from Bobby and Little Jim, Jimmy could hear the chants of his fellow POW's . . . "Fight Jimmy Fight! Don't ever give up. Fight like hell, Jimmy. Lord give him the strength to survive."

As they continued to chant, however, their voices were competing with the even louder voices of Bobby and Little Jim, "I hate you. Why didn't you die?" "Till death due us part." Those were the chants he was hearing the loudest. Those were the chants that were pounding in his head.

He then heard his fellow POW's sounding a different chant, as though now in retreat . . . "Take him Lord. Take him home to You. He has suffered far too long. His fight is over." The voices were unanimous. The pain and suffering and the torture he had been through in Vietnam and here at home were winning out. Once it was unanimous, he knew he would die.

As Bobby and Little Jim continued their taunts of "I hate you . . . Till death due us part . . . it's the only way", Jimmy saw the North Vietnamese officer walking toward him.

Meanwhile, inside the house, the others were ready to continue their session and noticed Jimmy's prolonged absence. They all walked to the back door thinking he was sitting on a swing on the back porch. As Bobby opened the door, a bolt of lightning lit up the night sky and the woods behind Jimmy's house. There, in an opening about 40 yards into the woods, they saw Jimmy. He was on his knees with his left hand behind his back and his right hand holding the pistol under his chin.

As they raced to save his life, the last words they heard Jimmy say were "Shoot me you son of a bitch . . . shoot me!"

Bobby was running toward his friend, but as the single gunshot rang through the trees, he stopped, frozen in his tracks. Katie instantly let out a scream and fell to the ground, pulling her knees up to her chest and closing her eyes tightly. The psychologist called 911.

After arriving, EMT's were confronted with two traumas . . . a self-inflicted gunshot wound, and a traumatized bystander, still frozen in a fetal position. After Jimmy's body was removed, Katie was taken to the hospital, still frozen in the same position and treated for shock.

Bobby and the psychologist were left to provide statements to law enforcement as to what they had witnessed. Once released by the law enforcement officers, Bobby proceeded to the hospital to tend to his wife. When he arrived at the hospital, he was told they were keeping her overnight for observation. Seeing her in her hospital bed, Katie was still in the same fetal position with her eyes tightly shut, her body rejecting the reality of what had just happened.

Though her mother was heavily sedated, Kim, her daughter, insisted on staying in the bed with her. She remained with her all night, constantly brushing her hair and reminding her how much she loved her. When Katie eventually awoke the next day, it was to the sounds of her daughter telling her she loved her. She was still groggy and barely able to piece together the events of the previous night. But she could not escape the cruel irony of the situation . . . 'The love her daughter was expressing to her, was the same love that started everything so long ago, and caused Jimmy to take his life.'

She held her daughter tightly and wept.

# CHAPTER 25
## The Final Goodbyes

S UICIDES ARE NOT a common occurrence in a small community like Black Oak. And especially when it involves one of the community's favorite sons.

Jimmy Wrann was a legend in Black Oak. He was a high school sports star, but beyond that, he was a clean cut, lovable kid whose future seemed unbound. Jimmy Wrann had dreams. But, his dreams were not his alone. They were the dreams of the entire community. He was legendary from his earliest days as a Little League pitcher, and later as a three-sport star in high school. He was destined to take that legend to college and beyond. He would become famous, and in turn, make the entire community famous.

He carried on his shoulders the dreams and aspirations of virtually everyone in town, and he did so gracefully and with that unmistakable 'Jimmy Wrann grin.' He was everything heroes are supposed to be . . . a multi-sport superstar, he had the smarts, the looks, the personality, and the girl. He was Black Oak's hero. His path was a foregone conclusion . . . one of scholarship, college, and of fame and stardom.

Yet, in classic 'Jimmy Wrann' style, he chose a different path. Instead of going off to the comfortable existence that was put before him, he chose to accompany his friend to war. The two would fight that war, then come home to travel their path together. But first, he would marry. Then, he, his wife and his best friend would all three pursue that path together. Jimmy Wrann didn't abandon his dream . . . he just deferred it.

'All for one and one for all', they said. 'We're all in this together', they said. 'Til death due us part', they said; and they meant every word of it. They just didn't know the price they'd have to pay.

Jimmy Wrann was now, finally free. There would be no more pain or suffering, no more nightmares. His war was over. The war of those he left behind, however, lingered on, haunted by his memory.

The funeral service, which Bobby arranged at Katie's request, was a study in contrasts. It had the informal and candid remembrances from members of the family and community, some of which would warm and some of which would jar the mourners' sensibilities. And, intertwined with the pomp and circumstance of a somber, but formal military procession. This would be the final farewell and tribute to Jimmy Wrann, and Katie and Bobby wanted it to capture those two dimensions of his life.

The pastoral grounds of the local cemetery provided the perfect backdrop from which to bid farewell to one of the town's favorite sons.

As mourners arrived, there was a large tent containing a flag-draped coffin, a podium, a large portrait of their local legend, looking regal in his formal military uniform, and flags of the U.S. and the state of Indiana on either side. Given the circumstances of Jimmy's self-inflicted wound, the family had opted for a closed casket.

The scene was reminiscent of gathering in the local gym to watch Jimmy play basketball those many years ago . . . an overflow crowd with standing room only. The chairs were quickly filled, leaving others to gather behind them. The only remaining chairs were those positioned to the left of the casket and podium, reserved for family.

The gatherers weren't there just to honor Jimmy Wrann, the local legend. They were also there in hopes of putting this long crazy nightmare to an end, once and for all. Jimmy, Katie and Bobby were at the center of this nightmare, but the entire community had lived through it with them. They were there to celebrate when Jimmy and Katie were married. They were there to watch Jimmy and Bobby go off to war. They were there when Jimmy was declared missing, and Bobby came home alone. They were there when Jimmy was pronounced dead. And while they mourned his passing, they were also there to celebrate as Katie and Bobby wed.

They were also there when it was discovered that Jimmy was still alive, and witnessed that traumatic, aborted reunion between Katie and Jimmy on the airport tarmac. The community lived through all the anguish and the trauma of that moment, and all that followed afterwards. Along with Jimmy, Bobby and Katie, they wondered what now?

They watched as the three attempted to sort through the complex and emotional issues of two best friends being married to the same woman, all while warding off the haunting memories of war.

No, the crowd that gathered at the cemetery that day was not there just to pay tribute to their fallen hero. They were there, hopefully, to put an end to a decade-long nightmare. After this day, they hoped, everything could return to normal.

Father Fusco started the service the way priests traditionally begin a funeral service. He began with a prayer, followed by the traditional messages of peace, and forgiveness, and how God was an all-loving and all-forgiving God. He told the congregation that anything is possible when you put your faith in the Lord.

He reminded the congregation of Jimmy's undying faith; of how his unrelenting message to his fellow POW's was, "We must never lose faith in God, our Country or our family." He told the congregants, 'That is what sustained Jimmy through all he had endured all these years, and eventually brought him home.'

Though he was saying all the things you would expect a priest to say at times like this, Father Fusco struggled with his words. This was no ordinary man the priest was talking about, and these were not ordinary circumstances. This was one of the town's favorite sons who had undergone one of the most dramatic and bizarre episodes in the town's history.

Father Fusco was a seasoned priest, he had conducted many funerals. But this one, for all those reasons, was different. He struggled for the right words. His sentences were interrupted by periods of long pauses. He stared out at the congregation, his face, glassy-eyed and full of sadness. He searched for words that refused to come. Without completing his thoughts or introducing the next speaker, he concluded and stumbled his way back to his chair. In his effort to provide comfort, his confusing rumblings seemed to reflect what the entire congregation was feeling.

Sister Margaline stepped up next and appeared to get the flow of events back on track. She was Jimmy's grade school teacher and followed the local hero all through school. She greeted Jimmy, Katie and Bobby every Sunday in Church, which they very rarely missed. She told stories of the dodge ball games they played and how Jimmy was an altar boy for so many years. She told of the time when he was in second grade and had rheumatic fever, which lasted nearly a month. Bedridden and unable to attend school, she described how she would walk to his house every night with his homework assignments and stay and help him complete them.

She told of how his fever returned two years later, and she and several other nuns made the same daily trips to help him remain current with his schoolwork. That time, she told the congregation, was much worse and lasted much longer, but the nuns persisted. That's how much, she said, anyone who ever came in contact with him, loved Jimmy Wrann.

Sheepishly, she told of the time when Jimmy got caught telling a joke that he thought was dirty. It went like this she said, "What caused Mrs. Tomatoes face to turn read? She saw Mr. Green pea." Jimmy was ashamed and embarrassed and cried endlessly when I told him how disappointed I was in him, she told the crowd, 'while all the time I was trying not to laugh.'

Sister Margaline's tributes seemed to lighten the mood of the entire congregation, which made it much easier for townspeople to pay their final respects with their own Jimmy Wrann stories. Family members and friends took turns telling stories about Jimmy's many qualities and much touted athletic abilities. Red the Barber, a renowned storyteller in Black Oak and life-long follower of Jimmy's many athletic feats, talked as if he were sitting in the empty chair of his barber shop.

"I can see him now, the way he did that night when he dropped 50 on those Panthers from Griffith. They were double and triple teaming him all night. But he couldn't miss. Nothing but swish all night long!" Red was on a roll, giving little attention to those who were waiting to pay their tributes. He continued.

"And that time he took our boys all the way to the state finals where we lost to the Lowell Red Devils, 14-7. Geez, that was a tough one! It wasn't just Jimmy and the rest of the team that lost night. The whole town lost that night. I'll tell you. That's the night we all learned to hate the chant of "RDP" which meant Red Devil Pride. Remember? Jimmy Wrann ... Man, there'll never be another one like him!" Then, looking at Jimmy's son seated in the congregation, Red caught himself. "Well, maybe there will be. I sure hope so."

As others followed Red to the podium, everyone had a favorite Jimmy Wrann story. When they all finished, the only ones left were the family members. Bobby and Kim sat together crying and holding hands comforting each other. Little Jim was sitting with his Mom holding her, literally supporting her, it seemed Katie didn't have the strength to even stand up.

Father Fusco gestured for Bobby to speak. He slowly shook his head no. Then he turned to Little Jim and Katie. Little Jim rose to speak, and as he walked to the podium Bobby moved closer to Katie, maintaining the support Little Jim was providing. Jimmy's son, who was now a sophomore in high school and following in his father's footsteps as a local sports star, was both sad and angry.

He started by asking the congregants a question.

*"Who do you want me to talk about? The Jimmy Wrann that came home and destroyed my life? Or my Dad who fought like hell just to see me again. I didn't know the man that came home from Vietnam ... but you did. I didn't want anything to do with him ... but you told me story after story about how much he loved my Mom, and how much she loved him ... but I already had a Dad ... one of the greatest men I will ever know. A man that gave his arm and half of his leg and his soul for this country ... that's who my Dad was ... not some guy who just showed up one day.*

*But then, slowly but surely I started to see this man you talked about. This man didn't push his way back into my life ... he let me come to him. And when I did, I began to see the person that everyone talked about. I saw how kind he was. I saw how much he loved Mom and I could feel how much he loved me. I began to see him differently. I began to see my Dad.*

*My Dad . . . the one that fought like hell just to see me and Mom
again . . . the man who lived through years of torture and abuse to
come home to a family and town he thought would welcome him
home with loving arms. But we didn't. We all gave up on him and
we did nothing as this unsolvable problem began to kill my Mom,
my Dad, Bobby, and this stranger that I now am proud to call my
Dad.*

As Little Jim paused to take a breath, Bobby had a change of heart.
He, too, was angry and wanted to be heard. He was tired of all the
talk behind his back. Stories about him had been spreading wildly
throughout the town, changing just a little every time it was told. Some
say he left Jimmy to die and did nothing to try and save him. Others
had heard he ran like a coward leaving his best friend behind to die.

Bobby endured all of the stares and the shaking of the heads from
townspeople he thought knew him, and loved him. He never once
stooped to respond to the rumors to clear his name. He tried to maintain
his dignity throughout. But now it was over, Jimmy was gone, and he
wanted people to know the truth.

He rose and motioned to Little Jim that he would like to speak. His
son invited him to the podium, and then returned to his seat. When
Bobby began to speak it was with a voice no one had ever heard from
the gentlemanly school administrator..

*For the last several years I have lived in a town that hated me . . . a
town that once loved me . . . hell, a town that once loved all three of
us. I've listened to rumors about how I did nothing to save Jimmy,
or that I ran from the fight and left him there to die.*

*You all began to believe this was all my fault. You blamed
me . . . you blamed me for Jimmy dying. And you blamed me for
what this has done to Katie, Little Jim and Kim. Well the hell with
you all he screamed. Every last one of you can go straight to hell. I
fought with every ounce of energy I had to save Jimmy Wrann that
day, and so did every man that was there. There was nothing else
I or anyone could have done to save him, as his voice lowered.*

*War . . . he paused . . . .war is unlike anything any of you have ever experienced. That day, that very moment I woke up and saw Jimmy crawling on the ground, has never left me. Every day, I relive that fucking nightmare over and over again.*

With that, the crowd visibly gasped, shocked at hearing Bobby speak this way. And, during a funeral!!! He was always the ultra-professional, dignified school administrator, who conducted himself in a calm unruffled manner. But there were two Bobby Bower's there that day, and up until now, the town had only seen one of them. Everyone knew the chubby catcher from little league, or the defiant soldier that naively toasted Jimmy and Katie at their wedding. They knew the President of the School Board. But no-one there knew the Bobby that sacrificed so much in Vietnam for this country. The only one that could have possibly understood was Jimmy and he was gone.

No one knew the Bobby that protected Katie, Little Jim and Kim, as if they were in a war zone, constantly scanning the area looking for danger. No one knew that the nightmares and flashbacks Bobby was dealing with, that would confuse their sleepy little hometown with the same dangers he experienced in Vietnam. No one knew the nights he would be up at 4 in the morning, telling Katie he was catching up on paperwork, when actually he was fighting off the nightmares of battle and other demons of the night.

Bobby did things in Vietnam that were wrong. He knew it. But he did them to survive. He saw innocent men, women and families die. He held his own friends in his arms, rocking them and begging them to hang on. He begged them to fight to survive, knowing they only had minutes of life remaining. And when death came there was no time to grieve. There was no time for funerals or 21-gun salutes. You just moved on and hoped the nightmare would soon be over.

Bobby was like the many veterans who survive war. They change, but pretend to be the same person that everyone knew before they went to war. They live a lie of being the same person they always were, when in reality they are never again the same person. Bobby had been living that lie since returning to Black Oak. He was everything everyone wanted him to be. He was a great husband to Katie. A wonderful father to Little Jim and Kim. But he couldn't forget. He couldn't forget the things he had seen; and, he couldn't forget the things he had done. They were forever etched in his soul. And listening to Little Jim speak, he was done!

He was done being what everyone wanted him to be. He was done pretending, living a lie. The town now knew the other hidden side of Bobby Bowers.

As the crowd continued to murmur from the harshness of what they had heard from Bobby, a sudden hush washed over them as they saw Katie rise and approach the podium.

Given what they had just heard, what could she possibly have to add. Would she agree with Bobby? Would she rebut what he had to say? Would she give *her* side of the three-way saga? The crowd waited in suspense.

Katie paused as she stood at the podium, seeming to build her strength as she waited to speak. She began . . .

*Friends let me tell you about my storybook life . . . a life of unconditional love . . . a life of friendship, understanding and commitment. I can remember Jimmy in little league. I remember how much he loved Bobby and how they were always together. I remember the day I challenged him, and he threw me the curve. I can still remember when Jimmy, myself and Bobby on the ground wrestling . . . Jimmy and Bobby were laughing, but I was mad as hell. But it was right then . . . right there on the ground that this wonderful life that I would live began . . . oh what a life I have had.*

*I can remember the first time Jimmy and I made love. It was after a basketball game over in Central Park. It was full of love, and passion, we use to lay together for hours, just holding on to each other without saying a word. We really didn't have to say anything just touching him was enough. He meant that much to me. Then all of the proms and homecoming dances, the football games and the basketball games how could life have been any better.*

*I remember laughing as I tried to sew all of his patches on his lettermen's jacket, there just wasn't enough room. Little Jim still has it. It's a little worn out . . . a little beat up . . . but just looking at it . . . just holding it close to my heart brings back the very essence of Jim . . . his smell, his touch and his smile and all those memories we shared. I remember the first time I saw him in his uniform . . . how handsome he was . . . how proud he was to serve his country. When you see pictures of him and Bobby together they both looked great.*

*But looking back on the time he was home on leave before he went to Vietnam I noticed he was different. He didn't laugh as much as he used to, and he seemed more serious all the time. Sure there were great times when they told stories on each other . . . you know about what happened in boot camp and the fun we had at our wedding. What a day that was . . . you were all there . . . you all remember how happy we all were . . . I remember when I found out I was pregnant. I think I ran to every house in town telling everyone that would listen that I was pregnant and with the help of God above we will have a healthy baby boy and his name would be Jimmy Wrann.*

*Then there was the wedding, how could anyone be happier than we were. I was surrounded by love . . . not only by my new husband and best friend, but by all of you . . . what could have been better for us . . . God was with us and seemed to bless this marriage and our future. I can remember the Congo line at our reception in the park, it seemed to go on forever. Do you remember our vows to each other? She asked as the tone of her voice began to fade . . . Till death due us part . . . Till death due us part . . . we all said it . . . we all meant it . . . but little did we know that those vows would become reality . . . that one of us was going to die.*

*I've told you about a fairytale life that a princess once had, full of everything good . . . God, an abundance of love, and family. Now let me tell you how the story ends.*

*As soon as Jimmy and Bobby left for Vietnam things began to change. The security I felt with them home was replaced by the constant worry of their safety. The letters I received told of a world I didn't know . . . A world I couldn't understand . . . I began to count the days until their return. When the news came about Bobby and the injuries he had sustained my heart was broken. I cried for days . . . and I prayed to the God that had given me so much happiness to heal Bobby, both in mind and body . . . then bring him home to a town that would love him, and take care of him. I thanked that same God for saving his life. But what about Jimmy?*

*I hadn't heard from Jimmy in over a week and my sleepless nights were full of worry and constant prayers. Then came the news that Jimmy was listed as MIA/POW. (Missing in Action, Prisoner of War). This was the first time I truly felt as if the love and kindness that I had been blessed with my entire life, was sucked out of my soul and replaced with dark clouds and with many questions and anger. God where are you I would ask? How could you let this happen?*

*I thought to myself . . . Our Government didn't declare him dead so they must have some type of evidence that he is still alive, and if there is one person on the face of this earth that could make it back home on his own it was Jimmy Wrann . . . so I took up the cross and began to push for the release of our POW'S, believing in my heart that my husband would be one of them returned.*

*In February of 73 when the first group of POW'S returned, Jimmy wasn't with them. The flights continued until late March . . . and again, Jimmy wasn't there. I so wanted that reunion at the airport when Jimmy would come home, and everything would be over. Everything would be just like it was before he went to Vietnam. But how could it ever be the same?*

*I finally got my reunion at the airport. I got to hold my husband in my arms once again. But who was this man? I was now Katherine Bowers. He really wasn't even my husband. But I knew deep down in my heart I still loved him just as much as I did that day in Central Park, the day we first made love.*

*When the Government declared Jimmy dead and Bobby came home for the funeral it seemed like everything was over. Bobby and*

*I shared so much together growing up we shared all the laughter and love that was possible. We also shared Jimmy. Because of the bond we had, our friendship turned to a different kind of love . . . a love we shared for Jimmy, and little Jim and a love for each other. Bobby Bowers is one hell of a man. A great husband, a wonderful father and provider. My children couldn't ask for a better father. And all of this was possible because of the love we shared for Jimmy. We believed that love could heal the wounds of a terrible war.*

*I remember the first time I made love to Bobby. We both cried. As we lay together, we both felt Jimmy was there with us, blessing this relationship, wanting his best friends to stay together and raise his son. I really felt that love. We believed our love for each other, given to us by God, had written the final chapter of this nightmare. But little did I know it was only the beginning.*

*I can't begin to explain to you how I felt when I received the news of Jimmy coming home. How could this be? What in the world is going to happen now? I cried and begged God for answers. Was I wrong to marry Bobby? Who am I now, Katie Wrann? or Katherine Bowers? Then it became clear to me . . . this was all my fault. I should have waited.*

*"I should have waited", she repeated. In a voice barely audible, she looked down and repeated for a third time, "I should have waited."*

She remained at the podium, continually looking down in silence for more than a minute before returning to her seat. The prolonged silence was then interrupted by muffled sounds coming from behind the mourners, 'Left, left, left-right-left.' A military honor guard was marching up to the coffin where, in precise military fashion, two of the soldiers began to remove and fold the flag into a crisp, military triangle. In the moving presentation, the commander of the honor guard then presented the flag to Katie, who was back in her seat and crying, overcome by the ceremony.

As Katie sat crying, the folded American flag in her lap and being comforted by her family, she, and the rest of the crowd, were surprised when daughter, Kim, stood and moved next to the podium. Without fanfare or accompaniment, she proceeded timidly, not to speak, but to begin singing . . .

> *Amaaaa-zing grace, how sweet thou art*
> *that saved a wretch like meeeeeee.*
> *I once was lost, but now I'm found*
> *was blind, but now I see.*

Katie was dumfounded by her daughter's singing, as was the rest of the gatherers. This was something only Bobby knew would occur. She was further surprised when, by the end of the second verse, members of the congregation were beginning to stand and sing with her daughter. By the end of the song, everyone in the cemetery was standing, singing, and crying.

While still standing, another sound echoed from behind the gatherers. 'Detail . . . Ten-*HUT*! Ready, Aim. *Fire!*' The military command was, followed by the loud, solitary sounds of gunfire, which jarred audience members. The traditional 21-gun salute had launched its first volley, followed by a second, after hearing the rifles cock and re-load, '*Fire*', then a third, '*Fire*'!.

The sounds of the 21-gun salute were still reverberating through the trees, when the solitary sounds of a bugle began playing *Taps*. While the military bugler played from the crest of the adjacent hill, the remaining members of the honor guard began to slowly lower Jimmy's coffin into the ground.

The final goodbyes to Jimmy Wrann were coming to a painful close.

At Father Fusco's motioning, the crowd rose and slowly began to exit, somewhat overwhelmed by what they had just witnessed. Some of them ventured over to once again offer their condolences to the family, who had remained at their seats. Bobby and Katie, both numbed by the accumulation of events over the past week, tried their best to respond graciously to the sympathizers.

Having thanked the final array of community members, the strain of Katie's and Bobby's relationship once again emerged. The two had agreed to present themselves as a united front through the service, to honor Jimmy, and for the sake of Little Jim and Kim. Bobby organized the service, just the way Katie requested. They sat through the service together as a family. They refrained from expressing anything negative or critical of each other. But the distance between the two of them had increased over the past months, and with the service now completed, that distance once again resurfaced.

Without as much as a verbal acknowledgement or even eye contact with each other, they proceeded from the grounds in opposite directions... Katie with Little Jim and Kim, toward the funeral limousine; and Bobby, toward his car. Within a year, the two were separated, divorced, and had moved away from the town they so loved.

Bobby's departure was immediate. Less than a month after the funeral, the proud, up-standing veteran and school administrator, left the community and his friends and family still talking about how he left Black Oak in shock with those final words at the funeral.

Katie remained in the community with Little Jim and Kim for several months. She had hoped her parents and the townspeople who loved her, would be a source of healing for her and the children. But nothing seemed to remove the same anguish that had haunted her since that fateful night. She finally moved, taking with her the tragedy of that night and the nightmares of a war in which she never fought.

Jimmy received the full military honors he so deserved at his funeral, but, unjustly, his name was never placed on the wall of the Vietnam Memorial in Washington. Though he took his own life, he was, without question, a casualty of the war that claimed some 58,000 fellow Americans.

# Author's Note

LOVE STORIES DON'T always have happy endings, and love triangles seldom if ever do. They invariably run their course and collide with the cruelest of outcomes. And when you pit a love triangle against the tragic uncertainties of war, the odds of a satisfying ending are reduced even further. This love story is about all of that, and what the ravages of war can do to that love, how it can destroy that love . . . how it can destroy hope.

I would like to leave you with some statistics on our heroes that fight and sometimes die to keep us free. But first, a little background . . .

I am a combat veteran with a Purple Heart and a Heroism medal for Valor. When it comes to war and politics, I am neither a "hawk" nor a "dove." But if we come under attack, if we need to defend our liberties and freedoms that so many have fought and died for, I hope and pray that we fight with the unleashed fury of the Lord. I hope we end it quickly and decisively, and bring our fighting men and women back home and treat them like the heroes that they are.

When their military duty has ended, the vast majority of our war veterans find their way back into society leading happy, healthy and fruitful lives. Yet, there are many who continue to struggle with their personal battles, as evidenced by the following . . .

Every day, 20 veterans who have fought for us, and have been willing to give their lives for us, take their own lives by suicide . . . 20 every day! *Our Suicide Prevention Hotline number is 1-800-273-8255.*

On any given night here in the United States of America there are approximately75,000 veterans who are homeless.

Addiction, divorce and depression, , accompanied by feelings of isolation, guilt and anger, among returning combat veterans are among the highest in the country.

Emotions such as love, and hope, can be lost and even destroyed by war. But, fortunately the human body is resilient. Those feelings can also be resurrected with love, understanding, and the belief that you are not alone in your fight. Which you are not.

Whatever you may be suffering from, be it PTSD, or any other physical, emotional or moral injuries, you are never alone. You are, as is the very flag we fought for, a symbol of freedom, liberty, and the American way of life. And for that, we salute you, and support you in your continued journey. Your battle was and continues to be an honorable one, and we are there, walking arm in arm with you.

I was once asked during an interview "What is it that America can do for our veterans when they return home? "Respect us," I replied. "Respect us for what we have given you." The interviewer looked at me with a puzzled look on her face and said, "What is it you have given me Mr. Chancellor?"

I replied, "I have given you part of my soul. I have given you part of my piece of mind. I have given you part of me, so you and all America can live the life you do. I will never get these things back . . . none of us who have served will ever get these things back."

Stay Strong,

*Jim Chancellor*

CPSIA information can be obtained
at www.ICGtesting.com
Printed in the USA
LVHW112042260720
661578LV00008B/57/J